THE BACK OF THE NET

A STORY OF RESCUE, RENEWAL, AND REWARD

LARRY FITZGERALD

Published by hope*books
2217 Matthews Township Pkwy
Suite D302
Matthews, NC 28105
www.hopebooks.com

hope*books is a division of hope*media

Printed in the United States of America

First paperback edition.
Paperback ISBN: 979-8-89185-170-2
Hardcover ISBN: 979-8-89185-171-9
Ebook ISBN: 979-8-89185-172-6
Library of Congress Number: 2025931425

Scripture quotations taken from the (NASB®) New American Standard Bible®, Copyright © 1960, 1971, 1977, 1995, 2020 by The Lockman Foundation. Used by permission. All rights reserved. lockman.org"

A NOTE TO THE READER

This book contains discussions of sensitive topics, including gun violence and assault. These themes are intended to encourage thoughtful reflection and conversation about their real-world consequences. However, they may not be suitable for all readers, especially those under the age of 13 or those who have had personal experiences with similar events. If you or someone you know is struggling with the topics presented, we strongly encourage you to seek guidance from a trusted adult or counselor. Reader discretion is advised.

CONTENTS

CHAPTER 1

The bleachers were packed. The fans were raucous. It was the opening game of the season for both teams. Barrymore was playing Langford at Langford, and the second half of the game was about to start. Barrymore was up by a goal, and the players were anxious to get back to the action ahead as they rushed onto the field to start the second half.

There was no rushing onto the field for Barrymore's Michael Shepherd, however. His position was, and always had been, the team bench. Michael only played when the game's outcome had already been decided. He could have played more; he certainly had the tools to do so, at six feet and still growing. Michael was lean, muscular, and smart-he simply did not care enough to put in the work required to be a good soccer player. Soccer was not that important to Michael, especially that night. What was important to Michael that night was that it was his eighteenth birthday. His dad and mom had given him a beautiful sports coat, and he looked forward to showing it off on a date with Ashley Templeton at the next school dance.

Michael looked up fondly at the snow-capped mountains of Eastern Oregon above the farmland surrounding the soccer field. Mom's voice echoed in his head: "You're a senior, Michael! You need to figure out your college plans." Michael's plan, however, was quite simple: "I'll figure it out this summer."

Michael took a quick break from his thoughts to glance at the game action. *Wow! Still a close game, which means I won't get in. Oh well. Not a biggie. Let's see, Dad said he and Mom wanted us to have a serious talk tonight after the game. What's that all about? Tomorrow, I caddy for Mr. Trotter in LaGrange. That'll net me a cool fifty bucks plus tip, which, if he wins, will be another fifty. I'll have to get up early and hope old Lizzy has 20 miles in her to get me to LaGrange.*

At that moment, the intensity of the game began to increase as the clock wound down to the final few minutes. The crowd began to ramp up the noise as Langford pushed all of its players, including their goalkeeper, forward in a desperate effort to pull the game back to a tie score in its final minutes.

Langford's center midfielder, number ten, collected a perfect pass from his mid-field teammate and barreled down the left side of Barrymore's defense with the ball on his right foot. Splitting two defenders, he darted into the top of the box and once again squared off against Barrymore's big center back, Austin Davis, who had successfully countered his drives into the box the entire game. This time, it would be different. With a sudden faint to his left and slick left-foot-to-right ball movement, the Langford player juked Davis, which opened the way for a clear shot on goal. He pulled the trigger. The ball blew past the goalkeeper and into the right corner of the net, tying the score one to one with ten minutes of game-time remaining.

The band played. Home team fans cheered. The players charged back to midfield to restart the game. Players who had been on the field rushed to their assigned positions. Suddenly, Barrymore's coach, Kyle Patton, was on the field running toward Austin Davis, who was down, holding his knee and writhing in pain. Minutes later, Patton and his assistant coach, Aaron Agular, with support from some players, helped Davis off the field. Once the coach knew Davis was not badly hurt but unfit to continue playing, he turned to Agular and asked, "What do you think, Coach?"

"Well, the only healthy defender we've got is Michael. Tommy's only about fifty percent because of his sore knee. Brian's okay in midfield, but I don't think he can hold off their striker. That leaves Michael," Agular responded.

Coach Patton shook his head and grimaced. "So, I guess we'll go with Michael. Why not? He's big and has a decent left foot."

"You're right, but Michael's still Michael, Coach."

"Yeah, I know." Coach Patton looked over at Michael, who was, at the moment, aimlessly gazing at the crowd. "Put him in at left back and move Quinn to the middle."

Agular sighed. "Yes, sir."

At that moment, the referee pointed at Coach Patton and blew his whistle. "Let's go, Coach!"

The restart was furious. Both teams attacked and defended their goals with equal vigor well into the final minutes of the game. The Barrymore defense struggled with Alexander Pittman at center back in place of Austin Davis and Michael Shepherd defending the team's left flank.

The Barrymore coaches were nervous, and so was Michael. His chest rose and fell rapidly, fear coursing through his body. He had never been in a game when the outcome was on the line before; he always played during the "garbage" minutes, where outcomes were already decided before he was subbed in. But here he was in a game when the result was in doubt, fighting for his team and the school's honor.

It's my birthday. Wow! What a great birthday present this is! I can't blow this, Michael thought to himself.

Michael hunkered down and extended his arms, hoping nothing of consequence would come his way. The game was momentarily delayed while Langford made a substitution. Michael grabbed the opportunity to scan the crowd, looking for Ashley. She was out there somewhere. His mind wandered to their recent conversation after he had finally worked up enough courage to ask her for a date.

"I'll go out with you on one condition," she finally consented. "If you score a goal in the game against Langford, I'll go out with you. That's the deal, Michael Shepherd. Take it or leave it." She chuckled to herself as she walked away.

It was a safe bet on her part, Michael thought. *She knew I probably wouldn't even get in the game, let alone score a goal. I hope she at least sees I'm in the game now. I wonder where my folks are. Dad's probably filming the game. He always does, even when I don't play. I wonder what "important thing" they want to talk to me about.*

"Heads up, Michael!" Coach Patton screamed from the touchline.

Michael snapped to attention. Langford's number ten was barreling toward him at full speed. He looked like a finely tuned Corvette in complete control of the ball and the entire offensive right side of the field.

Oh crap! What do I do now? I've got to get in front of this guy!

Michael charged forward, but number ten easily flew past him. He cruised into midfield, where he fired a missile shot on goal. Barrymore's goalkeeper, Matt Arnold, deflected the ball over the top of the goal at the last second. The clock was ticking. Langford wasted no time as they retrieved the ball and rushed to the right corner flag. Players from both teams gathered in the penalty box for what might be a game-deciding corner kick. Michael was confused, not sure where to go. He ran toward the middle of the players crowded together in the box.

Above the commotion, he heard Coach Patton scream, "Far post, Michael! Go to the far post!" Michael ran for the far post just as the Langford player put the ball in play. The well-delivered corner kick curved inward toward the goal, ricocheted off the back of Michael's head, and sailed past the goalkeeper's outstretched hands into the back of the net.

The Langford fans went crazy. They began celebrating, dancing, and laughing while the Langford players gleefully began patting Michael on his back. "Thanks, man. Great goal! You should get the game ball." The contest ended minutes later with a final score of two to one in favor of Langford.

Michael was beside himself in grief. He knew the loss was on him and was already feeling ostracized as the players made their way to the team bus. To make things worse, just as he stepped forward to enter the bus, he heard someone holler, "You're a loser, Michael Shepherd!"

Michael climbed aboard and immediately went to the back of the bus. His heart was heavy as he fought back tears.

That really hurts, but he's right. I am a loser. How am I going to go to school on Monday morning? The kids will either hate me, laugh at me, or both. I'm all by myself. I wish I was dead.

"What is wrong with me?" Michael murmured as he leaned back and stared at the bus ceiling.

"There's nothing wrong with you, Michael," Coach Patton said as he sat down beside him. "You just had an unfortunate moment today, that's all. It happens to all of us."

Michael looked at Coach Patton briefly and then down to his feet. "I know, Coach. But I can't believe what happened. I didn't need this, especially tonight. I feel so stupid! After what happened tonight, I have to be the most hated kid in the whole school."

Coach Patton stared sympathetically at Michael, then said, "Let me tell you about a young man I read about in my Bible recently, Michael. His name was Joseph, and he lived a long time ago, a very long time ago. Joseph grew up in a large family. He had eleven brothers. They hated him because he was their dad's favorite son, so they plotted how to get rid of him. It was so bad that some of them even wanted to kill him. When the opportunity came, they grabbed him and dumped him into a well. They kept him there until they made up their minds about what to do. Finally, they decided to sell him as a slave to some men traveling to Egypt. These men took him to Egypt, and Joseph eventually became a slave to an Egyptian police officer named Potiphar."

"Over time, Joseph earned Potiphar's trust, so he put Joseph in charge of his entire household. Joseph worked hard to please his master, but Potiphar's wife tried to entice Joseph into an immoral relationship with her. When he refused, she lied to her husband that Joseph had tried to seduce her. So, Potiphar imprisoned Joseph. Despite this tragedy, Joseph hung tough. He worked diligently and soon became a model prisoner. Then, one day, because of his miraculous ability to interpret Pharaoh's perplexing dream, Pharaoh released him from prison and put him in charge of the whole country. Joseph soon became the most powerful man in the world. Joseph was a young man who didn't worry about being hated. He kept doing what he knew was right, and everything worked out for the best."

The coach paused to gather his thoughts once again. Then he continued: "Here is the most surprising part, Michael. God had given Joseph all this power and prestige, but when he saw his brothers again a few years later, he forgave them for what they did to him. He was not bitter. He did not seek revenge. He wept over them, and he forgave them."

Coach Patton paused, sat back in his seat, and after a few minutes, turned to Michael and said, "Joseph was a gifted young man. He had abilities no one knew about until he decided to put them to work." Patton paused for a moment, then said, "I might add, Michael, I believe you have a lot of abilities as well."

Michael smiled and said, "Thanks, Coach, that really helps."

Coach Patton stood. "So, hang in there, Michael. Like Joseph, you can turn this experience into something positive. It's all about attitude."

Michael reached out and shook his coach's extended hand. "Thanks, Coach."

Coach Patton smiled and asked, "So, what've you got going for tomorrow? I'm going to work with a few of the players. You'd be welcome to join us."

"Can I rain-check that coach? I'm driving to LaGrange tomorrow for a caddy job."

"Okay, no problem. We'll be back next Saturday as well."

"I'll remember that. Thanks again, Coach."

***

Michael was the last player off the bus. He grabbed his duffle bag and walked the four blocks to his house. His dad and mom were waiting for him in the living room. Michael dropped his bag beside a fabric chair and sat down.

"What did you think of the game?"

Dad picked up his cocktail and sipped from the contents. Then he said, "Well, it didn't go well for Barrymore, or you either, for that matter."

 Michael glared at his dad. "What's that supposed to mean?"

Dad paused momentarily, sipped from his glass again, and said, "Let's just say it had an unfortunate ending."

Mom quickly jumped in. "You did fine, son. I was worried when that ball hit you on the head. Are you okay?"

"I'm fine, Mom," Michael said quietly.

Dad butted in, "Let's not talk about the game. It's over and done with. We have something important we need to discuss with you, Michael."

Michael slouched back in his chair. His eyes darted back and forth between both parents. "So, what's up? Are we moving or something?"

Mom replied, "No, son. We're not moving. Where would we move to, for goodness sake?"

Dad cleared his throat. "Michael, we have purposefully kept a vital secret from you for a long time, which now we feel you are old enough to hear and understand. It is a critical detail, something you should know."

At sixty-two years old, George Shepherd was the CEO of one of the few large businesses in Barrymore. He had been with the company since its inception, having risen from plant accountant to its top position in over thirty years of service. George was known as a hard-nosed manager at work and at home with his family.

Cupping his drink in both hands, he looked at Michael and began to speak. "Several years ago, your mom and I decided to shield you from some facts about your birth until you reached your eighteenth birthday, and, well... You are eighteen years old today. You'll soon graduate from high school and, more than likely, be off to college. You are no longer a child, so it is time we made you aware of something."

Michael's heart began to speed up. His mouth went dry, and he started to rock back and forth slowly, *for crying out loud, Dad. Please get to the point! You're killing me here!*

Dad looked at Mom and then back at Michael. "First, we want you to know that we love you very much – as if you were our own son. We want you to know that."

Michael stopped rocking. His eyes darted back and forth between his mom and his dad. At an elevated pitch, Michael asked, "What do you mean, as if I were your own son? I am your son!"

George paused. He sipped his drink and set the glass down on a side table. Mom stared at him, obviously anxious for him to continue. Michael's mouth dropped open as his blue eyes locked onto his dad's hazel-brown eyes. Mom adjusted her posture, removed her glasses, and wiped them with a tissue.

Finally, Dad said, "Yes, you are our son, Michael, but you are our adopted son."

"Adopted son? What are you talking about? I'm adopted, and you're just now telling me? That's not right! That's not fair!" Michael paused and took a deep breath. "Okay, Mom and Dad. Please tell me then, who the heck are my real parents?"

George sighed, "We don't know, Michael. You came to us as a baby. There was no parental disclosure."

Michael stared at his parents, shook his head, and looked down at his shoes. "I can't believe this."

"I understand why you're upset," George continued. "We had three girls. We wanted a boy so badly that we decided the only sure way we could have one would be to adopt. So, we applied, and after a long wait, we got you."

"Michael, we're very glad we got you. Very glad," Mom added.

Michael looked at his dad. "How about you, Dad? Are you glad you have the son you have?"

"Of course," George responded.

"Even a son who makes a fool out of himself in front of hundreds of people. Like tonight?" Michael asked, eyebrows raised.

"This isn't about tonight, Michael. "What happened tonight doesn't matter. What matters is for you to know the truth."

"Maybe so, but it's unfortunate that you are disowning me today," Michael muttered.

George's face reddened. "We're not disowning you! Don't be a fool, Michael."

Michael stood. "I'm sorry I've been such a big disappointment to you, Dad!"

"Michael, I'm telling you, I love you, son, I..."

"Do you love me, Dad? Do you know this is the first time I've ever heard you say that to me? You have never told me that you loved me—ever!"

Awkward silence filled the room. Thirty seconds later, Michael departed.

CHAPTER 2

Early the next morning, Michael left his home in his pickup truck and headed for LaGrange, Oregon, thirty minutes away. Michael was a regular caddy for one of the top golfers in the valley, Carson Trotter. Carson was playing in the Annual Children's Charity Golf Tournament. Carson was an attorney and owned a law firm in LaGrange. Over the years, he and Michael had become close friends.

Maybe I can get some advice from Carson on all of this. He's a pretty smart dude. Michael turned onto State Highway 22, heading south toward LaGrange. Just as he reached the Barrymore City Limits, his truck's engine began to sputter and lose power. He quickly pulled into an empty fast food parking lot where the truck totally shut down. After several failed attempts to restart the vehicle, Michael gave up and got out of the truck.

Why is all this happening to me? Dad's working today. He can't help me. After last night, I probably wouldn't ask him to anyway.

Michael walked back to the highway and stopped next to the "LEAVING BARRYMORE sign near the bridge over Stevens Creek. Stevens Creek flowed into the Grande Ronde River near the Blue Mountain foothills. Michael stood with his arm extended in the air and his thumb out. This was not the first time he had hitch-hiked to LaGrange, Oregon.

Michael had plenty on his mind as many vehicles passed by

him that morning.

What else could go wrong in the life and times of Michael Shepherd? I've got problems with my dad, who really isn't my dad, after all. So, who am I? Where did I come from? What good am I? I'm a benchwarmer on the soccer team. Ashley doesn't really care about me. Why am I such a loser? I don't know why – I just am. Why can't I be like Joseph, the guy Coach Patton was talking about? He was hated, but he overcame it. He went from loser to winner. Why can't I be like Joseph?

Michael checked his watch. He only had an hour before Mr. Trotter's tee time. Once he caught a ride, the trip to LaGrange would take half an hour. He couldn't afford to be late. Mr. Trotter was a good man, but he was also impatient, especially when it came to his golf game.

Come on, people. I'm not going to hurt you. I need a ride to the golf course, that's all. I promise you; I'm not armed. I'm just a dude trying to make a buck.

Michael stayed the course, but his anxiety level was ticking up rapidly. Finally, a beat-up pickup truck with an outlandish orange, green, and rust color scheme rattled to a stop in front of him. Inside were two passengers plus the driver. The back door swung open, and a young man with a beard and a stringy ponytail leaned forward and asked, "Where are you headed, dude?"

"LaGrange," Michael replied. "Where are you guys going?"

"We're going that way, too! Hop in."

With a sigh of relief, Michael jumped into the truck and closed the door. "Thanks. I appreciate this."

The driver shifted into low gear and spewed a bucket of gravel into the air as he pulled back onto the highway. Then he gunned the engine, pushed in the clutch, and shifted into second gear. He gained speed as he engaged the clutch once more and dropped into high gear. By now, the speedometer was at seventy, with the engine screaming and every nut and bolt in the truck rattling angrily.

Two of the young men looked to be in their late teens. The driver was older, *probably in his mid-twenties,* Michael thought. They all had facial hair in different stages of growth, stringy head hair, and heavy tattoos. The inside of the car reeked of alcohol. A sickening feeling began to creep into Michael's gut.

The front-seat passenger looked back at Michael and asked, "You live in Barrymore?"

"Uh-huh," Michael answered nervously as he peeked over the front seat and checked the speedometer. "I've lived here all my life. Um, say, could you slow this thing down a little bit?"

The driver grinned at Michael through a cracked rear-view mirror and said, "What's the matter, bruh? Are you scared?" He then put the gas pedal to the floor and started weaving the vehicle from side to side on the narrow highway.

Michael's heart began to pound. His mouth went dry. He grabbed the inside door grip and tried to keep from sliding across the seat. His body contorted side to side and front to back as he held the hand grip with his right hand and the back of the front seat with the other. A load of acid dumped into his stomach. He wanted out!

His fellow passengers began to laugh. They were having a good time.

"Come on, guys. Please stop and let me out. You all are crazy!"

The driver immediately slowed the vehicle down and looked back at Michael. "What did you say? Are you calling me crazy? Is that what you're calling me, boy?" He angled the truck over to the side of the road and stopped. Looking back at Michael, he said, "I'm going to ask you one more time. Are you calling me crazy, boy?"

Michael froze. He looked at the driver and tried to speak. Nothing came out.

"He said we were all crazy, Derek," one of the passengers volunteered.

The driver, Derek, got out of the car, walked around, and jerked open the door where Michael was sitting. He grabbed Michael and started to pull him out of the vehicle.

"What are you doing? Knock it off!" Michael leaned back against the passenger in the rear seat and used his legs in an attempt to rebuff Derek.

"Hold his arms, Joker," Derek screamed. Then he grabbed Michael at his belt line and tried to jerk down his pants. Michael kicked his legs at Derek, sputtering, "Stop it, you idiot!"

But between Joker's pushing and Derek's pulling, Michael finally came out of the car, landing with a thud on the edge of the road. By this time, the third youth was out of the vehicle, and between the three men, they soon had Michael barefoot and stripped down to his shorts.

The three youths gathered over him. "What's your name, boy?" Derek demanded.

Michael lay flat on the ground. He didn't answer.

Derek picked up his pants, removed his billfold, and handed it to the third youth. Joker yanked off his watch.

"You got any money, boy?" the third youth queried as he rifled through the wallet. "Oh yeah, five bucks!"

"Five lousy bucks," Derek scoffed. "That's pitiful. You know what, boy? You're lucky I'm in a good mood. Get him out of here. We need to go."

Derek stood aside as the other two grabbed Michael's arms, dragged him off the edge of the road, and flung him into the ditch alongside the road. The three assailants then jumped back into the truck and drove away, leaving Michael lying face-down in the narrow ditch.

Michael rolled over onto his back and sat up. His arms and legs were scratched and bleeding. His face was swollen. Fortunately, he wasn't badly hurt, at least on the outside. His clothes, wallet, and watch were gone. He felt the worst about losing his new jacket. The other things could be replaced, but the jacket couldn't.

"Hey, nice jacket," Derek had taunted as he pulled it over Michael's head fifteen minutes earlier. He had held it to his chest and sneered, "I like it. Thanks, dude."

Michael staggered to his feet. He felt wobbly. Gravel dug into his feet as he hobbled back toward Barrymore, about ten miles away. He drew lots of attention as he stumbled along dressed only in his undershorts. As cars approached, he would stick out his thumb, hoping some kind soul would show him mercy. Most, however, just slowed down for a good look, maybe a horn honk, and then sped away. After he had struggled along for close to a mile, a car finally pulled over and stopped.

The driver lowered his window and asked Michael, "Would you like a ride, son?"

"Yes, sir. I sure would."

Michael breathed a sigh of relief as he hopped into the back seat. The driver pulled onto the highway and looked back at Michael. "Do you want to talk about it, son?"

"No, sir. I'd just as soon not."

"I understand. Where are you going?"

"Barrymore, sir."

"Do you live there?"

"Yes, sir."

"Okay. When we get to Barrymore, let me know how to get to your house, okay?"

"Yes. Thank you, sir."

***

Michael and his parents had a quiet meal that evening in lieu of the birthday celebration that had been planned. All invitations were canceled. No one in the Shepherd family felt like partying. "We'll just postpone it for now," Mom decided. "We can do it later." Everyone readily agreed.

Michael explained what happened in the hitchhiking incident but didn't go into any detail. Of course, the elephant in the room was the adoption issue, but no one wanted to tackle that subject on this dramatic night. There would be time for that discussion when Michael's nerves were not teetering on a thin edge.

"Did you film the game, Dad?" Michael asked as he pushed away from the table.

"Yes, I did. Would you like me to set it up so we could watch it together?" George asked.

"No, I'd rather watch it alone if you don't mind."

"I understand. It's in the study. Watch it anytime you'd like."

"Okay, thanks, Dad," Michael said. "I'll watch it in my room if that's okay."

"Sure, no problem."

Michael entered his room and turned on the overhead light. He placed his dad's camera next to the television receiver on his dresser and plugged it in. He then walked over to his bed, fluffed his pillows, and sat with his back against the headboard, cushioned by three pillows. When he was comfortable, he picked up his phone.

"Wow. Nine o'clock already," he muttered. "I hope she's still up."

Michael held his phone for several minutes and silently rehearsed his planned remarks for Ashley when she answered his call. Once he was satisfied, he hit the speed-dial button. After several rings, he heard Ashley's voice.

"Hello."

"Hi, Ashley. It's me, Michael."

"I know who it is."

"Oh, sure you do. How are you doing?"

"Good. Why are you calling?"

"Well, two reasons. I was just wondering how you're doing, and two…"

"I said, I'm doing fine."

"Two is," Michael cleared his throat and asked, "When are you going to keep your end of our deal?"

"Deal? What deal? What are you talking about, Michael Shepherd?'

There was a long pause. Finally, Michael broke the silence: "Don't you remember saying you would go out with me if I scored a goal in the Langford game?"

There was another pause. Michael's heart began to beat rapidly as he waited for Ashley to respond. It didn't take long. With a loud sigh, she said, "You scored a goal for the wrong team, Michael. You scored a goal for Langford."

Michael had prepared himself for that objection. "That doesn't matter. Our deal had no conditions. You said you would go out with me if I scored a goal, and I scored a goal. Nothing was said about which team. We made a deal, and I expect you to keep your end of the bargain. So, what day? How about next Saturday?"

There was another long pause. Then Ashley said, "Michael, I'm sorry. I'm not interested in going out with you, not now anyway.... Probably not ever. Good night, Michael."

"But we had a deal...."

"Good night, Michael." Ashley was gone.

Michael set his phone down on a bed cabinet, sighed deeply, and laid back against his pillows. He stared at his television for a few minutes, then reached over, picked up a remote, and turned it on. After a few minutes of manipulating the TV remote, the recorded game against Langford appeared on the screen.

Michael watched as the game proceeded to the first score when Barrymore went up one-nil on a well-placed penalty kick by Ian Gregson, Barrymore's striker. For the rest of the first half, there was plenty of action but no scoring.

During halftime, George Shepherd had spent several minutes filming the crowd, the school bands, and a few family friends. He also had some footage of Ashley and her friends. Michael wondered if his dad knew he had some interest in her.

Probably not. I never talked to them about Ashley.

The game was well into the second half when Langford scored its tying goal on the play just before Barrymore's center back was hurt. Michael's entry into the game followed that. Unfortunately, from then on, the camera focused on Michael's every move. Michael shuddered as he watched Langford's number ten blow by him with little effort, followed by his shot, which was deflected over the goal. He watched the corner kick and the ball ricocheting off the back of his head into the net for the winning goal.

Michael rolled his eyes as he watched the confusion that followed. He cringed at the mocking back-pats from the Langford players, the cheering from the home crowd, and the head shaking by the Barrymore team and fans as they walked away from the field. He was saddened to see Ashley staring at him with her hands on her hips and looking as disgusted as he had ever seen her. Michael watched this film segment several times, hoping to see at least one positive thing he could rejoice over. But there weren't any. Finally, he turned off the television, stretched out on his bed, and stared at the ceiling.

Michael lay there for hours, thinking through everything that had happened in the last two days. It was disgusting. He tried to sleep, but his heart and mind were so burdened that he could not. After all that consideration, Michael Shepherd came to a final conclusion:

Yes, I'm a loser!

Except for an occasional trip to the refrigerator or bathroom, Michael remained in his room that night and all the next day. His mind wandered to his unknown biological parents. *Who were they? Are they still living, and where? What do they look like? I wonder why they gave me up for adoption. I wonder if my real dad was an athlete. I wonder if they ever wonder about me. I wonder if I could find them and maybe get to know them. That would be pretty cool.*

"Michael, are you okay?" Michael's mom asked through the

closed door several times throughout the day.

"Yeah, Mom. I'm fine."

"Would you like some company?"

"No thanks, Mom. I'll be out soon."

"Can I bring you something to eat?" she asked, concern in her voice.

"Maybe later, Mom. I'm okay for now."

The hours ticked away, and by late Sunday evening, Michael finally realized he had arrived at a crossroads in his life. Something had to change. *So, what's it going to be?* Michael thought. *I hate my life. I'm a world-champion loser. I'm not a good teammate. I have no close friends. The girl I like thinks I'm a joke. My family's not really my family and has been lying to me for years. I've been beaten, stripped, and humiliated. My dad's disappointed in me. My life stinks. That about sums up the life and times of Michael Shepherd.*

So, what happens now? Where do I go from here? I can quit school, leave home, start taking drugs, and check out. Would anybody care? Well, yeah, my mom, of course. I guess my dad would, too. Coach, some of my teammates, maybe most of them, I don't know. I don't know any of them that well. Carson Trotter would have to find a new caddy. That's not a big deal. Oh yeah, I need to call him and apologize. I let him down. Yeah, that's right, Michael Messup strikes again.

Michael chewed on those thoughts multiple times as he lay on his bed and stared at the ceiling. Checking out would certainly be the easy way to go. He had known some who had chosen the psychedelic route. But as he thought of them and the pitiful lives they were now living, he decided they were still losers, even worse off than before.

Yeah, I could go that route.

Or, I could try to be like Joseph! Put all this stuff behind me and excel at something... like soccer, like becoming a leader. Coach Patton said I had the tools to be a good player. I'm certain Coach would not say anything he didn't really believe was true.

Yes, that's it, Michael! You are going to change. You are going to get serious. You are going to start working out, lifting weights, and running every day. You will become a starter on the soccer team. You will become a leader on the field and in the classroom, and you are going to win Ashley's heart. As a matter of fact, at the end of the day, she will be chasing you.

A smile crossed Michael's face as this final resolution came to mind. *Last but not least, Michael, you are going to hunt Derek down, and when you find him, you are going to beat him to the last inch of his miserable life!*

CHAPTER 3

The following Saturday morning, five Barrymore soccer players were in a circle on the school soccer pitch, passing a soccer ball back and forth as coach Patton walked from his car toward the players, clipboard in hand. The players paid no attention to the coach as they focused on the skills needed to receive and deliver crisp passes to one another. However, they did interrupt their routine when they noticed a sixth player emerge from his pickup truck, which was back in action due to a recently installed reconditioned carburetor, and jog toward them. That player was Michael Shepherd. Michael and Coach Patton reached the circle of players at the same time. Michael joined the players.

Coach Patton greeted the players, "Good morning, men. As you were, please."

The players began again, including Michael in their passing drill. Throughout the next two hours, Coach Patton took the players through several soccer drills, ending with a three-on-three scrimmage. Michael, though not the most skilled of the players, made an impressive account of himself and, by the end of the practice, had won a new measure of respect from his teammates.

After the scrimmage, coach Patton called his players together. "Thanks for coming out today, men. It's important to remember these Saturday get-togethers are on a volunteer basis, so you can work on your skills. I'm glad you're here. Take a couple of laps, and we're done."

The players began to run, mainly in pairs. Michael was not paired with anyone initially, but as he ran, he was soon joined by Jake Ledger, center midfielder and team captain.

"I'm surprised you came out, Mike. Glad you did," Jake said as they jogged together. "Are you pushing for more playing time?"

"Yeah, I want to get better," Michael said. "I know I've got a long way to go, but maybe someday I'll be able to help the team. I hope so, anyway."

"Good deal, man," Jake said with a smile. "I'd be glad to help you if you want to add extra time. Let me know."

The boys ran together in silence for several minutes. As their pace slowed on the final lap, Michael said, "I can stay a while today."

For the next three hours, Michael and Jake worked together one-on-one. Jake took the lead as they worked on ball control, shooting, marking, and tackling.

"Watch the ball," Jake insisted as he offered it with one foot, suddenly pulling it back and moving it sideways to get past Michael's position. "Never take your eye off the ball. Wait for your chance to disrupt your opponent, then move in quickly, always maintaining your balance. Tackle hard! Be aggressive! Use your body, but keep your arms inside."

Finally, Jake looked at his watch and said, "I need to get going, Mike. But you're doing great. You can do a lot of stuff on your own. You don't need me. Work on your juggling. Find a wall you can pound the ball against, and work on ball control. We'll get together again soon, okay?"

Michael held out a sweaty hand and said, "I appreciate this,

Jake."

"No problem, man. Are you heading out too?"

"No, I might hang around for a while longer. I need to do some work while I have a goal to work with. "Uh, do you want another go at it tomorrow morning?"

"Oh, no thanks," Jake said. "Tomorrow is church day for me and my family."

Michael, surprised at Jake's answer, was slow to respond. "Oh, okay. Do you go to church every Sunday?"

"Sure do. Would you like to go with me tomorrow?"

"Oh, no thanks, Jake. I'm not a church guy,"

"Hmm, I see. Well, I'm not as much a church guy as a Jesus guy. I'm available if you'd ever like to talk about it."

"Okay, thanks, Jake. See you Monday."

With that, Jake turned and headed for his truck. With a strong leg, Michael stepped up to his soccer ball and powered it into the back of the net. He retrieved his ball and did it again—and again—until he had taken fifty shots on goal. Michael finished his workout by running four laps around the soccer field and thirty minutes of juggling practice. Michael was tired but felt good about himself as he returned to his truck that afternoon.

As he drove home, two thoughts dominated his mind. The first was how he was going to spend tomorrow pounding his ball against the garage wall of their home, juggling, dribbling through a maze of cones, lifting weights, and running up to Horseshoe Bend and back a five-mile trek each way. The second was: *What was Jake talking about when he said he was not a church guy, he was a Jesus guy? What's the difference?*

***

The following morning, Michael's mom, Abigail, was busy in the kitchen. Michael entered the room, smiled at his mom, sat down at the breakfast counter, and started dishing himself up some dry cereal, which he topped off with some fresh strawberries and milk.

"Where's Dad?" Michael asked.

"He had an early tee time this morning. He should be home by noon," she responded with a smile.

"Okay, good." After gulping down a spoonful of flakes, he muttered, "Hey, Mom, I've got a question for you."

"Okay," she said, sitting down next to him. "What might that be?"

"Did you and Dad ever try to find out who my real parents were?"

"No, son, we never did," Abigail said with a sigh. "We were advised not to at the time."

"Why? Was it illegal or something?"

"No, I don't think it was illegal. They just advised against it. I guess it would be less complicated for everyone that way."

"So, you have no idea who it was?"

"No, we don't."

"Where did you adopt me then?"

"In Portland. We drove there, picked you up at The Good Samaritan Hospital, and brought you home the next day. We were very proud to have you in the family, and we still are. Your dad and I love you very much," she said, placing her hand over his.

Michael pushed his empty bowl aside and said, "I know you

do, Mom. I'm glad you got me." He stood up and put his bowl in the sink.

Mom wiped her already-dampened eyes with the corner of her apron and crept over to hug Michael.

As she walked away, Michael asked, "Mom, I've got another question for you."

"What's that?" Abigail asked.

"Did Dad ever play sports? He never talks about it if he did."

"No, son. Your dad lived on a farm. He never had time for sports when he was growing up."

"Okay, Mom. One final question."

"Michael, you are wearing me out," she laughed. "What?"

"Why don't we ever go to church?"

Abigail Shepherd paused to gather her thoughts. Then she said, "Well, we just never have, Michael. We weren't raised that way. Neither one of us. We never thought it was that important, I guess. Why do you ask?"

"Oh, Jake mentioned it at practice yesterday, that's all. He said his family goes to church every Sunday."

"Who's Jake?" Abigail asked.

"A player on our team. He asked me if I would like to go with him sometime."

"Well, that would be up to you, son. Like I say, we never wanted to join a church."

"Okay, Mom. I understand. I'm going to dig our old barbell out of the garage and pump some iron this morning."

"Hmm. Why are you going to do that?"

"It will make it easier to kill Derek," Michael muttered quietly.

"What's that, Michael?" Abigail asked.

"I'm just going to improve my skills, Mom," Michael responded as he left the kitchen.

"Okay, Michael. Be careful you don't drop them on your toe."

"Don't worry, Mom. I'll protect my toes," Michael called back, followed by a muttered, "I'll need them to kick Derek's teeth in."

***

The Barrymore Huskies had no game scheduled for the following week, so there were five straight days of hard practices, giving the injured players a chance to heal. It also gave Michael an opportunity to work on his soccer skills under the close supervision of Coaches Patton and Agular. He worked within a group of defenders coached by Coach Agular. Agular would play balls onto the pitch with the boys in small groups, pushing hard to win every loose ball and to put it into play to begin an offensive attack. These drills were repeated until Coach was satisfied with what he saw. Other routines included bringing the offensive players in one-on-one drills against the defenders from thirty yards outside the goal area. Michael worked hard to compete and showed enhanced improvement by the end of the week.

After the final practice on Friday, Coach Agular caught Michael by the arm as he was leaving the practice field.

"You're looking good, Mike," he said, clapping Michael on the back. "I like your renewed effort. Keep it up. We'll make a defender out of you yet."

"Thanks, Coach," Michael responded with conviction. Extra hours of practice, running, and lifting weights every day added to an ever-increasing sense of self-confidence. Michael knew his skill levels were progressing. He was building muscle, running faster, and his endurance was higher. All these factors were bound to result in his ultimate goal: more playing time.

The next Saturday, ten players were on the practice pitch warming up as Coach Patton got out of his car and walked to the field. Michael was there, and so was Jake Ledger. After some opening ball skill drills, Coach Patton pulled the boys together and said, "We're playing Willowdale next week. They are a decent team, but we can beat them if we open the field up and force them to bring their outside defenders out wide, opening the middle for our two strikers to have room to pressure their center back and their goalkeeper. That means we need maximum speed on the outside."

Coach Patton paused for a moment and thoughtfully studied the group of players standing before him. Then he said, "Line up, men. I'm going to let you do some wind sprints," which elicited several moans from the young men.

The players formed a straight line across the field. The coach moved down the field fifty yards, put his whistle in his mouth, and blew it loudly. The young men accelerated to their top speeds and covered the area in seconds. To everyone's surprise, Michael was the first player to reach the coach.

Coach Patton ran back to the starting line, turned, and blew his whistle. The players responded by racing to the starting line at their top speeds. Once again, Michael finished in first place. This running drill was repeated two more times. There were some differences among the top finishers, but Michael was the fastest runner each time.

The coach broke the players into small groups for ball control and shooting drills. He ended the practice with the outside wingers and midfielders attacking down the wings and crossing the ball to the strikers and midfielders. When Michael started toward his usual defensive position, Coach Patton hollered, "Mike, I want you to join the offense on the left side."

Michael was surprised by the change but immediately raced to join the wingers on the left side. At the end of the practice, Coach Patton called the team together. "Great job, men. Go home and get some rest. We'll pick it up from here on Monday."

Some of the boys began to gather their things together and head for the parking area. Michael sat down on the grass and thought about the practice he had just finished. He felt good about his performance as he watched the players depart. He was excited about the possibility of moving to a wing position, admitting that, at the same time, he needed a lot more practice working with the ball at his feet. Then, he thought about Ashley and wondered how she might respond if he called her again. Then an unwelcome thought interrupted him:

Should I try to locate my real parents?

He shook his head, trying to clear his mind. Instead, an image of Derek jumped into his brain.

I know one thing: if I ever see that guy again, I am going to kill him.

"Good practice, Mike. Our extra work paid off, right?" Jake said as he plopped down beside Michael. "You've got some serious after-burners, bruh. Where have you been hiding them all this time?"

"I don't know, it just didn't seem to matter before, I guess," Michael replied with a huge grin.

"Now it does? What happened?" Jake asked.

Michael paused thoughtfully. Then he laughed, "Joseph."

"Joseph?" Jake asked.

"Yeah. Look in your Bible, dude."

"Oh, that Joseph. How do you know about him?"

"Coach told me." Michael stood and challenged Jake. "Are you good for another hour or so?"

"Sure, why not?"

The boys stood and raced to the nearby goal with their soccer balls at their feet. Both struck their soccer balls at the same moment. Both balls rocketed into the back of the net, Michael's upper right and Jake's lower left. The boys high-fived one another. Michael felt the strength of a growing relationship with Jake and their shared excitement to reach a common goal.

CHAPTER 4

Morning classes started early in Barrymore. Michael's first class was American History, taught by Coach Patton. As was his custom, Coach Patton stood by the door as the kids entered the classroom. He greeted each student with a fist bump or a pat on the shoulder. It was obvious that Patton loved his students and, for the most part, was loved by them. As was also his custom, Coach Patton would have one of the students take roll once everyone was seated.

"Maggie will take roll and handle announcements this week," he announced from behind his desk. "Maggie, the floor is yours."

Maggie, a tall, slender girl wearing flowery, horn-rimmed glasses, stood with a clipboard in her hand and looked around the room. All the desks were occupied except for one, Olivia Cummings' desk.

All eyes focused on Olivia's desk, including Coach Patton's, who interjected, "I talked to her pastor yesterday. He said she wouldn't be at school for a while."

"Do we know what happened, Coach?" Maggie asked.

"All we know is that Olivia was coming home from a date, and the car she was in went out of control and rolled down an embankment," Coach said sadly. "She was not wearing a seatbelt and was thrown out of the car."

"Was the guy she was with hurt?" Jake Ledger asked.

"Apparently not. Just Olivia," Coach responded.

"We should send her a card from the class!" Maggie said.

Coach Patton looked at Maggie with a smile and said, "That's a good idea, Maggie. Will you get that started?"

"Yes, sir!"

"Thank you. Now, what about the announcements, Maggie?"

Maggie looked out at her classmates and then read from her notes, "There will be a Husky Highlights staff meeting after school Wednesday, a school assembly meeting Friday at 2:45 p.m., and, of course, a soccer game at home Friday night against Willowdale."

"Come out and support the team!" Coach Patton added as he stepped to the front of the classroom. "Good job, Maggie. Now, let's talk about our Constitution. Last semester and part of this semester, we learned a lot about our nation's Constitution. This month, and probably for the rest of our spring semester, we will be talking about our country's Bill of Rights and many of our founding fathers as well. So, who can tell me, what is this country's Bill Of Rights?"

"The first ten amendments to the Constitution," came a voice from the middle of the classroom.

"Right. Thank you, Gracie. So, Gracie, which amendment should we start with?" Coach asked.

"How about number one?" Gracie quipped.

"A wise suggestion, Gracie. Why don't you stand and read amendment number one for us, please?"

Gracie, a petite, dark-haired girl with braces, stood beside her desk and read from her notes: "Congress shall make no law respecting an establishment of religion or prohibiting the free exercise thereof, or abridging the freedom of speech, or of the press, or the right of the people peaceably to assemble, and to petition the Government for a redress of grievances."

"Wow, that's saying a lot, isn't it, Gracie?" Coach Patton remarked.

"Yes, sir," she said as she sat back down.

"Well, let's break that down into segments and see how far we get this morning." The coach looked around the room and spotted a student who seemed not to be paying attention.

"Baker!"

Grant Baker snapped straight up in his chair and replied, "Yes, sir."

"How are you this morning, Baker?"

"Uh, fine, sir."

"How do you take this beginning segment of the First Amendment to the Constitution?" Coach asked.

"The beginning segment, sir? Uh, well, I think it's a good one, sir," Baker stuttered.

"You do? Please tell the class what you think is so good about it."

"Well, if it's an amendment, it makes it better than what was there before it got there. Doesn't it?"

Coach Patton shook his head slightly with a disappointed look and said, "Baker, I suggest you stay alert while in my classroom. Okay?"

"Yes, sir," Baker said as he slumped into his chair.

"Rad, how are you this morning?" Coach continued.

Radford sat up straight in his chair. "Good, sir. Very good.

How are you doing?"

"I'm doing well, Rad. Thank you for asking."

"Oh, yes, sir. Anytime, sir."

Coach smiled and asked, "Rad, what are your thoughts regarding the First Amendment, particularly the first section?"

"I think it's right on target, sir."

"How's that, Rad?"

"Well, I guess what it's saying is, the government can't force you to adopt a particular religion that you don't believe in."

"Okay, Rad," Coach said with a smile. Give me an example of what you mean by that."

"Well, if I don't believe in God, the government can't put me in jail. Or if I don't believe in Muhammad, they can't take away my citizenship like they might do in a Muslim country."

At that point, a student named Wendy raised her hand.

Coach Patton looked at her and said, "Yes, Wendy. What are your thoughts?"

"What if the religion was anti-American and its purpose was to overthrow our government?" she asked.

"That is a great question, Wendy. What do you think?"

Wendy locked eyes with Coach and replied with confidence, "I don't think they should have the right to live in this country if they want to overthrow our government."

Coach Patton looked around the room. All the students were sitting up, showing great interest in the discussion. "What do you think, class? Should we allow folks to live here if they hate our republic and want to overthrow our government?"

From around the room, there were many utterances of "No. No

way, Coach!"

Coach Patton paced around the classroom. Then he stopped and asked, "But what about freedom of speech?"

"Yeah, what about that?" Baker spoke out loudly as he glanced at the coach.

"It still would be wrong. People shouldn't be allowed to undermine our government," Michael chimed in.

"If you believe that, you don't believe in freedom of speech," Maggie rebutted.

After a pause, Coach Patton said, "That's the problem. Here is a truth we Americans have had to deal with from the very beginning. Americans must recognize that a democracy like ours sows within itself the seeds of its own destruction. That is why we need to ensure we exercise our right to vote and vote for strong and righteous legislators who will fight to protect our freedoms. That is why we fought two world wars, and that is why we maintain a strong military. It is also why we cherish our right to vote for our leaders and then hold them accountable for how they perform their jobs."

The classroom went momentarily quiet again as the students were left to contemplate the points Coach Patton had made. That quietness was soon interrupted by the shrill sound of a bell signaling the end of the first period. "Okay, that's it for this morning," Coach Patton announced, "Your homework is to memorize the First Amendment by the end of the week. If you can say it to the class perfectly, word for word, you will bank 10,000 Husky Points. So, get on it. I'll see you in the morning."

The students all stood and left the room, followed by Coach Patton.

Michael headed down the hall to a long row of lockers. As he stopped at his locker, he noticed Ashley in front of her locker in the midst of several girls chatting together as they retrieved and deposited books and notebooks. Of course, she didn't notice him.

His short-lived trance was interrupted by a familiar voice coming from behind.

"Are you ready to move out to a wing position this afternoon?"

Michael turned to see Jake with a massive grin on his face.

"What makes you think that's going to happen?" Michael replied.

"Because it makes sense!" Jake said.

"Really? How's that?"

"Coach likes your left foot and your speed," Jake said with a smile. "It looks like Austin is ready to go back to center back, which will move Nolan back to the left side on defense, which means you could move up to wing on the left side."

"What about Taylor? Where's he going to go?" Michael asked.

"That will be up to you. You will have to win the job away from him. Coach is going to start the best player at every position. We all have to fight to keep our jobs, including me."

"I don't think you have anything to worry about, Jake. Nobody's going to take your job," Michael chuckled.

"You never know, my friend. I play for the Lord's pleasure, not my own."

Michael, taken aback by Jake's statement, was slow to respond. "I'm not sure I follow that."

"You don't? Well, let me put it this way. The Bible has a lot to say about pride, like pride being the 'root of all kinds of evil.' God hates pride. That's why I try not to get too puffed up about myself. Do you see what I'm saying?"

"Well, kind of. But I guess I'll have to think about it."

"Okay. There will be time for that. Meanwhile, we'd better get going or be late for chemistry."

Michael looked at his watch and closed his locker. "Yeah, we better step it up. We wouldn't want to upset Mr. Brooks. We might have to listen to his 'Word to the Wise' spiel for the umpteenth time. Let's go."

Ashley left her locker at the same moment and moved ahead of the two boys on their way to the chemistry lab. She looked nice, wearing a pink blouse and a short black skirt.

"Now, that's the kind of chemistry I'm into," Michael said with a quiet laugh.

***

Practice that afternoon and the following three afternoons was centered around ball control drills for all the players, free kicks, and corner kick defense, followed by a ninety-minute scrimmage. With the team divided into two squads of eleven, Michael got a lot of time at left wing. Both sides attacked from the back, moving the ball quickly through midfield where the mid-fielders could distribute the ball to the outside for long runs and crosses into the middle for shots on goal opportunities. The practice seemed unending, and the boys were grouped in bent-over positions as they waited between charges on goal. At the same time, though far from perfect, Michael felt confident in his own performance. He was also impressed by the masterful job Jake was doing directing traffic from his midfield position for the offense.

On Thursday afternoon, Coach Patton cut the practice short by half an hour. The players gathered around him, sitting on the ground and removing their shoes and socks.

"Well, I think we got everything we wanted to accomplish this week, men," Coach smiled. "I believe we are as ready as we can be. We've had a week to get ready for Willowdale. We have a long season ahead of us. We can square things up tomorrow night by beating Willowdale. I think we will do that. What do you think?"

"We've got this, Coach!" Austin Davis spoke out.

Jake stood up and quietly looked around at his teammates and then at Coach Patton. "This is the last year for me and many of us, Coach. This is going to be *our* year. We are going to get a win Friday night and then annihilate everybody else as we blow through the rest of the schedule. I feel it. I know it! We won't let you down, Coach, and we won't let the city of Barrymore down. Do you agree with me, guys?"

All the boys rose to their feet and shouted out, "Go! Huskies! Go! Huskies!" Their voices echoed across the playing field as they fist-bumped and clapped each other on the back. Michael felt his heart swell with pride.

Coach Patton stepped into the middle of the group and put his hands up to quiet the uproar. "Okay, men. Go home, eat a nice meal with your family, and get a good night's sleep. Oh yeah, and don't forget your homework. Game time is 7:00 p.m. Be here at 6, ready to lace up your boots and play some soccer." Pumped up, the Huskies left the practice field.

CHAPTER 5

Michael and his parents sat at the kitchen table for dinner. Mom had prepared a family favorite: stew with vegetables, cornbread, and corn on the cob. Michael loaded up his stew with a thick covering of tomato ketchup and, when everyone was seated, dug in.

Mr. Shepherd smiled as he looked at Michael's plate, "Did you get enough ketchup, Michael?"

"Yeah, I think so, Dad," Michael said with a laugh. "You should try it."

"I don't think so, bud," George said. "Not today, anyway."

Michael took another bite, then looked at his parents. "Dad, Mom, I've been thinking, you know... about being adopted."

Both parents stopped eating and looked at Michael. George asked, "So, what are your thoughts?"

"Well, I can't stop wondering about my biological parents; you know, who they are and what they look like. I know you are my mom and dad, and you raised me. Nothing can change that. But I would like to try to find them..." Michael hesitated. "Would you mind if I did that?"

Mr. and Mrs. Shepherd exchanged quick, uncomfortable glances at one another and then looked back to Michael.

Mr. Shepherd cleared his throat, looked again at Abigail, and finally said, "I guess we would have no objections to that, Michael. However, I'm not sure how you would do that."

"Well, didn't you go through an adoption agency?" Michael asked.

"Yes, we did. But we used a lawyer who specialized in adoptions. He worked for a law firm in Portland," Abigail explained.

"What was the name of it?" Michael asked.

"Hmm, I'm not sure right now, but we have it in our files, of course," George said.

"So, you don't mind if I check it out?"

"No, of course not. However, I'm sure there will be some costs involved. That could be a problem. Lawyers don't come cheap," Mr. Shepherd responded.

"Hmm," Michael said. "I hadn't thought about that. That might be a game-changer."

"Might be, Michael. We would need a clear estimate of those costs before we began."

"That's okay, Dad. Let me think about it."

"Okay, as long as we have that understanding," George said before changing the subject. "So, who do you play tomorrow night?"

"Willowdale. "Should be a good game."

"We'll be there," Mr. Shepherd said with a smile.

"I know you will. Thanks, Dad. Oh, by the way, the coach has moved me up to a wing position."

"Really? Why did he do that?" George asked, surprised.

Michael paused for a moment, not sure how to answer. Then he said, "Coach Patton just wanted to try me at a different position."

"Hmm, okay, and how do you feel about that?"

"Good," Michael said, excited for them to see him play.

"We'll be proud of you whatever position you play, Michael," Abigail said.

"Thanks, Mom."

***

Friday night was game night. To Michael, it seemed like the whole town had turned out as he and his teammates ran out onto the field and began their stretches and personal warmup routines. Within minutes, the team formed two lines at midfield and took shots on goal, with Matt Arnold in goal and Coach Patton and Coach Agular distributing the balls.

It was a cool, clear night, perfect for soccer. Willowdale players were at the other end of the field doing their own warmups. Their team looked sharp in their black uniforms and precise ball control. They also typically looked bigger and older than the Barrymore squad. But that didn't dampen the enthusiasm for Barrymore. Their fans were loud and boisterous, anxious to see the referee march to the center of the field and blow his whistle to start the game.

As the starters were announced, Coach Patton and Coach Agular gathered with the players on their touchline. The lineup was the same as it had been against Langford two weeks earlier.

With sixteen players suited up for the game, Coach Patton addressed the team: "Okay, men, we have ninety minutes of soccer ahead of us. Stay under control. Play the ball to open spaces. Be patient. Move the ball around in the back and play it forward when you see an opportunity. Force them to the margins. Okay? Let's go!"

The team broke away after a loud shout of "Go Huskies!"

Michael had mixed emotions as he returned to the bench: disappointment and relief. He was disappointed that he wasn't starting, but he was also slightly relieved. He knew he would be given some playing time and vowed to himself that he would make the most of it when he did.

The game got underway with an immediate attack by Willowdale charging down the right side, making a dangerous cross into the Barrymore penalty box. The tall center forward for Willowdale headed the ball to the far post, which took a miraculous save by Matt Arnold, who punched the ball out to the right to the feet of a Barrymore defender, who then played the ball into the middle to the feet of Jake Ledger who began an attack on goal by swinging the ball to the right midfielder, Loronzo Gonzales. Loronzo quickly played the ball into the feet of right-wing Chris Carson, streaking down the right side for an excellent cross into the penalty box, but unfortunately, intercepted and played away by a defending Willowdale center back.

For the remainder of the first half, the game flowed back and forth up and down the pitch. When the whistle sounded, ending the first half, both teams went to their respective dressing rooms. The halftime score was zero to zero.

In the dressing room, Coach Patton gave his players time to gather their thoughts and drink some liquids before stepping to the middle of the room. He held up his hand to stop the chatter.

"I'm seeing some good things out there, men. You are keeping the ball in front of you on the defensive side, and everyone is defending well. That's great. Good defense wins games. But it looks to me like we are playing not to lose. We are making it too easy on them. We attack but ease up the pressure when we should be increasing the pressure. I want you to play this second half, giving them no mercy. Press them. Don't let up. Defenders, you are hanging back, waiting for them to come to you. Don't do that! Press forward! Attack! Keep them under constant pressure. Listen to your goalkeeper. He can see the whole field and take care of his area at the same time. Get back when he tells you to, but then push forward. You got it? Let's play to win, okay?"

The team stood as one. It was clear they bought into what Coach Patton was saying.

"Our only lineup change is that I'm putting Mike in at left wing to bring us more speed down the left side. Most of our attacks have been from the right. This change should give them something to think about if we swing left with a new player on the pitch. So, work it around in the back through midfield, then BAM, up the left side where we can put their right back under some real pressure. Okay, let's go, Huskies!"

"LET'S GO, HUSKIES!"

The Barrymore Huskies charged out the dressing room door and onto the field, greeted by scattered cheers from their loyal Barrymore fans.

As Barrymore took to the field, Willowdale was already lined up and ready for them. The second half began slowly, with Barrymore controlling the ball from the back as they had picked up ball possession from a failed Willowdale charge down their right sideline. Several minutes passed before left-back Alexander Pittman controlled the ball and played it forward to Jake. Jake received the ball at midfield and relayed it to Lorenzo Gonzales on a give-and-go. Lorenzo barreled down the right side and then sent the ball back into the middle, where Jake controlled it and then played it into space, where he saw Michael streaking down the left side to fill. Michael trapped the well-played ball near the touchline and sped past a hesitant right back toward the corner flag. Then suddenly, Michael played the ball with his left foot into the box, where striker Ian Gregson buried it with a rocket shot into the back of the net. The home crowd roared their approval. Barrymore was up by one goal with thirty minutes left in the game.

For the remaining time, Barrymore played the game Coach Patton had drawn up for them. They kept Willowdale under constant pressure by moving their defenders into forward positions and only retreating when goalkeeper Arnold called them back. Michael's speed was a definite factor in keeping the Willowdale right-back on his heels for the remainder of the game. The final score was one to nothing, Barrymore.

Michael felt good about the game and how he had played. However, his spirits took a sudden downturn as he left the field. He looked for Ashley, hoping to talk with her about the game and ask her out again. His hopes were dashed when he spotted her leaving the game hand in hand with Daniel Fountain, a local drifter known to have a rough reputation and sour attitude.

"Great win, men," Coach Patton commented in the dressing room after the game. "We controlled the game in the second half and got the win. Did we play a perfect game? No, and we never will. However, we moved a step in that direction, and you should feel thankful for that. Did I say proud? No. Pride always leads to destruction. I said, be thankful. Go home, listen to Mom and Dad, be gracious to your siblings, and have a good weekend. I'll see you next week."

***

When Michael opened the front door to the Shepherd home,

he was greeted by his parents. George Shepherd was seated in his leather recliner, and Abigail was in a recliner nearby.

"Well, the victor has arrived!" George said, grinning profusely as his son placed his bag down and sat on a fabric armchair. Great game, son."

"Thank you, Dad."

"It was a close game," Abigail remarked. "What did the coach say about it?"

Michael smiled, "He was glad to get the win."

"Of course!" George exclaimed.

Mom interjected, "Carson Trotter called. He'd like you to caddy for him tomorrow."

"Really? I'm surprised about that after I stood him up a few weeks ago."

"You called him, didn't you?" she asked.

"Yes, I did."

"Well, I told him you would call him. Do you want to caddy tomorrow?" Abigail asked.

"Not really. I hate to miss soccer practice, but I probably should, considering the circumstances..." Michael hesitated.

"You can take the car tomorrow if you'd like," George offered.

"You're not playing golf tomorrow?" Abigail asked.

"Nope. No tee times were available because of the golf tournament."

Michael stood. "I'm going to turn in. I'll text Mr. Carson about tomorrow. Good night. I'll see you in the morning."

"Good night, son. We're proud of you," George said.

Michael's parents studied him as he left the room.

"Something seems to be bothering him," his mom said when Michael was out of sight.

"Yeah, you'd think he would be pleased about the game," George replied. "He's probably upset about that girl he likes."

"Yeah, maybe so," Mom agreed. "I wish he would move on."

"That's what your mom told you, right? 'I wish you would find someone else other than that Shepherd kid.'"

"If only I'd have listened," Abigail quipped with a wink as she rose from her chair. "Good night, dear. I'm going to bed."

"Good night, dear girl. I'm going to watch the game film."

CHAPTER 6

Michael parked his dad's Lexus 350 in the LaGrange Country Club parking lot and walked toward the clubhouse. It was a lovely sunny morning, complimented by a cool northern breeze. Michael was glad he had worn a sweatshirt, which would be helpful until the day warmed up. Some golfers were already on the practice green and the driving range. He spotted Carson Trotter on the putting green as he approached the clubhouse and walked over to an area near where Carson was practicing.

When Carson saw Michael, he came off the green. "Good morning, Michael," he said as he walked toward his young caddy.

"Good morning, Mr. Trotter."

"How have you been, son?" Carson said fondly. "I've missed seeing you out here each week. I'm glad you're back."

"Thank you, sir. It's good to be here. Can we talk for a few minutes?"

Carson glanced at his watch and said, "I don't have time right now, Michael. They will be calling me any minute to head for the tee box. If you want to grab my clubs, we should head that way now. We can talk after the match. I'll have time then."

"Yes, sir," Michael said as he hit a fast pace to grab Carson's clubs. Then Carson struck out ahead, joining other players on their way to the first tee box.

The game went well for Carson. His irons were working for him as he regularly put himself in good green positions on each hole. His putting, always a vital part of his game, kept him in the money. He led his group at eight under par at the end of the round.

Carson was in a good mood coming off the eighteenth green. He shook hands with his competitors and handed Michael his putter as they left the green together.

"Let's go check in the clubhouse for a minute, grab a drink, and find a place to talk," Carson said.

"Sounds good, sir," Michael responded.

Minutes later, Michael and Carson were seated in a shaded patio area near a small fountain surrounded by a flower garden of roses, gardenias, and fresh-blooming rhododendrons. Carson lifted his glass of iced tea, looked at Michael, and said, "So, tell me. What's going on, Michael?"

"Well, sir..." Michael began hesitantly. "First, please let me apologize and explain what happened to me."

"Yes, please do. I was put in an awkward situation. I'm sure you realize that. You were mugged or something?" Carson asked.

"Yes, sir, I was, and I apologize. I am very sorry. I have no excuse for not calling you." Michael paused, stirred his drink, and then looked Carson in the eyes. "In some ways, my life has been turned upside down these past few weeks."

"I accept your apology, Michael," Carson said kindly. "So tell me what's going on."

Michael described what happened to him the day he hitchhiked to LaGrange: the wild car ride nightmare, losing his clothes (including his new coat), and the embarrassment of hitching a ride back to Barrymore in his underwear.

Carson Trotter sat in quiet disbelief as Michael related his story. "Michael, I am so sorry you had to experience that," he said. "Do you have any idea who those men were? Did you file a police report?"

"No sir, on both counts," Michael responded. "Should I file a police report, or is it too late?"

"Let me look into that. I'll get back to you," Carson said. "Is there anything else you'd like to tell me?"

Michael looked down at his drink, took a sip, and set the glass back on the table. "No, there is some other stuff going on, but most of it is personal." He sat quietly for a moment, staring at his empty glass.

"I understand," Carson said quietly.

Michael looked up at Carson again. "Well, there is one thing."

"What's that, Michael?"

"I also learned that I was adopted as a baby," Micahel said slowly, looking back down at his drink.

"Really? I imagine that was a major surprise."

"Yes, sir. It was."

"So, your folks revealed that to you?"

"Yes, sir. They said it was time that I knew."

Carson paused, looked thoughtfully at Michael, and asked, "How do you feel about that, Michael?"

"Well, I was upset at first," Michael admitted. "But I'm okay with it now. Truthfully, I'm kind of excited about it. I asked them if they knew who my biological parents were, and they said they didn't. So, I'm wondering how I might go about finding that out. Would you have any advice for me on that since you're a lawyer?"

Carson sat back in his cushioned chair. Then he looked at the young man sitting before him and asked, "How old are you, Michael?"

"I just turned eighteen."

Carson paused for a moment, then pushed back in his chair.

"Well, unfortunately, in Oregon, you have to be twenty-one to initiate the process."

Michael's countenance visibly dropped at that piece of information. He didn't respond, and silence filled the table.

Carson leaned forward, looked into Michael's eyes, and said, "I'm sorry, Michael."

Michael gripped his drink with both hands. "Me too," he replied. "Do you think they ever make exceptions on that point?"

"I doubt it. But here's what I suggest we do. I will send you some paperwork to fill out, giving me all the information your mom and dad have about the adoption. Then, we'll have everything we need to move forward when the time is right. How does that sound?"

Michael looked down, stirred his drink, and then looked back at Carson. "I'm not sure how much we will be able to pay. That may be a problem."

Carson smiled, took a last swallow of his drink, and stood. "Let me worry about that. It won't be an issue, Michael." Carson reached into his pocket and retrieved a business card.

"Here you go. Write your email address on the back of this card. I'll send you the paperwork you will need to fill out. Will that work for you?"

"Yes, sir, it will," Michael said with a sigh of relief.

Carson extended his hand to Michael, and as the two shook hands, Carson said, "Don't worry, Michael. Trust the Lord. It will all work out."

As Michael drove back to Barrymore, those words kept running through his mind. "Trust the Lord, and it will all work out?" he wondered aloud.

Like, yeah. I wish it were that simple. He and Jake must be reading from the same script.

CHAPTER 7

Derek Steinman exited his house and climbed into his junky pickup truck. He slammed the vehicle into reverse and spewed five feet of gravel in the air as he ripped the truck through progressive gears. He was soon hurtling toward the city of LaGrange at seventy miles per hour. He turned onto Atlantic Avenue and continued the pace until he reached Charbonneau Park, where he pulled into a parking lot next to a black two-door 2010 model Dodge Charger. Both front doors opened on the Dodge, and Nick Foster and Joker Duff stepped out, the two friends who were with him when they abused Michael on the way to LaGrange a few weeks earlier.

Derek cranked down his window. "You got the stuff?"

"Of course," Nick smirked.

"So, what you got?"

"We got weed to tweak your illusions and a quart of Wild Crow to whet your appetite. What's your pleasure?" Joker laughed.

"A little of each," Derek said as he slid into the back seat of the automobile. By the time Nick and Joker got back in the car, Derek had already spun the cap off the bottle of Wild Crow and devoured several gulps.

The young men enjoyed reminiscing as they drank the booze and smoked their weed. Joker displayed a huge grin, exposing his lack of a few front teeth. As he looked at Derek, he said, "Hey Derek, do you remember the night we were at that Rodeo dance outside of French Camp, and we stole some dude's horse and rode it through town, hoopin' and hollerin' at everybody?"

"Yeah, man. I sure do," Derek laughed. "That horse dumped your butt in the middle of downtown French Camp. We barely made it out of town before those cowboys got their posse together and came after us. That was a close call, bruh."

Nick immediately chimed in with, "That ain't nothin'! I remember when we stole a cop's car that night outside of Blinken, Idaho."

Derek winced. "Shut up, man. I'm trying to forget that." Derek held up his right hand and pinched his thumb and middle finger together. "I came that close to goin' to the slammer' over that deal."

"Yeah, that wasn't cool, man. I agree," Joker said.

Over the years, the three boys had continually managed to stay out of jail due to sheer luck. They had never intended to be incorrigible lawbreakers—they weren't at that level yet. They just liked to get high and stir up trouble. What they enjoyed most was playing tough guy and intimidating people, especially young men they could force into a fistfight.

Derek lived in Tomika, a small town twenty miles south of LaGrange. His dad, now deceased, had been a brawler himself and taught Derek how to fight. Derek never made it past tenth grade in school. His dad made him go to work in a small sawmill where he pulled lumber from the green chain for stacking and shipping. He learned to chew tobacco, cuss, and live an undisciplined life. His two friends were a little more civilized, but they were hypnotized by Derek's leadership. Their problem was an addiction to booze, drugs, and mayhem. People who crossed paths with these three thugs usually got hurt.

After about an hour of smoking and drinking, Derek said, "Okay, it's getting dark. Let's go."

Nick asked, "Where to?"

"I don't know. Let's find some action. You brothers are boring me," Derek growled.

"Yeah, me too," Joker said. "Let's go make something happen in downtown LaGrange."

Derek took one last swallow of Wild Crow and said, "You got the keys, dude."

Joker turned the ignition on, and the three men set off to make trouble in downtown LaGrange, Oregon. It didn't take long. Just one pass down Market Street was all they needed.

Jacob Nichols, walking with his girlfriend, Madison Philips, turned from Market Street down 12th Avenue, an unlit narrow alley. They were holding hands and talking about the movie they had just seen, "The Boys in the Boat." They moved aside when a dark automobile pulled up behind them. Two of the three occupants hopped out of the car and confronted the young couple.

The two were startled and fearful. Jacob asked, "What's going on?"

"I saw you make an obscene gesture to me and my friends in the car," Derek said. "Am I right about that?"

"I didn't make any gesture at you. I didn't even see you," Jacob replied.

"My man Nick here; he saw it too. Didn't you, Nick?"

"I sure did. I was embarrassed and shocked."

Derek pushed Jacob up against the wall of a bank building.

"Don't lie to me, sonny. I don't take to liars. I want an apology."

Meanwhile, Joker had parked the car and walked into the middle of the group. Instead of joining in the confrontation with Jacob, however, he went straight for Madison Philips, according to plan and previous encounters the three had participated in many times. Joker grabbed Madison, locked her into a crude embrace, and pushed her up against the same wall.

"Leave her alone," Jacob screamed as he struggled to get away from Derek's hold on his arms and shoulders. Derek responded by pounding Jacob with his fists. Jacob fought back, but he was no match for Derek's street-fighting abilities. He was soon on the ground, where he became the recipient of Derek's severe body kicks.

Joker's assault on Madison continued until a few people began to gather, curious about what was going on. When Derek saw several in the gathering crowd activating their cell phones, he stepped away from Jacob and hollered to his two friends, "Let's go!"

Grabbing Joker's arm, he pulled him away from Madison. The three of them ran to the Charger, jumped in, and, with screeching tires, fled the scene. Several of the witnesses rushed to aid the young couple and began comforting them. Some of them ministered to Jacob, who was bleeding from his nose and had cuts on his face.

"I'm okay," he said. "Thanks, everyone." He stood quickly and walked over to Madison, who was weeping. He put his arms around her and held her quietly for several minutes. In short order, several people were in the alley, and police vehicles were howling in the distance.

Someone in the gathering crowd asked, "Did anyone get a license plate number?"

The people stared at one another for a few minutes.

"I guess not," another person said.

The bystanders continued to help the young couple as they escorted them to their car.

CHAPTER 8

Monday morning, Coach Kyle Patton stood at his classroom door, greeting his students as they entered the room with the usual high-fives and pats on the back. Once they were all in, Patton closed the door, entered the room, and sat at his desk. Ethan Maybre, a senior, stood and took role. All the students were present except for Olivia Cummings.

"Does anyone have an update on Olivia you can share?" Coach Patton asked.

"My mom talked to her mom last week," Jake offered. "She has been put in an induced coma. It's still pretty iffy. She's badly hurt. Her mom is asking for prayer."

"Okay, thank you for sharing that, Jake." Coach Patton paused and looked down momentarily, then said as he raised his eyes and looked around the room. "Okay, as you know, we spent all last week discussing the First Amendment to our Constitution. All of you were able to memorize that important amendment—some of you, perfectly. So, we are ready to move on. But before we do, I want to make sure all of you understand the amendment and its importance to this republic. Are there any questions or comments you want to make before we leave the First Amendment behind? Or does anyone want to try for the 10,000-point word perfect bonus before we move on?"

Coach Patton surveyed his class, looking for a last-minute convert. His gaze stopped at Baker, who fidgeted as if he wanted to say something. "How about it, Baker? Are you ready to move on?"

Grant Baker slowly rose to his feet. He looked at Coach Patton momentarily, scanned his classmates, cleared his throat, and began speaking. "Congress shall make no law respecting an establishment of religion or prohibiting the free exercise thereof, or abridging the freedom of speech, or the press, or the right of the people peaceably to assemble, and to petition the government for a redress of grievances." Then he bowed at the waist and sat down. His classmates were frozen in place as their eyes went from Baker to Coach Patton and back to Baker. Then Jake began to slowly clap his hands, which soon built into a full round of applause from the rest of the class.

For a moment, Coach Patton was lost for words. Then he said, "Wow! Grant, great job. You just earned yourself 10,000 points, son. I'm proud of you."

Grant Baker sloped down into his seat, grinned, and said, "Thanks, Coach."

"You're welcome, Grant."

Coach Patton turned his attention back to the class. "Now we will tackle the remaining amendments, one per day, until we get through them all, which should take us into next week. Who wants to recite the Second Amendment to our Constitution?"

After a short silence, Samantha Springside raised her hand.

"Yes, Sammy. Go ahead, please," Coach said.

Sammy stood and read from her notes: "A well-regulated Militia, being necessary to the security of a free State, the right of the people to keep and bear Arms, shall not be infringed."

"Thank you, Sammy. Can you tell me, in your own words, what

this amendment is saying?"

Sammy put her hand on the back of her chair for extra security. Then she said, "Well, I guess it says our nation needs to be able to defend itself in case there's a war or something, right?"

"That is right, Sammy," Coach Patton agreed. "Our nation must be able to defend itself against outside aggressors and, as you know, has had to do that several times. However, Article Two of the Bill of Rights doesn't refer to that. Can anyone help Sammy out here?"

Maggie raised her hand and immediately said, "The militia in the Ten Amendments refers to the independent state's militia, doesn't it?"

"Very good, Maggie," Coach Patton said. "Please go on."

"Well, the individual states were worried about having to defend themselves against their own federal government, so these amendments were designed to do that. Isn't that right?"

"That is precisely right, Maggie," Coach replied. "We were a new country, and the individual states needed to ensure they had the protections they needed as independent entities."

The coach looked around the room, waiting for follow-up commentary. Michael Shepherd raised his hand. "Yes, Mike," Coach said. "What's on your mind regarding our Second Amendment?"

"A lot of stuff is being said about the second part of that amendment," Michael began.

"Which is?"

"The right to bear arms."

"Yes, the right to keep and bear arms. You are right, Mike. "What are your thoughts about that?"

"Well, there are a lot of guns out there," Michael said.

"Yes, there are. Why is that, do you think?"

"Well, partly because people like to hunt and stuff."

"Yeah, but they sure don't need an AK-47 to do that," Avia Schuster, a diminutive blonde student wearing a western-style shirt, contributed from the middle of the room.

Several people murmured in agreement.

Coach Patton interjected, "So, for those of you who agree, are you saying we should change the law and confiscate these types of weapons from our citizens? Could we even accomplish that if it were legal?"

Again, from the back of the room came, "Not without a lot of people getting killed." This remark was closely followed by, "Nobody should be allowed to have guns at home."

"Why do people have guns anyway?" Coach Patton asked.

"To protect themselves," Matt Arnold answered.

"From whom?" Coach Patton asked, looking at Matt.

"From the bad guys," Matt responded.

"Who are the bad guys?" Coach asked.

Matt paused, then grinned. "Everybody who disagrees with me. Those are the bad guys."

Everybody in the class laughed at that remark.

Coach Patton slowly scanned the room. "Let's have some more input here. This is a subject that's on everybody's mind these days. Some folks say all guns should be turned in. Should we pass a law to confiscate all guns?"

"Yes, guns kill people!" Jayden Gilmore spoke out from his desk on the left side of the room.

"Come again, Jayden? You say *guns* kill people?" Coach asked.

"Yes, guns kill people," Jayden said, but not as forcefully as he said it the first time.

"So, Jayden, you say we should do away with all guns because guns kill people. Is that your position?"

"Yes, sir," Jayden said.

"Hmm, okay, Jayden. Let me ask you this: If you turn in an essay paper you have written, and it has several spelling errors, did your pencil make those errors?" Coach asked.

Jayden remained silent, causing an awkward tension in the room. He let out a deep sigh and slumped back in his chair. He said, "You got me coach. Sorry." Then, after a few seconds, he thrust his pencil into the air, shook it a few times, and said, "Stupid pencil!"

The class erupted into laughter.

Coach Patton waited for the noise to abate, then said, "Before we leave this morning, I want to make sure you all understand that the Bill of Rights was written on behalf of the states to protect them from incursion by the United States government. So, they were allowed to have their own militias. The Constitution of the United States provides for the United States Military, and it is there for us to deal with foreign enemies. Does everyone understand the difference?"

Several "Yes, sir"s rang forth.

"Right now," Coach Patton continued, "We have the strongest military in the world. This has cost our taxpayers billions of dollars. As a future taxpayer, that burden will be on you someday. How do you feel about that?" Coach glanced at the wall clock.

"Well, I guess we will have to tackle that question tomorrow. Good stuff, class. But we need to draw it to a close. So, here's the deal. Because gun crimes are being committed in this country at an increasing rate, should our government pass new legislation that takes away our right to keep and bear arms? Your homework assignment is to take a side, supporting your position with clear and logical arguments. Please submit a written statement to me by class time on Thursday, in five hundred words or less, defending your position. The best argument on both sides wins the writer 10,000 points."

Patton glanced again at the clock on the wall, nodded, and said, "See you tomorrow." The students stood and, not so quietly, filed out of the classroom. When they had all departed, Coach Patton gathered his papers, the book he was reading called *Fault Lines* by Voddie Bauchman, and started to leave the room. At that moment, a very attractive lady with auburn hair who looked to be in her early thirties barged through the door. The coach stopped in his tracks, surprised by the sudden interruption–and the beauty of the culprit.

"I am so sorry," she said. "But I need some help."

"Sure," Coach replied, placing his papers and books back down on his desk. "What can I do for you?"

"I'm trying to set up a video for my students, and I can't figure out how," the lady laughed. "Are you a techie by chance?"

"Somewhat. "I'd be glad to try. Um, are you a new teacher here?"

"I'm a sub, filling in for Mrs. Allen while she is on maternity leave."

"Oh, I see. Okay, let's go have a look at what you're doing," Coach Patton replied.

The coach followed the lady out the door and across the hall into a nearby classroom. At the front of the room was a television hooked up to a receiver with several unconnected electrical cords, many serving no purpose as far as the coach could determine. He checked the receiver and confirmed there was a disc inside. Then, after experimenting for several minutes with the cords, he had the video playing correctly.

By then, students were entering the classroom and beginning to sit in their assigned seats. The substitute teacher walked to the large whiteboard and wrote:

"Good morning, students. My name is Miss Leanard."

Then she turned to the class and said with a smile, "I will be substituting for Mrs. Allen for the next several weeks until she can return from her maternity leave. I'm excited to be here! Today, we will be focusing on Short Story Writing. We will start by watching a short video." With that, Miss Leanard looked at the coach and nodded.

Coach Patton could see some confusion in the student's eyes as they bounced back and forth between Miss Leanard and himself. He also sensed some nervousness in the new teacher's voice and body language. He knew the kids could sense it too and might put her to the test if given the chance. He pushed the remote's on-button and eased into a chair in the back of the classroom.

With the coach in the room, the students paid rapt attention to the video and became actively involved in the discussion that followed. When he was satisfied that Miss Leanard had everything under control, Coach Patton departed.

***

Michael Shepherd was seated at the dining room table, eating from a bowl of vanilla ice cream with his left hand and writing in a notebook with his right hand. Even though he was born left-handed, he always wrote with his right hand–a perfect combination for eating ice cream and studying at the same time.

Mrs. Shepherd entered the dining room, ostensibly to check on her son's progress.

"What 'cha working on, son?" Abigail asked.

"Homework, Mom."

"I know that," Abigail rolled her eyes as she sat down next to Michael. "But homework for what?"

"It's about guns," Michael replied, his mouth full of ice cream.

"Guns! What kind of homework is that?" Abigail exclaimed, leaning over Michael's notebook.

"It's about the Second Amendment. Should a citizen still have the right to own a gun or not? We have to state our position and then defend it. Five hundred words or less."

"Hmm," Abigail said. "And what is your position?"

"Yeah, I think people should be able to own a gun." Michael took another bite of ice cream. "What do you think?"

"Well, it depends on..." Abigail began.

"Hold on," Michael interrupted. "It has to be in five hundred words or less, Mom."

Abigail sighed. Then she continued, "Well, maybe one gun, but not an arsenal like some people have. You know, some people want to overdo...."

"Hey, Mom, did you know we are out of chocolate syrup?" Michael interrupted.

"Oh, no, I didn't know that," Abigail replied. "I'll put it on the grocery list."

"Thanks, Mom."

"You're welcome, son. "Now, where was I?"

Rising to his feet, Michael said, "Not sure, but I need to call it a night. Thank you, Mom. Thanks for your input. Love you."

"Love you too, son," Abigail answered.

***

Michael Shepherd was at one end of a dimly lit street. At the other end stood Derek. Derek was dressed in black pants, a black shirt, and the coat he stole from Michael several months ago. He had in his hand a nine-millimeter Glock handgun, holding it at his side in his right hand. He slowly moved toward Michael. The two men were locked in a deadly confrontation.

Michael moved forward; his eyes were on the large gun in Derek's hand. Michael wore his school soccer uniform, which was also black with the number 8 emblazoned on the front of the jersey, and the name SHEP-HERD stitched on the back. Michael's armament consisted solely of a soccer ball at his feet. He inched the ball forward with each step. Michael never took his eyes off the gun in Derek's right hand. Derek never took his eyes off Michael's intense stare. In perfect harmony, the two young men moved forward one step at a time until they were fifteen yards apart. Then they stopped. Neither man spoke.

Derek slowly raised his Glock automatic pistol and aimed it at Michael's chest. Michael did not cringe in fear. Neither did he hesitate. He pushed the ball slightly forward and drew back his left leg, striking the ball's sweet spot and sending it at a blinding speed of over 100 m.p.h. into Derek's crotch. Derek's gun exploded, but it was off-target. Derek doubled over in pain and dropped the gun. Michael closed the gap, picked up the weapon, and fired a round into Derek's right ear. Derek fell back, dead.

Michael looked down at his fallen enemy and said, "Keep your eye on the ball, idiot!"

Michael's body suddenly jerked up into a sitting position. His heartbeat pounded in his ears as he hurried to the kitchen, grabbing a bottle of water out of the refrigerator. As he took huge gulps, allowing the cold refrigerator air to blow onto his sweaty forehead, he only had one thought: *How weird was that dream?!*

CHAPTER 9

Brittany Cummings stared through the window at her daughter, Olivia, who was heavily sedated and lying in a hospital bed in the surgical center at University Hospital. She turned to Dr. Patterson and asked, "So, what's the bottom line here, Doctor?"

"Well, the bottom line, if she gets bad enough, we amputate her leg..." Dr. Patterson said slowly. "But we are not anywhere near that decision yet."

Brittany Cummings gasped in horror as a tear dropped down her cheek, unheeded. She cried, "She's a soccer player. She loves to dance! My baby girl doesn't deserve this–a young girl can't handle that! Is there no hope in saving her leg?"

"Sure, there's hope, Mrs. Cummings," Dr. Patterson said gently. "That's what I'm saying. We are not yet at the point of making that decision. We have stabilized the leg and will watch the blood supply and soft tissue condition over the next few days. We'll be looking for signs of improvement in those two areas. We should also be able to tell if there's any nerve damage. Meanwhile, we'll continue treating her with antibiotics and pain medicine. IV fluids should help keep her blood pressure at ideal levels."

"She is fortunate to be where she is, considering the extent of her injuries," Dr. Patterson continued. "If we see improvement over the next several days, we will consider reconstruction instead of amputation. However, you should know that they have made wonderful progress in prosthetics if it does come to that. She should be able to lead a normal life, including playing soccer and dancing. We'll take it one day at a time. I assure you we will give Olivia the best care possible and make the right choices when the time comes."

"Thank you, Doctor," Brittany said softly as her gaze returned to her daughter.

"Certainly. Please feel free to step back inside and visit your daughter. Call me if you have any questions."

"Yes, I will, sir."

***

On Wednesday afternoon, Michael hurriedly stopped in front of his high school locker. He yanked open the door, reached in to grab his gym bag, and closed the door with a bang. He was close to being late for soccer practice. As he spun the dial on his combination lock, he heard a familiar voice.

"Hi, Michael."

Michael whirled around and was face to face with Ashley Templeton and her best friend, Heather Whitmire.

Michael tried to hide his surprise with a smile and a nonchalant shrug. "Hi, Ashley. Hi Heather. What's up?"

"Nothing," Ashley said with a giggle. She turned and looked at Heather, who joined in the giggling. Then she looked back at Michael and said, "I haven't seen much of you lately. I thought maybe you were mad at me or something."

Michael looked at his watch and said, "I'm not mad, but I can't talk now. I'll be late for soccer practice. Big game this week."

"Yes, I know, against St. Pat's," Ashley said. "Are you going to score a goal?"

Michael smiled and said, "Maybe. Hope so. I've got to go, sorry."

Michael took off for the gymnasium. Then he looked back at Ashley and hollered, "I'll call you."

Both girls giggled in response.

Things are looking up! Michael thought to himself as he double-timed it down the hall and through the gymnasium doors.

Michael was pumped as he ran onto the practice field that afternoon. He found Jake Ledger and flopped down beside him as the players began their stretch routines.

"So, what's up, my friend?' Jake asked. "You're looking a little hyper."

"It's just a momentous day, Jake" Michael smiled. "That's all, just a momentous day."

"Well then–God is good, isn't He?"

Michael hesitated, looked quizzically at Jake, then said, "Yeah, I guess so."

"What do you mean you guess so? You need to own it, man!"

Jake jumped to his feet and ran to join the rest of the team, leaving Michael alone to lace up his boots and ponder Jake's latest remark.

Soon, Coach Patton stood before his team, which was kneeling or sitting in rapt attention to every word Coach was saying: "St. Pat's is good. Their defense will be the best we have faced so far. Their defenders are big and rangy. They are not afraid to push forward, and they score many goals themselves. We need to stop them at midfield by forcing them to give up the ball early. So, midfielders, Jake, Lorenzo, Seth, you have your work cut out for you."

"We can handle it, Coach," Seth replied.

"I have every confidence you can, Seth," Coach Patton said with a smile.

Coach Patton took a moment to study his players' faces. Satisfied with what he saw, he said, "This was our last hard practice. Tomorrow, we'll go through game strategy and set-piece work. Have a great evening, gentlemen. Also, do not ignore your homework."

That night, after a dinner of fried chicken, mashed potatoes, green salad, and a piece of apple pie a la mode, Michael retreated to his room, ostensibly to study, but as soon as he closed the bedroom door, he sat on his bed and punched the keys on his phone.

"Hello," came Ashley's voice.

"Hey, Ashley. This is Mike. How are you?"

"I'm fine," Ashley responded. "What's on your mind tonight?"

"Well, right now, you are."

Ashley giggled.

"Are you ready for our date?" Michael asked.

"Hmmm, maybe."

"There's a dance after the game Friday night. We could go to that. What do you think?" Michael asked.

"Well, maybe. If you score a goal–for the right team, of course," Ashley said with a laugh.

"So, you're saying we go to the dance together on the condition I score a goal? What happens if I don't? Because the reality is, I probably won't. How about we make it just if I play well?"

Ashley hesitated, then said, "Okay, as long as you play well."

"How about we make it if I get to play, period?" Michael countered.

There was another pause, and Ashley finally said, "Okay, I guess."

"Good deal," Michael said. "By the way, what's with you and Dan Fountain?"

"Dan Fountain?"

"Yeah. I saw you leaving the game with him last week. "He's bad news, Ashley. You need to stay away from him?"

"Oh, so you're my protector now?"

"No, I'm just saying Dan has a bad reputation. Is he trying to date you now?"

"Of course. Everyone is trying to date me."

"Really! And where do I stand?"

"You're moving up. Congratulations."

"Thanks," Michael chuckled. "See you tomorrow. Goodnight."

"Goodnight, Michael."

Michael stared at his phone. *This girl is driving me crazy.*

***

Five minutes after Ashley said goodnight to Michael, her phone rang again.

"Hello," she said impatiently.

"Hello, Ashley. This is Dan."

"Oh, hi, Dan. How are you?"

"I'm good," Dan replied. "I was wondering if we could get together tomorrow evening."

After a slight hesitation, Ashley said, "I'm sorry, Dan. I have a date for tomorrow night. Maybe another time."

"Who's your date with?"

"Well, Dan, I don't want to be rude, but that's really none of your business."

"Maybe I think it is," Dan replied, raising his voice slightly.

"Dan, I don't know what makes you say that. I haven't...."

"Goodbye, Ashley," Dan said sharply. "See you around."

Ashley's phone beeped and went silent.

***

The game against St. Pat's was the last home game for the next two weeks. Barrymore and St. Pat's were locked in second place in league standings behind Langford, who had beaten them both in close games.

Barrymore took an early lead on a nice header by Jake Ledger from a corner kick by Michael, who took the left-footed kick from the right corner to ensure the ball would swing in towards the goal from Michael's left foot. Michael had entered the game at the thirty-minute mark and had played well enough to give the team a boost in offense down the left touchline. St. Pat's tied the score early in the second half, and the game remained tied for forty minutes. Play was hectic as the players were near exhaustion on both sides.

In what had to be the closing minutes, Michael received a nice pass from Jake at midfield and streaked down the left touchline. The defender for St. Pat's hunkered down and challenged Michael just outside the box. Michael drew close and popped the ball over the challenging defender's head, a move he had been practicing for weeks. When he secured the ball again, Michael was alone with the goalkeeper, who rushed forward, ending with a diving charge to Michael's feet to smother the ball. Michael maintained control and shot the ball past the goalkeeper's outstretched hands into the lower right corner of the net.

Minutes later, the referee blew his whistle, signaling the game was over. The Barrymore players and fans flooded the field, many reaching out to Michael with hand clasps and back slaps.

****

Three hours later, Michael and Ashley were sitting in Michael's dad's car, parked on an overlook on the outskirts of Barrymore, a popular spot for young couples to park. The view of the city was outstanding as the lights twinkled from below, and the full moon added to a romantic setting.

Michael was nervous but willing to gamble. He put his arm around Ashley and attempted to pull her close. Unfortunately for Michael, Ashley resisted.

"What's wrong, Ashley? No kissing on the first date?" Michael jested.

"Maybe," Ashley replied as she scooted away. "That's part of it, anyway. Michael, you need to understand that I'm my own woman. I don't need anybody to lead me around, especially a man. Actually, it would be best if you didn't get your hopes up about me at all. I'm not sure we could have a relationship. You are a nice guy; I don't want to hurt you. Do you know what I mean?"

"So, you're saying I'm not your type of guy?"

"I'm not sure," Ashley replied.

"So, what type of guy turns you on? A guy like Dan Fountain, maybe?"

"Well, Dan certainly isn't a clinger," Ashley replied. "He's more of the 'rugged' type."

"So you like rugged?"

Ashley snickered, "Sometimes."

"Did Dan kiss you on your first date?" Michael asked.

Again, Ashley snickered. "I'm not going to tell you that. That's none of...."

Suddenly, Michael's door was yanked open, and he was jerked from the front seat by Dan Fountain, who planted a hard kick into Michael's ribs when he hit the ground.

"Hey!" Michael screamed as he struggled to his feet, only to be the recipient of hammering fists to his head delivered by Dan. "What's going on?!"

Ashley launched herself from her side of the vehicle and screamed at Dan: "What are you doing, Dan? Stop it!"

Dan continued to throw haymakers at Michael's head. Michael threw his arms up to protect himself. But after absorbing a few punches, he began to fight back. His fists connected with Dan Fountain's head, staggering Dan and curtailing his aggression. He took a step back and looked at Michael.

"Stay away from my woman," he screamed, taking another wild swing at Michael's head. Michael saw that one coming and ducked under it. Then he responded by stepping forward and throwing a left hook into the right side of Dan's head, dazing him momentarily. Michael, gaining confidence, began to pound Dan with both fists. Michael's many hours lifting weights had added a lot of muscle to his arms and upper body. His fists began to take a toll as his barrage of punches punished Dan severely. The fight in Dan suddenly vanished, and he dropped to his knees, putting his arms up in a gesture of surrender.

Michael stood over his vanquished foe. "Are we done here, Dan?"

"We're done," Dan muttered.

"Good. Now do me a favor and move your car so my date and I can go home. Okay?"

Dan nodded, struggled to his feet, crawled into his car, and disappeared.

Michael then walked to the car's passenger side and held the door open for Ashley to enter. Ashley looked up at Michael and slipped inside without uttering a word.

Michael said nothing as he backed the car from the overlook and drove onto the highway leading back to Barrymore.

After several miles of torturous silence, Ashley uttered, "I'm sorry, Michael."

"Sorry about what?" Michael asked.

"Sorry about what happened. What Dan did."

"Were you surprised?"

"Yes, very surprised," Ashley said, turning her head to look at Michael. "Weren't you surprised?"

"Not really," Michael replied. That's the way 'rugged' guys act."

"I just can't believe he's like that," Ashley said.

Michael paused and looked at Ashley, "Well, that's too bad, Ashley. I'm sorry you can't."

Michael pulled the car onto the driveway and idled up near the front porch of the Templeton home. He got out and opened the passenger door for Ashley.

Ashley exited the car. Michael closed the door and walked around to the front of the vehicle, leaving Ashley standing by herself.

"Aren't you going to walk me to the door?" Ashley asked.

Michael glanced at the door and then back to Ashley. "I don't think so, Ashley. Remember, you are an independent woman who doesn't need anyone to lead her around, especially a man." Michael popped open the driver's side door. As he stood by the open door, he looked at Ashley and quipped, "See you around."

He got in, cranked the engine, and pulled quietly away, leaving Ashley standing alone on the driveway.

CHAPTER 10

Michael was finishing breakfast Saturday morning when his dad came into the kitchen dressed for his Saturday morning golf game.

"Hey, Dad, what's up?" Michael asked.

"Not much," Mr. Shepherd responded. "How was your date with ah, with ah…"

"With Ashley?" Michael asked. "Good. We went to the dance after the game. It was fun."

"Super. Why don't you bring her around sometime so we can meet her?"

"Not likely, Dad," Michael replied, continuing to eat his breakfast. I probably won't be seeing much of her in the future."

"Really! That's interesting." George then leaned over and looked closer at his son's face. "Say, what happened to you?"

"Nothing. It's just a disagreement with somebody. It's all okay,"

"You don't want to talk about it?"

"No, sir."

"Okay. That's fine," Mr. Shepherd responded. "So, what do you have going on this weekend?"

"Soccer practice," Michael replied. "After that, I might hang out with some of the guys and maybe go to a movie. I've got a lot of homework I need to get done. I need to do some lifting and some ball work. Tomorrow, I'll sleep in and then go for a long run-up to Cricket Flat."

"That sounds like an ambitious way to spend a weekend. Okay, I'm out of here," Mr Shepherd said, grabbing his car keys.

"Hit 'em straight, Pop," Michael said, raising his orange juice glass in a salute.

"I'll try," Mr. Shepherd chuckled. "See you tonight."

* * *

That Saturday morning, Coach Patton got into his car to leave for the soccer field when his cell phone went off. He didn't recognize the caller's number and was tempted not to answer but thought better of it.

"Hello?" he asked.

"Hello, coach. This is Andrew Sharpe. I'm not sure if we have ever met, but I'm the athletic director of Unity University here in LaGrange."

"Yes, Andrew. We haven't met, but I know who you are. What can I do for you, sir?"

"Well, I wonder if we could meet sometime next week in my office. I don't want to go into any details now, but we are looking to hire a new assistant coach this fall and would like to talk to you about any interest you might have in joining our coaching staff."

Coach Patton's heart jumped in surprise and excitement. It took a few moments for the suggestion to sink in. Then he said, "Of course, I would like to talk to you about that. When would you like me to come in?"

"Would you be available for an extended lunch meeting, maybe this coming Wednesday around 12:30?" Andrew asked.

"Yes, I could do that," Coach replied.

"Great. Bill Cathey, our head coach, will join us, of course, as will Preston Hardy, our university president. Just come into the Ad Building and ask for me."

"Okay, thank you, sir," Coach replied.

"You're welcome, Coach Patton," Andrew replied. "See you then."

With a wide grin and a surge of pride, Coach Patton sat back in his seat, hit the ignition switch, and backed down his driveway. Of course, he would need to hear a lot more details, but he was extremely excited about the prospect of coaching at the university level.

As Coach Patton drove along Florence Avenue on his way to the practice field, his mind raced through a myriad of "what ifs:" *What if this really happens? What will I tell my kids? I'm not sure if it will even happen, of course. But what if it does? There's no doubt I am just one of a half dozen or more coaches they're probably considering. What about the rumors that will inevitably come if I start talking to the university when people know they are looking for a new soccer coach? Well, I guess we'll cross that bridge if and when we get to it. It's great to be considered, that's for sure.*

Coach Patton pulled his car into the soccer field parking lot and parked. He looked out at his players, who were already at work warming up for the two-hour practice ahead. *Man, I would miss these kids. We have been together for a long time. What would happen to them?*

Coach Patton got out of his car and jogged across the parking lot to join his players.

***

Two hours later, Michael and several players were on the ground, unlacing their shoes. They were all drenched in sweat.

Jake looked up and said to the group, "Man, Coach was on fire today. He must have eaten a bunch of energy bars for breakfast."

"Yeah, either that or drunk ten cups of coffee," Austin responded.

The players all chuckled in agreement as Coach Patton walked over to where they had gathered.

"Good work, men," Coach Patton affirmed. "We've got a lot of work to do this week to prepare for Pilot Ridge. Get some rest, eat healthily, and do your homework. I'll see you Monday, okay?"

"Sounds good, Coach," Jake responded. Then he added, "Get some rest yourself, Coach."

Several players stood and began to follow the coach to the parking lot. Michael and Jake stayed on the ground, both feeling the stiffness setting in. Finally, Michael looked at Jake and asked, "What's up with you today, Jake?"

"You'll never guess," Jake said with a sly grin.

Michael stared at Jake for a moment and said, "You're going to church!"

"Nope."

"You're going to a revival!"

"Wrong again," Jake laughed.

"Okay, I give up. Where are you going?"

"Well, after I go home and shower, I'm going to visit Olivia Cummings at the hospital. Actually, Mr. Wise Guy, you can go with me if you'd like."

"Can she have visitors?" Michael asked in surprise.

"Yep. I talked to her mom this morning, and she told me Olivia had been moved to a private room and would love to have visitors," Jake replied.

"Wow. That's cool, Jake. Sure, I'd like to go."

"Great! I'll pick you up at your house at 2:30. Does that work for you?"

"Yes, it does. Thanks, bruh."

Four hours later, Jake pulled his pickup truck onto the driveway of the Shepherd household. Michael was waiting for him on the front steps of the large porch. As Michael opened the truck door, Jake repositioned a large bouquet of roses to give him room to sit down.

"Cool," Michael said. "Are those for me?"

"No, dumb butt," Jake laughed. They're for Olivia. Now, don't mess them up, okay?"

"So, are they from both of us?"

"Wrong again, dude," Jake said. They are from me. If you want to give her flowers, you can buy some at the gift shop in the hospital."

"Hmm. Okay then, can you loan me five bucks?"

"Five bucks?" Jake chuckled. "That might get you one stem, and no, I can't loan you five bucks."

"Bummer. What kind of friend are you?" Michael snapped his seat belt in place and said, "What are you waiting for, bruh? Let's go!"

A little over an hour later, Michael and Jake slowly opened the door to room 4935 on the fourth floor of University Hospital.

With the door partially open, Jake made their presence known: "Anybody home?"

"Yes, come in!" Mrs. Cummings answered.

Olivia was in bed, propped up against two pillows. She smiled as Jake and Michael entered the room. Her left leg was heavily wrapped and resting on a large cushion.

Jake walked over to the bed and presented the flowers to Olivia. "Oh my, they are beautiful," she gushed. "Thank you, Jake and Michael. This is so special."

"Well, you are kind of special, too," Jake replied with a slight blush.

Mrs. Cummings stepped over, took the flower vase, and placed it on a nearby table. Then she hugged both boys, wiped a tear away from her eye, and sat back down. Michael sat in the other available chair, and Jake sat on the edge of the bed.

"So, how are you doing?" Jake asked as he looked at Olivia.

"Pretty good, all things considered," Olivia replied.

"Is there a plan in place to treat your injury?" Jake asked.

"They are still doing some tests," Mrs. Cummings interjected. "We should know something in the next few days. We aren't worried. The Lord's in charge. It will all work out."

Jake smiled, "Romans 8:28. Right?"

"That's right, Jake," Mrs. Cummings replied. "Romans 8:28."

Olivia glanced at Michael and said, "Mike, thanks for coming with Jake. How are you doing?"

Michael grinned. He was glad to be brought into the conversation. "I'm good."

"I've been hearing great things about you playing soccer," Olivia said.

"Really? Have you been talking to my mom or something?" Michael joked, standing and walking over to the hospital bed to join Jake.

"No, silly," Olivia laughed. "Just my friends."

"Uhm, that's a rowdy bunch." Michael mocked. "Better not listen to them."

The three visited together for close to an hour, discussing school activities, soccer, friends, and homework.

Finally, Jake stood up and said, "We should probably get out of here and let you get some rest."

He walked to the bed's top edge and stretched his hand to Olivia. "Let me pray for you before we leave, Olivia."

Olivia reached out to Jake. "Please do, Jake."

Jake prayed, "Our heavenly Father. We lift Olivia Cummings up to you in prayer. We know you can heal her, Lord, and we pray that you will. Give the doctor wisdom to make the right decisions and the ability to do what needs to be done to restore her back to her family and her friends, completely healed and well, Father. We entrust her to you, Father, and thank you for what you are going to do. In Jesus' great name, we pray, Amen."

"Thank you, Jake," Brittany Cummings whispered.

After receiving hugs from Mrs. Cummings, Jake and Michael said goodbye to Olivia and left the room.

***

Fifteen minutes later, the boys were back in Jake's truck on their way to Michael's house, about an hour's drive from the hospital. At first, their discussion was lighthearted, centering around their hopes for Olivia's full recovery. Then Michael posed a deeper question.

"Romans 8:28. That's a Bible verse, right?"

"It sure is," Jake replied.

"So, what does it say?"

"It says, 'And we know that God causes all things to work together for good to those who love God and are called according to His purpose.'"

"That's in the Bible?"

"Yep. It sure is."

"So, you believe what happened to Olivia is good?"

"That's not what the verse says," Jake explained. "Listen again: 'And we know that God *causes* all things to work together for good to those who love God and are called according to His purpose.' It is saying that God has the power to make every event in life beneficial and accomplish what He wants for us."

"I don't know, Jake..." Michael said. "There's a good chance Olivia could lose her leg. Tell me how that could be good."

"We will have to wait, Mike," Jake replied. "That's part of trusting God."

Jake pulled up the driveway at Michael's home, parked the truck, and shut down the engine. He turned to Michael and said, "There's one more part to that verse we shouldn't overlook, Michael."

"What's that?" Michael asked.

"It only pertains to certain people. The part that says, 'Those who love God, and are called according to His purpose.' Did you catch that?" Jake asked.

"Yes, I did," Michael replied. "So what is that all about?"

Jake leaned back against the door and started to speak just when his phone rang.

"Hello, Dad. What's up?"

After a few moments, he said, "Sure, Dad. I'll be right there."

Jake put his phone down and looked at Michael. "I need to get home. We'll have to finish this conversation later. Sorry."

"Oh, okay. Is there anything wrong at home?" Michael asked.

"No. I forgot we were having company for dinner, that's all. I'll catch you up on Monday. Okay?"

"Sounds good," Michael said as he opened the door and exited the truck. He waved goodbye to Jake as he backed his truck down the driveway.

Maybe that call was a case of fortunate timing. Michael smiled to himself as he walked up the steps to the front door of his house. *I don't think I want to get into the weeds of Bible talk. It doesn't make any sense, anyway.*

***

It was Monday morning, and American History class was already underway. Tori Zinser, known as TZ, had just taken roll and covered the announcements. Jake gave an update on his and Michael's visit with Olivia Cummings at the hospital.

"She's doing okay," Jake reported. "They are still waiting on some test results, but she is in good spirits and hoping for the best."

"Would she want visitors?" a student asked.

"Yes, but you should probably call her mom first and make sure it's okay," Jake explained.

Coach Patton rose and walked to the front of his desk. He surveyed the students and said, "Last week, your homework assignment was to write a summary of how our Bill of Rights came about and what they do. They were all good, and you can see that I have placed a copy of your submission on your desk. So, I would like one or two of you to stand and read your paper to the rest of the class. Don't be bashful. I'm putting 3,000 points on the table as an incentive."

Immediately, Teresa Zinser was on her feet, her paper in hand.

"Yes, TZ. What do you have for us today?" Coach asked.

TZ smiled and stood confidently beside her desk. She was an auburn-haired girl, about five foot two. She took a deep breath and read from her paper: "The Bill of Rights is the first ten amendments to the Constitution of the United States. It was adopted by Congress in 1791. These amendments are a collection of guarantees for individual rights and limitations on federal and state governments that were put into play to protect the states from the federal government because there was a huge concern that the Constitution was too limited in those areas. Over the years, these ten amendments to the Constitution have been used countless times and proven the wisdom of our founders to put them in place."

TZ looked up from her paper, smiled, and sat back down.

"Great job, TZ," Coach Patton proclaimed. "Thank you." Looking around the room, he added, "Anyone else?"

Blank stares from every student answered his question.

After a few seconds of silence, Coach Patton offered a new proposal. "Okay, please get a clean sheet of paper. We will close out our study of the first ten amendments to the Constitution with a pop quiz."

"Oh, come on, Coach," several students uttered. Others just groaned.

"Wait, Coach. I'll do mine," Grant Baker called out.

"Nope, too late," Coach Patton responded. "Please have paper and pencils at the ready." Coach Patton then stepped to the whiteboard and started writing as he commented aloud.

"Please remember to put your name and date on the paper. Today is the first day of April. Every incorrect answer will cost you five hundred points. Please read each question carefully because some of them are meant to trick you."

Coach Patton turned back toward the class and asked, "Are you ready?"

More than a few students loudly exclaimed, "NO!"

The coach picked up a black marker and wrote in large letters: "APRIL FOOLS!"

Most of the students reacted by throwing their pencils down and laughing.

All of them were relieved. And all of them loved Coach Patton.

CHAPTER 11

t was after 6:00 p.m. when Michael entered his house that evening. His mom greeted him as he walked into the kitchen. He dropped his book bag down on the kitchen floor.

"Hello, son," Abigail said with a smile as she stirred a pot on the stove. "How was your day?"

"Good," Michael replied. "What's for dinner? I'm starving."

"We're having spaghetti tonight, Michael. Can't you see that, my dear boy?" she laughed as she lifted her spoon, spaghetti dripping back into the water of the boiling pot.

"Yeah, I can," Michael laughed too. "I just like to hear you say it, Mom. Spaghetti, uhm... Gracias."

Abigail smiled and jested, "Okay, Mr. Lingo man, '*Vai a lavarsi le mani.*'"

Michael was obviously stumped. "'*Vai a lavarsi le mani?*' What does that mean?"

"It means, 'go wash your hands and face,'" Abigail said. "Don't spare the soap. They're quite dirty."

Michael raised his hands and looked them over.

"And call your dad for dinner while you're at it."

"It means all that?"

Abigail sighed and said, "Of course not. Now go call your dad for dinner, and..."

"And what, Mom?" Michael asked.

Abigail paused for a moment, then said, "And, and... Oh dear. I almost forgot what I was going to tell you. You received some mail today from the lawyer, Mr. Trotter. It's on your desk in your room."

"Oh great," Michael said. "I'll go..."

"No, you won't. I'm ready to put dinner on the table. Call your dad and wash up for dinner. You can read your mail later."

"Yes, Mom," Michael groaned as he strode to the door leading into the living room. Peering into the living room, he said, "Hey, Dad."

"Hey what?" Mr. Shepherd replied, his nose buried in a newspaper.

"Mom says it's time to eat."

After dinner that evening, Michael and his parents sat at the kitchen table. Michael held up a letter from Carson Trotter. "Mr. Carson would like us to send him all the papers relating to the adoption. I wonder why he needs all that. He told me we could do nothing until I turned 21."

"I don't know," Mr. Shepherd said. "Maybe he needs it for his file for future reference. Three years isn't so long, you know."

"Three years is forever," Michael moaned. "I might not even be around in three years!"

"Nor may any of us, my boy," Mr. Shepherd said briskly. "But do it anyway, okay?"

***

The following Wednesday, Coach Patton parked his car in a

visitor's parking slot in front of the administration building at Unity University. Dressed in gray slacks, a white shirt, and a blue blazer, Kyle Patton strode through the front doors of the building, looking sharp and feeling good about his upcoming interview. He had spent much time praying and reading his Bible before school that morning. He knew he had nothing to worry about. His trust was in the Lord.

A young receptionist behind an oak counter asked, "May I help you?"

"Yes, I have an appointment with Mr. Sharpe this morning," Coach Patton replied.

The lady looked at her computer monitor, pushed some buttons, and said, "Oh yes, Mr. Patton. Please have a chair. I will let them know you are here."

"Thank you," Coach said and walked over to one of several lobby chairs available.

After he had sat there for several minutes, tension began to creep into Patton's psyche. He suddenly felt uneasy. The scope of this opportunity began to dominate his thoughts and erode his confidence.

This is so huge. Could this be real? From high school soccer coach to university level coach? Am I up to this? Are they serious? Who else are they talking to? I'm pretty sure I'm not the only candidate for this job. Lord, I hope I'm not just wasting their time this morning. Help me with this interview, please. Help me do well, Lord. Please.

After several minutes, a young lady approached and broke the silence. "Mr. Patton?"

Coach Patton stood. "Yes, that's me," he said.

"Mr. Sharpe will see you now. Just follow me, please."

Patton stepped forward and dropped behind the young lady as she strode forward past several offices and to an open door to a large conference room. She stepped inside, then stood and nodded to the coach to come in.

Three men were standing in the room as Coach Patton entered. He was greeted by Andrew Sharpe, a large man who stuck out a huge right hand. "Hello, Coach. I'm Andrew Sharpe. Thanks for coming in this afternoon."

"Glad to be here," Patton replied.

"This is Jason Cathey, our head coach," Andrew said, gesturing to his left. "He tells me you two haven't met."

"Hello, Coach Patton. It's good to meet you," Cathey beamed as he extended his hand.

"My pleasure," Coach Patton replied.

"I want you to meet our president, Preston Hardy," Andrew continued, gesturing to the man on his left.

Just finishing his first year of employment at Unity, the university president stepped forward and offered his hand to Patton. Hardy was short in stature but had a strong handshake and displayed an engaging smile.

"Pleased to meet you, Coach. We are glad you are here. We are all looking forward to learning more about you."

"Thank you, sir," Patton replied. "I certainly appreciate meeting all of you."

Andrew Sharpe said, "Please be seated," as he pulled an oversized leather chair away from the table and motioned for the visitor to sit down.

The four men sat and exchanged information for the next hour and a half. Patton had prepared a resume, which he handed to

Sharpe early in the meeting. Coach Patton was impressed that President Hardy seemed more interested in his philosophy regarding player respect and relationships than the other two men. They were more into the X's and O's of coaching soccer.

I guess that's a natural contrast, he decided after giving it some thought.

"Sure, we want a winning team," President Hardy said at one point. "But more importantly, we want a team that will bring honor and dignity to our university and Christian maturity to our student athletes."

"I certainly understand," Coach Patton responded. "Those ideals have always been important to me in my career as well."

The university president picked up a document from his desk and looked at the coach. "I see that you have an outstanding record in your coaching and are highly regarded in your classroom work. You teach American History, correct?"

"Yes, sir."

"So, tell me, Coach Patton," President Hardy continued, "how do you account for this success? It's quite outstanding."

"I serve a mighty God," Coach Patton quickly responded.

President Hardy tucked his hands under his chin and smiled.

After a quiet thirty-second delay, Andrew Sharpe looked at Coach Cathey and said, "I know you two might want to get together later on, but for now, do you need any more information from the coach, Jason?"

Coach Cathey shook his head. "No sir, I'm good for now."

Sharpe then looked at Coach Patton. "Do you have any further questions, Kyle?"

"No, sir," he replied.

President Hardy looked at his watch and asked, "Is that it Andy?"

"Yes, sir. That's it. Thank you for joining us."

President Hardy then stood and reached out his right hand to Coach Patton. "It has been a pleasure, sir. I'm glad to have had the opportunity to get to know you. Thank you again for coming in."

Kyle stood, clasped the president's hand, and said, "Thanks very much for your time, sir."

When President Hardy left the room, Andrew Sharpe turned to Kyle. "Thanks, Coach. I appreciate your coming in. Give us a few days to get back to you. We will let you know if we need any further information."

"That will be great, Andrew. Thanks for having me," Patton replied.

"It was our pleasure."

Led by Coach Patton, the three men exited the room. Coach Cathey pulled up beside Kyle in the hallway and said, "I hear you will be playing a 'friendly' with LaGrange High School in a couple of weeks. Is that right?"

"Yes, sir, we will," Coach Patton replied. "We are looking forward to that."

"You're playing up two divisions," Cathey replied with a whistle. "That's a gutsy move."

"Yes, I know that," Patton chuckled. "We'll see what we're made of."

"Indeed, and how well those boys are coached."

Coach Patton smiled and said, "Yes, that too. Do you plan on being there?"

"Sure do. I wouldn't miss it," Cathey said with a smile.

"Great, Coach. I'll see you in a couple of weeks."

Coach Patton's mind was working overtime as he drove away from Unity's campus. If this opportunity happened, it would mean a serious change for him, so his thinking began to sift through several ramifications:

Do I even want this? I'm happy coaching at the high school level. I love the teaching aspect of my job, the kids, and the school. They would have to pay me a truck full of money to come and coach at the university level... or would they? This would be a step up. A significant step up. Wow! Andrew will be at our game against LaGrange. More pressure that I don't need. Hmm, I wonder if they are looking at the LaGrange coach, too. I'll bet they are. He's done an excellent job. It could be between the two of us. Who knows? Super vibes from President Hardy. I'm pretty sure he liked me. Anyway, there's a lot to think about. But no worries. Anything this big is in God's hands.

Besides, tonight, I have a date with a beautiful lady to look forward to.

***

Joker Duff was driving in his car along Park Avenue that Wednesday afternoon, waiting for a school bus to pass through the intersection of Park and Overview. When the bus cleared the intersection, Joker turned left and began to follow the bus. The bus made frequent stops along Overview Street, and Joker stopped behind the bus each time and waited for the young people to exit and head to their nearby homes. All were carrying heavy-looking bookbags. Joker became impatient with the slow progress until, at one stop, he noticed an attractive young lady depart from the bus, hitch up her book bag, and walk down a side street that intersected with Overview.

Annie Smith did not normally ride the bus to school. Her usual ride had been provided by a young man who had recently moved from the neighborhood, necessitating her to take the bus, which she hated. It wouldn't matter for long, however, as the school year would soon be over. Annie would turn eighteen in a few weeks and graduate from high school. She was more than ready and looking forward to the next chapter in her life. She had been accepted by Unity University for the fall semester and was very excited at the prospects of college life.

Annie paid scant attention to the sleek-looking black car that pulled to the curb several feet behind the school bus.

Annie walked up a sidewalk leading to a modest two-story brick home approximately fifty feet back from the street. She smiled when she heard the familiar excited barks and whines from her dog Biscuit, a pit bull mix rescue dog her parents had given her as a puppy on her twelfth birthday. She walked up the porch steps, swung her book bag to the porch floor, and dug around until she found her key to the front door. Her dog's excitement increased as he waited for the door to open.

"Hold on, Biscuit. I'm coming," she announced as she turned the key and opened the door. She remained unaware of the leering curbside lowlife watching her every move and making plans for a future encounter. Joker checked his watch, took a mental picture of the front of the house and the house number, and drove away.

***

Coach Patton stood at the front door of a small house in a modest neighborhood on Alder Drive in the south part of Barrymore. The neighborhood appeared to be family-friendly, and indeed, several children were playing outside their houses on this somewhat chilly April evening. Kyle noticed a small bicycle leaning against the wall at one end of the porch.

Hmm, that's strange.

He held a bouquet of pink roses in his hand. He was nervous, more nervous even than he was as he had waited earlier in the day for his meeting with the officials of Unity University. Coach Patton had not been on a date since his fiancée Christine Merryman had lost her life in a car crash two years earlier.

This is it, he thought as he reached up and pushed the doorbell button.

In a few seconds, Kayla Leanard stood at the open door. She was wearing a black dress, a pearl necklace, and a white button-up sweater. Kyle Paton was once again overwhelmed by her presence.

"Come in, Coach," she said with a smile. "Those flowers are so beautiful! Thank you very much."

Coach Patton stepped inside and handed the bouquet to Kayla. "I'm glad you like them," he replied with a broad grin.

"I'll go find a vase for these," Kayla said. "Please have a seat. I'll be just a minute."

The coach walked to a sofa and sat down. He noted that the room was neat and clean. As he waited, he reached over and picked up a children's puzzle magazine.

That's also strange.

In moments, Kayla was back. She placed the flowers in the vase on a fireplace mantel. "Looks nice," Kyle said.

"I love roses," Kayla replied. "Thank you again... uhh, please tell me what you would like me to call you: Coach, Kyle, or...."

Kyle smiled. *Actually, You can call me anything you want, lady.*

Just be sure to call.

"Uh, just call me Kyle," he replied.

"Okay, Kyle. Thank you."

"So, do you like Italian food?"

"I love Italian!" Kayla exclaimed.

"Good. I have some two-for-one coupons at a local pizza parlor," the coach said with a wide grin. He quickly followed with, "I'm just kidding. Are you ready to go?"

"Yes, I just need to get my jacket."

"Okay, sounds good," the coach said as he walked to the front door.

Two hours later, Kyle and Kayla were sharing a divided slice of Italian cream cake at The Mountain View Diner, Barrymore's most popular restaurant. Coach Patton finished his last bite and leaned back in his booth. "So, Kayla, we've spent a lot of time talking about me and coaching soccer. I'd like to hear more about you and your story."

Kayla leaned forward, put her elbows on the table, and cupped her chin in her hands. After a few thoughtful seconds, she said, "Well, I grew up in Portland. I graduated from Portland State University in 2020. I have a master's degree in English education and a minor in business. As you know, I'm paying the bills by substitute teaching."

"So, why are you substituting? Why not teach full-time? I know there's a real need for good English teachers," Kyle asked.

Kayla leaned back, paused, looked at Kyle momentarily, and then back at her unfinished cake. Then she looked back at Kyle. "I can't do that right now, Coach. I have a child to look after."

Coach Patton was not entirely surprised. "Oh. That explains

the bike on the porch and the children's book. So, uh, you've been married before?"

Kayla smiled. "No, I've never been married. But I do have a little boy, my eight-year-old brother, Joshua. He lives with me. Our mother passed away about a year ago, so I am raising him myself."

"I see," Kyle said kindly. "What about the father? Where is he?"

"He's around at times," Kayla began, "but he doesn't play a role in Joshua's life."

"Is he your dad too?" Kyle asked.

"No, but my dad is still alive. He remarried, and, uh, let's say his wife is not interested in raising somebody else's son," Kayla said with a wry chuckle.

"So, where do they live?"

"San Diego."

"Okay." Kyle paused as he considered Kayla's family. Then he said, "So, how are you dealing with all this?"

"One day at a time," Kayla said, putting the last bite of cake in her mouth.

"I get it," Kyle smiled. "So, where is Joshua tonight?"

"He's staying with a friend."

"I'd like to meet him sometime," Kyle said.

Kayla smiled. "I would like that too."

"Maybe Saturday. I could come by after practice. What do you think? Oh, wait. There's no practice on Saturday. We called it because we will be getting in late from our game on Friday against Venture. So maybe I could come by early Saturday afternoon. How does that sound?"

"Sounds fine, Kyle," Kayla replied. "Joshua will be excited when

I tell him."

Kyle smiled at that. He lifted his near-empty glass of Pinot and said, "To Saturday."

Kayla lifted her glass and clicked it against Kyle's. "To Saturday," she repeated with a chuckle.

As Kayla placed her glass down, she looked at Kyle and said, "What about you? How come you haven't married and settled down?"

Kyle was slow to respond, measuring his words. He finally answered, "I was close once, but God intervened. He took her home before we could close the deal. I haven't been able to start a new relationship, or even wanted to, for that matter, since I lost her."

"Oh, I'm so sorry, Kyle," Kayla replied, eyebrows furrowed. "How long ago was that?"

The coach paused and thought for a few moments. Then he said, "Two years ago last month."

"That's a long time to mourn. She must have been special."

"She was," Kyle said wistfully.

Kayla changed the subject. "So, do you like what you do, coaching soccer?

"I love it," Kyle grinned. "I like the opportunity to influence kids. To be a positive role model for them. Especially kids who have no dad in their lives."

"So, it's not the money?" Kayla chuckled.

"Ha! Very funny. No, it's not the money," Kyle replied.

Kayla smiled. "Who do you play Friday?"

"Venture."

"Are they good?"

"Yeah. This year, they all seem to be good. We will have to play well to beat them on their home field. Are you interested in going to the game?" Kyle asked.

"No. Thank you, Kyle. I'll stay home and get ready for my company," Kayla said with a wink.

"You're having company?" Kyle asked.

"I am. On Saturday. Remember?" Kayla laughed.

"Oh yeah. That's right. Thanks," Kyle smiled.

"I suppose we should head for home," Kayla said,"Workday tomorrow, remember?"

"Yes, I do," Kyle replied as he stood and picked up the receipt for dinner.

Thirty minutes later, Coach Patton parked his car against the curb in front of Kayla's house. He walked around to the passenger door and opened it so Kayla could exit the car. The two walked up the sidewalk to the front door. Kayla dug around in her purse, searching for her house key, finally producing it and inserting it into the key slot. She turned to Kyle.

"Thank you, Kyle. I had a wonderful time," Kayla smiled.

"Goodnight, Kayla. I'll see you tomorrow morning, okay?"

"Yes. Goodnight, Kyle."

Both Kyle and Kayla locked eyes for a moment. Then Kayla pushed open her door and disappeared inside her house.

CHAPTER 12

The town of Venture, Oregon, is snuggled deep into a valley between the high ranges of the Wallowa Mountains in Eastern Oregon. A farm and lumber town, their high school was slightly larger than Barrymore High School. Like Barrymore, local citizens strongly supported the high school and turned out in large numbers to cheer for their soccer team.

The Barrymore Huskies were on the field and ready for their game against Venture. Coach Patton made one significant change in his lineup. Michael Shepherd would start at left wing.

For the first several minutes of play, the game could best be described as sloppy. The Barrymore players were slow and impatient in executing their offense. Every time they took control and began a drive past midfield, Venture would win back the ball and begin a drive of their own. Several times in the first twenty minutes of the game, Venture came close to scoring. The Barrymore goalkeeper was forced to handle the ball several times, which was not a good sign for the visiting team.

In the sixteenth minute, a ball was played into Barrymore's penalty box, and unfortunately for Barrymore, it careened off the lower arm of Taylor Burns, Barrymore's left back. The referee immediately blew his whistle and awarded Venture a penalty kick, a questionable call in the minds of the Barrymore fans.

Both teams positioned themselves outside the box and waited

for Venture's right midfielder to line up and take the penalty kick. Goalkeeper Matt Arnold stood on the goal line and waited for the kick. The home crowd screamed in anticipation.

"Come on, Noah! You're the man! You got this, Noah!"

Noah walked to the ball, picked it up, and spun it a few times. Then he put it down and took a few steps back.

Several Barrymore fans had made the trip to support their team, quiet in this intense moment. All eyes were on the two players, waiting for the outcome—which came quickly.

Noah moved forward and, for a split second, looked left, which caused Matt to shift his weight slightly to the right. Then Noah blasted the ball into the back right corner of the net. Matt had bought the fake, dived right, and came up with two armfuls of air.

After the restart, Barrymore's offense slowly began to take control of the game. The score did not remain at one to nothing for very long. Barrymore tied it up with a nice breakthrough by striker Ian Gregson, who took the ball just over the mid-field and juked his way into the Venture goal area, drilling a shot at the top of the box into the top right corner of the net.

After that, the game belonged to Barrymore, who scored once more in the first half on a nice cross by Lorenzo and a header by Jake. At the end of the game, the score was six to two in favor of Barrymore.

"I'm proud of you, men," Coach said to his team as they assembled near their team bench after the game. "We played as a team on both ends of the field tonight. Defenders, you got the job done. They had few opportunities to get off an uncontested shot. Offense, you were outstanding, moving the ball quickly through midfield and through to our strikers. Good going, guys!"

Coach Patton took a deep breath before continuing: "Next week will be a huge challenge. This is the game I've been looking forward to since we scheduled it last year. You all know what I'm talking about: our 'friendly' against LaGrange. I want you to understand that I would not have scheduled this game if I didn't think we could win it."

The coach paused as the team went quiet. "Yes, they are 5A, we are 3A. Yes, it has already been called a mismatch. We have no business playing LaGrange. I've heard that. You've heard that. They are a good team, well-coached and highly regarded. People are saying that it will be a blowout. What do you say?"

Matt Arnold immediately popped off, "Yeah, well, we may not blow them out, Coach. But we'll beat 'em. Especially if we play like we did tonight."

Matt's comment drew a few chuckles. He surveyed his teammates, then added, "I'm serious."

Coach smiled and said, "I'm glad you are serious, Matt. I'm serious too. So, let me say this to every one of you. If you don't go into that game believing we will win it, don't bother to show up for practice on Monday. Do you understand me? If I see you at practice Monday, I will know you are convinced–meaning, you know that we will beat LaGrange, Friday night, on their home field! TEAM! DO YOU UNDERSTAND ME?"

"YES, SIR!"

As the team loaded onto the bus for the return trip to Barrymore, Michael and Jake headed to the back of the bus and found their seats. After several noisy minutes of bravo talk about the game, the interior noise began to settle down. The passengers, a mix of team members and high school supporters, grew silent and settled in for the two-hour ride home.

"So, what's going on this weekend, Jake?" Michael asked as the two players sat down together.

"Sleep in, goof around, study a little bit on Saturday. Church on Sunday. That's about it," Jake replied. "What about you?"

"About the same, I guess," Michael said. "Except for Sunday, of course."

"Yes, of course," Jake said. "So, what will you be doing on Sunday?"

"Well, lately, I've been going for runs up Cricket Flat," Michael replied.

"That's good, Michael. Keeping that old body tuned up. Yes, sir. That's important. Yes, sir, Michael Shepherd. You keep that up!"

Michael looked quizzically at Jake. "Why the mocking, bruh?"

"Well, let me put it to you like this, Mike. In this life, we understand that our bodies consist of three parts: physical, mental, and spiritual, right?"

"Well.... Duh!"

"Okay then, listen to your priorities for the weekend. This weekend, you said that you are going to sleep in, i.e., give your body some much-needed rest. That's a good thing to do, physically speaking. Then you're going to study, which is good for your mind, of course. So, what are we missing here? Let's see, we've got the physical. We can check that off. Then, the mental. Check it off. But wait. What about part number three, your spiritual life? What about that?" Jake asked.

Michael remained silent, so Jake continued. "Okay, of the three of these, which one would you say is the most important, Mike?"

Then Jake went quiet as he waited for Michael's response, which didn't come. So, a minute later, he added, "Do you know why your spiritual life is the most important, Mike?"

"I'm not sure," Michael said. "But I'm guessing you're about to tell me, aren't you?"

"As a matter of fact, I am," Jake declared. "Your spiritual life is most important because it lasts forever. Your spiritual life lives on eternally, even after your physical and mental selves have died. Mike, you need all three elements to live a balanced life on this earth. Right? But you need a strong spiritual life, which, when surrendered to God, opens the door to eternal life in heaven."

Michael sat quietly. Jake waited patiently. Finally, Michael queried, "How do you know all this?"

"Because I read the Bible, man. Because I listen to my pastors at church. Finally, because I have the Spirit of Christ to guide me, that's how I know. So could you, if you wanted."

After a few minutes of contemplation, Michael quietly said, "I'll think about it, Jake."

Jake said with a slight grin, "Please do. Let me know if you have any questions. I'm praying for you."

"I know you are, bruh. Thanks."

***

On Saturday afternoon, Coach Patton once again parked his car along the curb in front of the small house where Kayla and her brother Joshua lived. Exiting the car, he reached into the back seat and retrieved the soccer ball he had stowed there. Then, he made his way to the front door of Kayla's house. Before he punched the doorbell button, he noticed the wooden blinds were separated and the eyes of a young boy squinting at him between the slats.

In a few seconds, the door swung open. Kayla was dressed in

jeans and a blue flowered blouse. Joshua was in front of Kayla, wide-eyed and grinning from ear to ear.

"Come in, Coach," Kayla said as she stepped aside, pulling Joshua with her.

Coach Patton stepped inside and said, "Hello, Joshua. I'm Coach Patton. I brought you something." He handed the ball to Joshua, who took it and flashed a wide grin before hiding behind Kayla.

His sister prompted, "What do you say to the coach, Joshua?"

"Thank you," Joshua murmured, still hiding behind his sister.

"You're welcome, Joshua. We'll go outside and kick it around in a little bit, okay?"

"Okay," Joshua said, smiling as he peeked around Kayla to look at the coach.

"You're welcome, son. You can call me Coach Kyle, okay?"

"Yes, sir."

Later that afternoon, Kyle and Joshua were kicking the soccer ball back and forth in the small backyard. Coach Patton interrupted the passing routine quite often as he instructed Joshua in the techniques of passing and trapping the soccer ball.

"Use the inside of your foot to trap the ball," he instructed, demonstrating the action each time. "Then use the same part of your inside foot to pass the ball. Do you see what I mean, Josh?"

"Yes," Joshua would say each time, but he had to chase the ball down most of the time because he couldn't get the hang of bringing it under control when it was passed to him. The first few times this happened, Coach Patton had to caution him about picking the ball up with his hands after he had cornered it.

"Don't pick the ball up, Joshua. That's against the rules in soccer," he explained. "Get the ball under control with your feet, okay? Then pass it back to me, okay?" After several passes back and forth, Kyle said, "That's great, Josh! Now you've got it. Good job!"

Kayla observed the soccer lesson her brother was getting from a lawn chair on a nearby patio. She cheered and encouraged Joshua several times as the session went on. Finally, she disappeared for a few minutes, then reappeared with ice-cold glasses of lemonade for the players.

Kyle came over and sat in the chair beside her.

"Wow. He's wearing me out," Kyle chuckled as he gratefully took the lemonade.

"He's loving it," she replied. "Thank you, Coach."

Joshua joined them. He took several drinks of lemonade, then, looking at Kyle, said, "Are you ready, Coach Kyle?"

"Pretty soon, Joshua," Kyle laughed. "Why don't you take the ball and practice juggling? Do you remember how I showed you how to juggle?"

"Yes, sir," Josh said.

"Good. That's something all soccer players need to learn," Kyle replied. "Go for it. Let's see what your record is."

"Okay, Coach. You watch me, okay? You too, Kayla!"

"I will, Josh."

"I can't tell you how much this is a treat for him," Kayla said as the two of them watched Joshua's many attempts to juggle the soccer ball. "I really appreciate it, Kyle."

"Glad to do it, Kayla. I feel bad that his dad isn't around. He doesn't..."

"I'm glad he isn't," Kayla interrupted. "He's hopeless. We don't need him messing up Joshua's life."

"Does he ever visit?" Kyle asked.

"He rarely does. Mostly because it costs him money to visit his son."

"How's that?" Kyle said, eyebrows furrowed in confusion.

"Because he has to be supervised when he visits, and he has to pay the cost of having that privilege," Kayla said grimly.

"That bad, eh?" Kyle asked.

"Yes, every bit that bad."

"Hmmm. Does he help you with expenses?"

"He's supposed to, but no. And I don't want him to," Kayla sighed as she took another sip of lemonade.

"Why is that?"

"Well, then, he might demand visitation rights, and I don't want him around Josh," Kayla explained.

At that moment, Joshua came up to Coach Patton's chair. "Do you want to play some more, Coach Kyle?"

Kyle looked at the boy sternly and said, "What's that in your hands?"

"The soccer ball," Joshua answered. When the boy saw the look on Kyle's face, the ball dropped to the ground. "Oops."

Coach Patton looked at Joshua, then at Kayla, then back again to Joshua. The three burst out laughing.

"I guess we can go for a little while, Josh," Kyle said as the laughter abated. "But then, I probably need to get going."

With a huge frown, Joshua looked at his sister. "Does he have to go, Kalya?"

Kalya looked at Kyle and said, "I have all the fixings for hamburgers, Coach. We would love to share them with you if you could stay."

"Do you have a grill?" Kyle asked, looking around the patio.

"No, I don't. But I can grill them inside. And we can eat outside."

"Sounds good. I accept," Kyle announced with a grin. Then he looked at his watch. "Okay, young man. Thirty minutes left in the game, and we are down by a goal. Let's go win this thing!" He stood, and before Joshua could make a move, Kyle played the ball back into the middle of the backyard. Joshua screamed excitedly and ran after the ball, followed by Coach Patton.

Three hours later, Kyle sat on Kalya's living room sofa, watching soft flames dance brightly from a small fireplace. Joshua had gone up to bed after a fun dinner of hamburgers and ice cream. Kalya plopped down on the other end of the sofa. They both stared silently at the flickering flames. Finally, Kyle turned to Kalya.

He said, "You know, Kayla. This has been a great afternoon. I hope there will be more to follow."

Kalya smiled and continued gazing at the fire, "It was wonderful. Thank you, Kyle."

"Would you like there to be more?" Kyle asked.

Kalya looked up and turned toward Kyle. "Oh, yes," she said. "Of course, I would."

Kyle took a noticeable deep breath and then scooted across the seat to Kalya. He put his arm around her, pulled her into his arms, and kissed her.

After several minutes, Kalya pulled away from the embrace and looked at Kyle. "So, Coach, I'm not sure. Where do we go from here?"

"Where would you like to go?" Kyle quipped.

"Well, I'd like to get to know you better, Kyle, and you get to know me, as well. But...if we begin a relationship, it needs to be done cautiously."

"Cautiously? Why do you say that?"

"I don't think we want to become the targets of gossip at Barrymore High School," Kayla explained. "That wouldn't be good, especially for you. I'm probably not going to be there after this semester, but you will be returning next year. Kids have a keen sense of what's going on, especially when teachers are involved, and even more so if one of the teachers is a popular coach."

"Yeah, you're probably right about that," Kyle sighed. "We do need to be careful, especially at school. If the kids get wind of things, they will probably start following us around. We don't need that, do we?" Kyle rose to his feet and said, "I probably need to get going."

Kalya stood and stepped close to Kyle, who took her in his arms and kissed her again. They walked to the door and embraced once more. After a final kiss, Kyle opened the door and said, "This has been a blessed day, Kayla. Thank you. I'll see you on Monday." Kayla waved from the door, a huge smile on her face, as Kyle got into his car and drove away.

CHAPTER 13

onday morning, Coach Patton sat at his desk as Ethan Maybre stood before the American History Class. It was his morning to take the role and handle announcements. Ethan was a short and overweight young man. He was the oldest of three boys in his family. Ethan played the violin and was good enough to play in the LaGrange City Orchestra. However, he was short on self-confidence and always appeared to be quite uncomfortable when he had to speak to the class.

Reading from a prompt sheet, Ethan began to speak. "This week, a student council meeting will be at 9:30 in the boardroom."

"Is that a.m. or p.m.?" someone asked from the back of the room.

"Well, I guess it's a.m. Doesn't say, really," Ethan replied as he looked down and scanned his prompt sheet. A few snickers emanated around the room.

With an embarrassed smile, Ethan referred again to his prompt and said, "The cafeteria will be serving meatloaf with potatoes and brown gravy and a green salad for lunch today."

Grant Baker snorted, "Um, yummy. Can I get some broccoli with that?"

Someone else blurted out, "With a hint of Oprah?"

"You mean okra."

"Yeah, that too."

Many chuckles broke out in the classroom. Coach Patton got up, walked around his desk, and sat back against the desk with his arms folded. The laughter stopped immediately. The coach looked at Ethan.

"Go ahead, Ethan. You're doing fine."

Ethan smiled at the coach and returned to his papers. "The soccer team plays LaGrange in LaGrange Friday night, and the game time is 7:00 p.m. If you are taking the bus, please be ready to board no later than 5:30 p.m. Finally, don't forget the junior-senior prom is a week from this Saturday."

Ethan looked at the coach. Coach Patton nodded to Ethan. "Good job, Ethan. Thank you."

Coach Patton walked to the front of the class.

"Okay, history buffs, you all seem in great spirits this morning. I'm glad to see that. When we left off Friday, we mentioned two early presidents in our nation's history, John Adams and Thomas Jefferson. Our discussion all last week touched on the dynamics concerning these two men. Who wants to elaborate on that for us this morning?"

Michael Shepherd raised his hand and said, "Their relationship was weird."

"What do you mean by that, Mike?"

"Well, they started out as friends but ended up not liking each other," Michael explained.

"Yes, that's right. Thank you, Mike. Can you tell me what happened to their friendship?" Coach Patton asked.

"Well, it just fell apart," Michael said.

"It fell apart, yes. But what *caused* it to fall apart?" Coach prodded.

"Politics, I guess..." Michael replied, unsure of himself.

"You're telling me these two great statesmen had a falling out over politics? What type of politics?" Coach Patton continued.

"I guess because one of them was a liberal, and one was a conservative," Michael said.

"Maybe so," Coach Patton agreed. "Sounds familiar, doesn't it? Thank you, Mike."

"Yes, sir," Michael replied.

Coach Patton looked around the room, finally focusing on Grant Baker. He said, "Grant, you look pretty energetic today. Do you feel okay?"

"Uhm, yes, sir. Pretty good," Grant replied.

"You just heard Mike say Adams and Jefferson had a falling out because of politics. Do you agree with that?"

"Uh, yes, sir, I do," Grant said.

"So, what happened between these two great statesmen?" Coach continued.

"Well, they both ran for president."

"Yes, they did. Who won?"

"Adams," Grant replied.

"So, who did Adams choose to serve as his Vice President?" Coach asked.

"Thomas Jefferson. But he didn't choose him."

"He didn't choose him?" Patton asked.

"No, sir. The way it worked then, the man who came in second automatically became Vice President," Grant explained.

"Very good, Grant. But doesn't that seem a little awkward for these two men who were elected to run the country?"

"Kind of," Grant replied. "But those were the rules, Coach. And as you are always saying, we need to play by the rules."

"That's right, Grant," Coach Patton replied with a smile. "So even though they didn't like each other much at that particular time, they had to work together for the good of the country. And thankfully, our nation was birthed under their leadership, theirs, and other brave men who stepped up to win the freedom we enjoy today. Good discussion, Grant. I can tell you've been studying. Keep it up."

"Yes, sir," Grant replied.

Coach Patton then turned his attention to the entire class. "Okay, class. From what we've learned, certain political issues and principles in the midst of major complications resulted in the building of our country into the most powerful nation in the world today. I want to read what you think about how our country built such a strong foundation and, secondly, how we Americans today can protect the freedoms these early statesmen secured for us. I am going to reward 10,000 points to the student who writes the clearest, most compelling, and most defensible paper on this subject. Please note that this part of the assignment can only have one winner."

"But, for an extra bonus of 5,000 points, I will award the best papers that describe the history of the relationship between these two men and what you know about what they shared. All of you must participate in the first assignment, but there can be only one winner. The bonus assignment can have multiple winners. For those who want to build up your Husky points, here's your chance. Any questions?"

Coach Patton paused as he waited for questions or comments. Jake raised his hand and asked, "What about the war, Coach? Does that need to be part of it?"

"Not to any extent, Jake. Good question, however," Coach replied. "You can refer to it, of course. It was the major event of the time, but I'm looking at it from a political perspective more than the military story. Do you see what I mean?"

"Yes, sir," Jake replied.

"Okay, good. Any other questions?"

The students exchanged glances. Some shook their heads. No one responded to the coach.

"Okay. Your papers are due by next Monday. I'll give you some class time each day for this project, but you will also have to work at home to come up with the quality report I'm seeking," Coach said.

He stood quietly until the students were quiet and paying attention.

"Okay, American history fans, we are ready to break some new ground this week. I think you will find this an interesting study as we look at the fourth and fifth presidents of the United States. Who can tell me their names?" Patton asked.

A few hands went up, including Matt Arnold's and a shaky one from Brydon Gilmore.

"Yes, Brydon," Coach Patton said.

"Roosevelt and George Bush," Brydon said.

Coach looked at Brydon and frowned. "Roosevelt and George Bush. Hmm. Which Roosevelt, Brydon?"

Brydon, with a quizzical look, asked, "Was there more than one?"

"Yes, Brydon. Neither one was the fourth or fifth president, however. Nor was George Bush."

"You sure, Coach? I thought for sure...." Brydon trailed off.

"I'm sure, Brydon," Coach replied.

Coach Patton then looked at Matt. "Who were they, Matt?"

"Well, Coach, I was thinking maybe Benedict Arnold was one of them anyway," Matt replied.

"No, Matt. Benedict Arnold was not ever president of the United States. In fact, we are going to study him soon. I might ask you to write an essay on him. Will you remind me?" Coach asked with a wry smile.

"Sure, Coach," Matt uttered with a red face.

Coach Patton gazed around the room, locking eyes with Tori Zinzer. "What do you think, TZ? Who was the fourth president of the United States?"

"Was it James Madison?" TZ replied.

"Yes, it was. James Madison was the fourth president of the United States and served from 1809 to 1817. Can anyone tell me what James Madison was known as? Anyone?" Coach asked.

Coach Patton surveyed the students, but everyone was quiet. Finally, he asked, "What have we been studying for the last six weeks in this class?"

Several voices rang out, "The Constitution!"

"Right, the Constitution," Coach Patton responded.

Jake raised his hand, Google visibly pulled up on his smartphone. "I've got it, Coach. Madison was called the Father of the Constitution, and James Monroe was the fifth president of the United States."

"Good job, Jake!" Coach replied. "Now, put your phone away, okay?"

"Yes, sir," Jake replied sheepishly, slipping his phone into his back pocket.

Coach Patton turned to the whiteboard and wrote "JAMES MADISON" and "JAMES MONROE" on the board. Under Madison, he wrote "1809 – 1817, Father of the Constitution." Under James Monroe, he wrote "1817 – 1825, The Monroe Doctrine."

Then he turned to the class and said, "These two men were great statesmen who served their country during some of its most difficult times. Over the next two weeks, we will learn more about these men, how they contributed, what they believed, and some of the major issues they faced while serving in the White House. Your participation in these discussions will impact your grade, so you may want to get a head start on our discussions, which will begin tomorrow."

"Are there any questions?" The coach waited a few moments and looked around for someone to speak. No one did, so he finished with, "Okay, you can start writing your reports on our nation's political foundation and how you view the relationship between Adams and Jefferson. Be ready tomorrow to talk about our fourth and fifth presidents."

* * *

Joker Duff was once again driving along Overlook Street, following a yellow school bus that lumbered down the busy street. The bus stopped several times along the way to allow students to exit and begin their short treks to their homes.

Joker was not disappointed when he saw Annie Smith step down from the bus, hitch up her book bag, and begin to walk to her home. As before, he edged his car over to the curb, careful not to be noticed as doing anything suspicious or unusual.

As Annie started up the steps to her front door, Joker opened his car door, stepped out, and began to casually walk up the side-walk in front of Annie's house. Annie fumbled through her book bag, looking for her house key. As soon as she had it and inserted it into the deadlock on the front door, Joker made a quick turn and arrived on the porch just as Annie got the door open. Before Annie knew what was going on, Joker had pushed her into the house and closed the door. Annie screamed as he grabbed her. Her scream, however, was not the immediate issue confronting Joker. He had a bigger problem. A 70-pound, four-legged, enraged animal named Biscuit was all over him with gnashing teeth and digging claws, making hamburger of his legs and arms.

"Call him off! Call him off!" Joker screamed at the girl as he turned back to the door and tried to shake off the vicious dog at the same time. By the time he reached the door, his hand was slick with blood, and he was unable to turn the door handle. He fought the dog off as best he could until he was able to reach his knife, which was in a sheath on his belt.

When Annie saw the knife, she screamed, "Don't you hurt my dog!" She charged the intruder, driving Joker against the door. As the dog tore at his legs and midsection, Joker raised his knife in an attempt to plunge it into Biscuit's body.

Annie immediately screamed, "Oh no you don't!" She grabbed her book bag and swung it at Joker, connecting with the left side of his head, altering but not preventing Joker's knife from opening a deep gash in Biscuit's neck and slicing off a portion of his right ear.

Joker shoved Annie away, then managed to get the door open and escape from the house. He left a trail of blood across the yard, the sidewalk, and the street to his car. He wasted no time getting into his car and out of the neighborhood.

Annie's entire body shook as she dropped to her knees to comfort her dog. Biscuit shook his head several times as blood ran into his eyes and about the room.

"I'm so sorry, Biscuit," she said as she tried to pat her dog's head and hug him, but Biscuit wouldn't hold still long enough for her to do that. She jumped to her feet and ran into the kitchen to secure a towel, which she soaked with cold water, hurrying back to apply to her dog's wound. "Biscuit, please don't die," she sobbed. Biscuit began to slowly settle down, allowing Annie to apply the damp towel to his wounded ear.

After several minutes of applying pressure and turning the blood-soaked towel over several times, Annie stood and ran to her book bag. She dumped out the contents, grabbed her cell phone, and dialed 911.

"It's my dog, Biscuit," she said in an emotional plea into her phone. "He's been hurt badly. Please, can you help me?"

"Your dog is injured?" the dispatcher asked.

"Yes, ma-am," Annie cried.

"Hold on, please."

The next thing Annie heard was a recorded message that said, "We're sorry. Please contact your vet or the nearest emergency animal hospital for animal or pet emergencies."

"But I don't have that number," Annie sobbed, accidentally allowing the phone to slip out of her bloodied hands. She grabbed it off the floor, wiped it against her blouse, and shouted, "Siri, animal emergency clinic near me. Hurry!"

She studied her phone as she heard the words, "I found this.

Shady Grove Animal Clinic." Annie quickly dialed the number provided.

"Shady Grove Animal Clinic. How can I serve you?"

Her entire body was shaking. Annie cried into her phone, "My dog, Biscuit. He's been stabbed. He's bleeding. Can you help me?"

"Is your dog under control?"

"Yes," Annie replied.

"Do you have a wet towel you can use as a pressure bandage?"

"Yes."

"What is your address?"

Annie quickly responded with her address.

"We're on our way," came the immediate response.

Annie carefully lifted Biscuit's head from her lap and headed into the kitchen. She grabbed a clean dish towel and soaked it with cold water. She squeezed away the excess water and returned to her seriously wounded pet.

"You're going to be okay, Biscuit. They are coming to take you to the dog hospital. You're going to be okay," she said again as she applied gentle pressure to the wound.

CHAPTER 14

Rain had been in the forecast, but school officials at LaGrange High School determined the soccer game could be played as scheduled. Both teams were on the field, under the lights, and soccer fans were finding places to sit or stand to see the game.

Coach Patton and Coach Agular stood together, watching their team warm up.

Coach Agular said, "We could have a pretty good crowd tonight, coach. I'm surprised…"

"Hold that thought," Kyle said. "I'm going to jog over and speak to our opposing coach while I have the chance." Kyle double-timed it across the field and squared up with Patrick Hill, the head coach of LaGrange's soccer team.

Kyle offered his hand to Patrick, who accepted the gesture with a high-speed handshake. "Good luck, Coach," Kyle said.

"Yeah, you too, Coach," Patrick replied. "Uhh, tell me your name again, please."

"Yeah, sure. My name is Kyle Patton. We're glad to have the opportunity to play your team."

"Glad to do it," he replied. "Good luck, hear." Coach Hill turned away from Kyle and walked away.

At that moment, the referee blew his whistle and called the team captains to midfield for pregame instructions, goal selection, and the coin toss. With those issues settled, the captains returned to their teammates and coaches on the touchlines. The Barrymore fans were making a lot of noise, while the LaGrange crowd was much more subdued.

Coach Patton knelt as his team huddled around him. "Okay, guys. Press the ball. Take the game to them. Play to space, and do not concede anything to these guys. We have proven we are a good soccer team. Tonight, we move from good to great. You got it? From good to great!"

"YES, SIR!"

"Then, go do it!"

"YES, SIR!"

The Barrymore Huskies charged onto the field to take on the LaGrange Tigers. The game was on. The fans were ready for action, and they weren't disappointed. Play was furious as the two teams battled up and down the pitch. An opposing player challenged every touch, up and down, side to side. Frustration began to build early for LaGrange due to the intensive pressure of the Barrymore team. Counterattacks by Barrymore turned back every attack by LaGrange, and LaGrange turned back every attack by Barrymore. That is, until the thirty-eighth minute when Lorenzo Gonzales, Barrymore's right midfielder, controlled a ball lobbed to him from goalkeeper Arnold. With lightning speed, Lorenzo barreled down the right sideline to about thirty yards out and blasted a high ball that surprised the LaGrange goalkeeper as it sailed over his head and into the upper left corner of the net.

"GOAL!" The Barrymore fans screamed as they celebrated in the stands and exchanged enthusiastic high-fives.

Coach Agular and Coach Patton high-fived one another. Patton whispered, with a grin out of the corner of his mouth, "I think that was meant to be a cross, not a shot."

"I think so too, Coach. But I doubt that Lorenzo would ever admit it."

"I'm sure you're right," Patton laughed. "Either way, we'll take it, right?"

"For sure, Coach, for sure."

The teams lined up again for the restart, and play resumed with even more intensity, especially on the part of LaGrange. But nothing changed, and by halftime, Barrymore led the game one to nothing. The back-and-forth ferocity continued throughout the second half until close to the end of the game. With nine minutes to go, LaGrange was awarded a corner kick on the left side. The Tigers brought their entire team into the box. They had a tall striker standing on the goal line. When the ball was played into the box, he elevated himself higher than any other player, and struck a beautiful header that went over Matt's outstretched hands and into the goal.

"GOAL!" The LaGrange Tiger fans screamed.

The game was tied one to one, and it stayed that way through regulation play, followed by a ten-minute overtime period. When it was obvious that the score wouldn't change, the coaches on both teams huddled to discuss post-game strategy.

Coach Patton stepped in close to his assistant coach. "This thing is going to go into penalty kicks, Aaron," he said. "I need our penalty kickers and their kicking order."

Aaron put his head down, thought for about two minutes, and declared, "I've got them, Coach."

"Who do you have?" Patton asked.

"Jake, Lorenzo, Austin, Ian, and Michael, in that order."

"Sounds good," Kyle said as the referee blew his whistle, ending regular play.

The players from both teams gathered around their respective coaches.

Coach Patton addressed his team. "Okay, men, we have chosen five of you to start the first round of penalty kicks. Hopefully, we won't need more, but if we do, please cheer for your teammates and be ready for the next round in case it happens. The rules regarding penalty kicks are that each team alternates kickers until one team is far enough in front that the score can't be tied. You've all seen this before. Step up, figure out where to place the ball without tipping off their goalkeeper, take a deep breath, and strike the ball. If you score, great; if you don't score, don't worry about it. We're a team; remember that. Okay?" The coach then looked at his goalkeeper: "Matt, no matter how this plays out, you are the best goalkeeper on the field tonight. This is a team win or a team loss. You got that?"

"Yes, sir," Matt replied.

The referee blew his whistle, and twelve players and two officials walked to the west goal. Jake Ledger walked to the ball, which had been placed on the penalty spot by one of the officials. The LaGrange goalkeeper took his position in the goal. Jake picked up the ball, twirled it in his hands, and sat it back down. He took three paces back and to his left. He looked at the goalkeeper, then at the ball, moved to it quickly, but unfortunately, blasted it over the top of the goal. Jake's shoulders immediately sagged. He turned and trotted back to his teammates.

It was now the LaGrange team's turn. Their tall striker had been chosen to take their first kick. He walked to the ball, picked it up, wiped it on his jersey, and sat it back in place. He then positioned himself a few steps to his left behind the ball, quickly strode to it, and struck it solidly. It went right. Unfortunately, Matt anticipated he would go left, so he came up empty-handed. The La-Grange crowd cheered as their team led the match, two to one.

The penalty kicks continued, kick after kick, until all ten players had taken their turns. Although Barrymore had played the much larger school even-up for one hundred minutes of intense soccer, they could not pull out the victory. LaGrange won the match by a score of five to three due to their superiority in the penalty kick segment of the game.

The players congratulated one another, as did the coaches, as they came together at midfield.

"Good game, Coach," Patrick Hill said to Kyle as they shook hands. "You have a very good team, well coached. You gave us all we could handle."

"Thank you, Coach," Kyle replied. "Maybe we can do another friendly next year."

The LaGrange coach moved on without responding. Kyle smiled—*I guess that's a big fat, "No way, Jose."* Coach Patton returned to his players, waiting for him on the touchline.

"I am proud of you, men," he said. "You showed tonight what kind of players you are and how good we are as a team. This is not your loss tonight. This one's on me. We lost tonight because I didn't prepare you properly. That won't happen again, I can assure you. Thank goodness it was in a game that doesn't count in the standings, but it was a game that shows us how good a team we are, and that's big. Go home, stay positive, and I'll see you soon."

"Coach, did we go from good to great tonight?" Matt asked.

"You bet we did, Matt. For sure! Thank you for asking that question," Coach Patton replied with a smile.

As the team drifted away, Kyle saw Andrew Sharpe, the athletic director at Unity, talking to the LaGrange coach. Not wanting to interrupt their conversation, he took a circuitous route out of the athletic complex. People were disappearing rapidly as rain clouds still threatened. As he started to leave, he saw a small familiar figure running toward him. It was Joshua, followed by Kalya.

"Hey, pal!" Patton laughed as Joshua engulfed him in a huge hug. "Did you see the game?"

"Yes, I did, Coach Kyle," Joshua puffed. "Kalya and I were here the whole time. Didn't you see us? We were over there, in those bleachers." Joshua pointed to bleachers behind the LaGrange bench.

"Why in the world were you over there?" Coach Patton asked, eyebrows furrowed.

"Because we didn't want to be a distraction," Kalya answered with a wink as she stepped in to join them.

"You wouldn't have been a distraction," Kyle replied. Then he looked into Kalya's beautiful eyes and said, "Yeah, well, maybe you would have been a distraction. So, would you like to go get something to eat?"

Joshua immediately said, "Yeah!"

"No," Kayla said sadly. I need to get him home. It's late, and he needs to get to bed."

"Are you sure?"

"Come on, Kalya," Joshua cried out.

Kalya put her hand on Joshua's head, sighed, and said, "Yes, I'm sure, Coach."

"How about if I swing by when I return to Barrymore?"

Kalya looked Kyle in the eye and sighed again. "Probably not a good idea, Kyle. I'm sorry."

Kyle paused thoughtfully, then said, "I understand. May I come by tomorrow afternoon?"

"I'd like that," Kayla replied with a smile.

"Me, too, Coach Kyle," Joshua said enthusiastically.

Kyle smiled and said, "Okay, I will see you two tomorrow. Be careful going home."

As Kalya departed, Andrew Sharpe approached, interrupting Kyle's planned exit.

"Hey Coach," Sharpe called as he drew near Kyle.

"Hello, Andrew," Patton replied as he shook his hand. "I'm glad you made it. What did you think?"

"I think, great game. Two well-coached teams. I'm impressed," Andrew replied.

"Thank you," Kyle said. "I'm not proud of our finish, but I'm glad it came up in this game so I can fix it before the next game."

"I have no doubt you will be able to do that, Coach. "Well, I just wanted to let you know I was here. I am impressed with your team. Let's stay in touch, okay?"

"Yes, sir. Thanks again for coming."

"I wouldn't have missed it. Good night, Coach."

"Good night, Andrew."

Both men departed. But Kyle wondered. *What does "Let's stay in touch" mean?*

On his way back to Barrymore, Kyle drove slowly, trying to put everything into perspective, coaching soccer and possibly a change in venue. Then there was Kalya. What surprised him most was that his thoughts were more about Kalya than coaching soccer...

***

Michael and Jake were together in Jake's truck as they left the parking lot of LaGrange High School. "We were so close," Jake groaned as he swung the car onto Parker Street and headed into the downtown area of LaGrange.

"Yep," Michael replied, "but close only counts...."

"In horseshoes and hand grenades," Jake finished with a laugh. "I know. Okay, enough about the game. How about springing for some frozen yogurt? There's a place right up here on the right. We're burning my gas, right?"

"Okay, that's cool. Half a pound limit, okay?"

"Sounds good," Jake replied as he pulled his car into an open parking spot in front of Frankie's Frozen Yogurt Shop.

The two boys entered the shop, picked up two small sample cups, and headed to the frozen yogurt dispensers.

Michael stood in front of the vanilla dispenser. But he was distracted by a very attractive young lady standing next to him in front of the strawberry dispenser.

"Too many choices, aren't there?" Michael proclaimed as he stepped up close to the girl.

"There are," she said. "But I know I will always get strawberry, so that's where I start."

"Yeah, I'm that way with vanilla," Michael replied. "Do you live here in LaGrange?"

"I do," she replied. "How about you?"

"I live in Barrymore," Michael said as he pretended to survey the flavors. "My friend and I just finished a soccer game. We were headed back to Barrymore and decided to reward ourselves with a frozen yogurt."

"That means you must have won," the girl said as she pulled the handle and dispensed herself some frozen strawberry yogurt.

"Nope, unfortunately not. We lost the game on penalty kicks," Michael replied as he filled his cup with a generous supply of vanilla.

The girl moved over to another bank of flavors. Michael followed her. He asked, "What's your backup choice going to be?"

"I guess I'll go with this dark cherry café latte. That looks good," she replied.

"Yeah, sounds good too. I'll follow you," Micahel said.

He stepped beside her and asked, "Um, are you here by yourself?"

"No, my folks are here. They brought me out for a treat, sort of anyway." She placed her cup under the dispenser and pulled the handle.

"Sort of? What does that mean?"

"Well, my dog was just badly hurt. They felt sorry for me." She choked up momentarily. "We're celebrating that he's going to be alright." She smiled weakly, then said, "I need to get back to them. It's been nice talking to you."

"Yeah, you too," Michael said as he watched the young lady walk away. *My next question was going to be, What's your name? But I didn't ask. That was stupid. Now she's gone. What an idiot you are, Michael Shepherd!*

"Man, she was beautiful," Michael said as Jake backed his truck out of the parking lot and turned onto Parker Street.

"Yeah, she was!" Jake replied. "Did you get her name?"

"No," Michael said dejectedly.

"Too bad, dummy. Well, at least you know she likes frozen yo-gurt."

"That's true, and she prefers strawberry. Hey, maybe the gal running the cash register knows her!"

"Probably not," Jake said sympathetically. It's too late to go back and ask. You'll have to sharpen your social skills in dealing with women, bruh."

"Like you, right?"

"Right."

Michael asked, "So, who are you taking to the prom, lover boy?"

"I'm thinking about asking Olivia," Jake replied as he pulled the truck up to a stop at a red light.

"Isn't she still in the hospital?" Michael asked, confused.

"So?" Jake replied, turning to look at Michael with his eye-brows raised.

"So, how can you take her to the prom if she is in the hospital?" Michael asked.

"I can't," Jake said, laughing.

"Jacob, once again, you are not making any sense." Michael shook his head in confusion. The light turned green, and Jake put his foot back on the gas.

"Sure I am," Jake laughed. I'm just thinking outside the box."

"How's that?"

"I'm thinking about bringing the prom to the hospital," Jake replied.

"Hmmm," Michael mused. "How would you pull that off?"

"I'll get back to you on that, bruh. How about you? Are you going to ask anybody?"

"Yeah. I hope to."

"Who?" Jake asked.

"The chick in the frozen yogurt shop."

"Yeah? How are you going to do that? You don't even know her name."

"Maybe I'll try praying about it," Michael replied, playfully punching Jake's shoulder.

"Now that's the smartest thing you've said since I've known you," Jake said, grinning. "There's hope after all."

"I'll let you know if I get an answer."

"You'll get an answer, bruh. Just may not be one you're expecting."

CHAPTER 15

On Saturday afternoon, Coach Patton backed a borrowed pickup truck up the narrow driveway at Kayla's house. He hopped out of the truck, strode to the front door of Kayla's house, and rang the doorbell. Within minutes, Kayla and Joshua were at the door.

"Kyle, you're here early!" Kayla exclaimed. "Is everything okay?"

"Of course. Everything is perfect. But I do need your help unloading something from the truck. You too, Joshua."

All three walked to the driveway. Kyle jumped into the back of the truck and carefully pushed a shiny new grill over to the end of the truck bed. Then he jumped back to the ground and, along with Kayla and Joshua, got the new grill down and into the backyard.

"This is so nice," Kayla said as Kyle lifted the hood and positioned the two-piece grill tops together.

"Oh boy!" Joshua shouted. "Can we use it tonight?"

"We sure can," Kyle said as he hurried back to the truck and lifted out a fully fueled propane tank. "We'll initiate it tonight. I hope you all like steak."

"Oh yes," Kayla beamed. "We love steak."

"Steak and baked potato. I thought you might like that."

"I've got the fixings for a green salad," Kayla added.

"Wonderful. We're all set, then. I'll get the groceries out of the truck," and then, looking at Joshua, he said, "I'm ready to play some soccer. How about you, partner?"

With a huge grin, Joshua bellowed, "I'm ready, Coach Kyle."

After dinner, Kyle and Kayla were seated in lounge chairs, watching Joshua do his best to juggle his soccer ball. After several tries, he managed to get the number of touches to four and a half.

"Great job, Joshua," Kyle called out. "That's a new record."

Kayla joined in the cheering, "Wonderful, Joshua. Keep it up." Joshua disappeared behind a lilac bush in the back corner of the yard near the fence. as he ran after the ball.

Kalya looked at Kyle. "You've made quite an impression on him, Kyle. Thank you. And thank you for the steaks. They were wonderful."

"My pleasure, Kalya," Coach replied with a smile. "I'm enjoying this more than you can imagine."

Kalya was slow to respond, then looked at Kyle and said, "I heard from Joshua's dad today."

"You did?" Kyle replied, eyebrows raised in surprise.

Kalya nodded, pulled her legs up, tucked them under her body, and murmured, "Uh-huh."

"Do you want to talk about it?" Kyle asked gently.

"Sure," Kayla replied.

"So, what was on his mind?"

"Well, I'm not sure, really," Kayla said hesitantly. "Somehow, he knows about you."

"Really! How?" Kyle asked, confused.

"I don't know. All I know is that he asked me if I was dating someone. He apparently has seen your car here, or maybe he has spies keeping their eyes on me. I don't know. Anyway, I don't like it, and I told him it was none of his business and to stay away from Joshua."

"So, what are you going to do?" Kyle asked.

"Just wait, I guess," Kayla sighed. He has no rights. If he continues, I'll take him to court."

"Kalya, I want you to promise me that if he contacts you again, you will let me know, okay?"

"I don't want you to get involved in my problems, Kyle."

"I already am, Kalya. So please keep me in the loop, okay?" Kyle said, gently placing his hand over hers.

At that moment, Joshua came running up on the patio, the ball at his feet. "Hey, Coach Kyle. My new record is five!"

"Good job, Joshua. Keep it up, buddy. You're doing great!" Kyle nodded encouragingly.

"Thank you, Coach Kyle. Do you want to do some passing?"

"That would be cool, man." Kyle stood, winked at Kayla, and kicked the ball away from Joshua's feet into the backyard. He chased after it, calling back to Joshua, "Come on, man. What are you waiting for?"

***

Brittany Cummings was seated in a side chair in her daughter's hospital room. She was reading a magazine as Olivia worked on a history assignment about the relationship between John Adams and Thomas Jefferson.

Olivia broke the silence by uttering, "Huh! That's weird."

Brittany put her book in her lap, looked at her daughter, and said, "What's that?"

"Both John Adams and Thomas Jefferson died on the same day, on the fourth of July 1826," Olivia replied.

"Really?" Brittany said. "I didn't know that. Didn't they have a falling out or something?"

"Yes, they did. They...." At that moment, Dr. Patterson entered the room after a short knock on the door.

Brittany stood up and greeted the doctor with a handshake. "Dr. Patterson. It's good to see you."

"Thank you, Mrs. Cummings. I'm glad you're here. I have an update for you on Olivia's condition."

Brittany's expression immediately changed to a look of concern. "Oh dear, I hope it's good news."

"We think it is," the doctor replied with a smile. "The lab results show improvement, and she seems to be healing. I think she's ready to move into a step-down room now. We will continue with the antibiotics, reduce the pain meds, and begin to get her on her feet."

Both Olivia and her mom teared up over that good news. Brittany stepped over to Olivia and hugged her.

"That's wonderful news, Dr. Patterson," Brittany said, wiping tears from her eyes. "Thank you so much."

"Think nothing of it," he said. Then, turning to Olivia, he said, "The staff here will miss you, young lady."

"I'm going to miss them, too," Olivia replied.

"Okay, ladies. Your nurse will be in soon to make the arrangements. I'll check in with you tomorrow."

"Thank you, Dr. Patterson," Olivia and her mom called out as he moved to the door and left the room. Both ladies, with teary eyes, hugged again.

"We're going to be okay, Olivia. We're going to be okay. I know it."

"I do, too, Mom. I do, too."

***

One week later, Coach Patton was tuned into English soccer on television at his house. He had a date with Kalya and Joshua that evening for a pizza dinner and was contemplating the need to get ready when his doorbell rang. He rose from his chair and went to the door just in time to see a courier driver walking back down his front steps through an entryway window. He opened the door and, on the porch, lay a large carton addressed to Coach Kyle Patton. Kyle reached down, cradled the package, and, with no small effort, wrestled it through the doorway and into his living room. He then opened the top of the carton and peeked inside.

"Perfect," he whispered to himself. "This should do the job." He grinned, closed the flap down, and pushed the box into a corner of the room.

Three hours later, Kyle, Kalya, and Joshua were seated in a back corner of Piero's Pizza Parlor in LaGrange. They were having fun as they tore into the house specialty, a family-sized "Piero's Monster" on thick crust and with extra cheese.

"Good stuff," Kyle said as he polished off his first segment and reached for a second piece. "How do you like it, Joshua?"

"Good," Joshua replied, barely audible with his mouth full of cheese.

"How about you, Kayla?" Kyle asked.

"It's very good, thank you, Coach," Kayla smiled.

"You're welcome." After a slight pause, Kyle continued, "I want to confide in you about something I think you should know, Kayla... you alone. So, bear with me for a few minutes, okay?" Kyle reached into his inner coat pocket, pulled out a comic book, and handed it to Joshua.

"Joshua, could you take your pizza to the next table and read for a few minutes while I talk to your sister? We'll be right here."

Joshua looked quizzically at the coach and then at his sister. She smiled and nodded, "It's okay, Joshua."

Joshua grabbed his drink while Kyle helped him carry his pizza and moved to the next table. When he was settled and started to read his new comic book, Kyle returned to his table.

"So, what's going on, Coach?" Kalya asked as Kyle settled into his chair.

"Quite a lot, actually," Kyle replied as he reached for his last piece of pizza. "This is confidential, of course, but I want you to know that there's a chance that I might be leaving my job at Barrymore High School."

With a shocked expression, Kalya gasped and said, "You're leaving Barrymore?"

Kyle signaled with his hand to keep the volume down and said, "No. I'm not leaving Barrymore, but possibly leaving Barrymore High." Then, in an even more suppressed voice, he said, "There's a fair chance I will be getting an offer to coach at Unity."

"Really, Kyle? Why, that would be fantastic... wouldn't it?" Kayla asked.

"In many ways, yes," Kyle replied. "But still, it would be hard. I would miss the kids and the teaching, of course."

"Well, wouldn't there be some teaching included at Unity?"

"I don't think so, but I didn't ask that question," Kyle said thoughtfully.

"Men!" Kalya laughed. "When will you know something?"

"Not sure," Kyle replied. "Must be soon because contract deadlines are coming up."

"So, will you take it if it's offered?" Kayla asked.

"Probably. I'm praying about it, Kalya." Kyle reached across the table and took Kalya's hand. "I'd like you to pray about it, too."

"I will, sweetheart. I promise."

Their sweet moment of pleasure was suddenly and rudely interrupted when Derek Steinman, Joker Duff, and Nick Foster rambled into the restaurant and chose to sit at a nearby table.

Immediately, the room was filled with loud and coarse talk as the three looked over the menus and bantered with one another about how things would be better if they were in charge. Once Joker laid eyes on Kalya, he let out a loud whistle and roared, "Would you look at the lady? Ain't she pretty?"

Kyle looked at Kalya and said, "We need to finish up here, guys. Okay?" He stood and motioned to a waiter, who approached their table. "Yes, sir," the waiter said to Kyle.

"Yes, we'd like a check and a to-go box," Kyle said.

The waiter replied, "Yes, sir. I'll get that right away."

As the waiter left, Derek looked over at Kyle, sneered, and said, "What's the matter? Are you too good to eat near us?"

"Not really," Kyle replied. "I just don't like my family here to hear the garbage coming out of your mouths, that's all."

With that, Derek stood, followed by Joker and Nick. Derek motioned to his two friends to sit back down, then turned to Kyle. Kyle looked at Kalya and Joshua, who were still seated and obviously frightened. He knew he needed to get them out of the situation before things worsened. He quickly prayed, *Jesus, how should I handle this?*

"Are you ready to go?" Kyle asked.

Kalya stood. She took Joshua's hand.

The two men stared at one another. Then Derek, a few inches shorter than Kyle, snarled, "Yeah, you'd better leave while you can still walk. You're a coward. I can't stand cowards, especially when I'm eating."

"The lady could stay," Joker sneered.

At that remark, Kyle stiffened. He stepped close to Derek and, eyeball to eyeball, said in a low voice, "Okay, tough guy, do you happen to know where the city water tank is on Mount Stevens?"

"Yeah."

"Do you know the road that leads up there?"

"Yeah."

"Good. I'll meet you there in two hours, at about nine o'clock. Okay?"

Derek paused.

"Is it a deal or not? Or are you a coward? Leave your two friends at home, of course. Can you do that?" Kyle stuck his right hand out in a handshake gesture.

Derek hesitated, then returned the gesture. Kyle clasped Derek's hand in a vice grip, causing Derek to noticeably wince. "Just make sure you show up, tough guy."

Kyle turned to Kalya. "Are you ready?"

"I am," she asserted. Kyle picked up the boxed-up pizza, and the three departed.

***

Jake Ledger knocked on the partially ajar door of room 1214 of University Hospital.

"Come in," came Olivia Cummings' voice.

Jake stepped into the room, holding a bouquet of pink roses. Olivia was sitting up in bed. She smiled radiantly as Jake came across the room to the side of the bed. Kelsey, the nurse on duty, immediately reached for the flowers and said. "I'll go find a vase for these if you'd like. They are so pretty."

"That would be great," Jake said as he handed her the bouquet.

"Thank you, Kelsey," Olivia called out to the nurse as she departed the room. Then she looked at Jake. "They are beautiful, Jake. Thank you."

Jake smiled and asked, "How do you feel today?"

"Perfect today, Jake," Olivia replied. "Thank you."

"So, what is the doctor telling you? I know you're better. Otherwise, you wouldn't be in this room," Jake said as he sat down on the edge of her bed.

"I am better, Jake, much better."

"I'm glad about that because I want to ask you something," Jake said, a light hint of a blush climbing up his neck and cheeks.

With a smile of anticipation, Olivia pulled her legs up and leaned forward. "You do? What do you want to ask me?"

"Well, I want to ask if you want to go to the prom with me?"

Olivia was clearly stunned. She paused as she looked into Jake's eyes. "You're asking me to go to the prom? How can I do that? The prom is less than two weeks away. I can hardly walk. I certainly can't dance. I can't even get out of this bed without someone helping me."

"None of those things matter," Jake said. "If you can't come to the prom, I'll bring the prom to you."

Olivia leaned back on the pillows stacked against the bed's headboard. With tears running down her cheeks, she said, "Oh, Jake. That is so sweet. Of course, I will go to the prom with you."

Jake stepped forward and took Olivia by the hand. "Super," he said.

Olivia picked up a tissue and wiped her eyes. Then she looked at Jake and said, "How are you going to pull it off, Jake?"

"Don't you worry about that. I'll bring the crowd and the music," Jake said with a wink. "You won't have to do anything."

At that moment, Kelsey returned to the room with the flowers in a purple vase. She brought them to Olivia for her approval. "Nice! Thank you, Kelsey," Olivia said as she took a deep breath and smelled the fragrance. She looked at Jake again. "Thank you, Jake."

Jake smiled and turned to Kelsey. "So Kelsey, will you be here next Saturday evening?"

"I hope not," she quipped. "Why do you ask?"

"Well, we are going to celebrate prom night for Olivia. I want to bring some friends over and have some music. Do a little dancing. What do you think?" Jake asked.

"Hmmm. I don't know about that. This is a hospital, you know," Kelsey said.

"I know," Jake replied. "But I promise to keep it under control."

Kelsey glanced at Olivia and smiled. "Would you like me to be here, Olivia?"

"Oh yes," Olivia responded.

"Well, in that case, I will be here." She looked at Jake. "Can I bring my boyfriend?"

"You sure can. No extra charge for boyfriends," Jake said with a wink.

"Okay, it's a deal then," Kelsey said as she placed the flower vase on a side table and walked to the door. "I'll be back," she said, then disappeared from the room.

Jake spent the next hour in Olivia's room, updating her on what was happening with their classmates, school activities, and the soccer team. Finally, Kelsey returned and announced it was time for physical therapy and that Jake should leave. Jake walked to the bed, took Olivia's hand, and whispered, "See you soon, Olivia."

Olivia smiled. "See you soon, Jake."

***

At 8:45 p.m., Kyle Patton drove his car up the gravel road leading to the city of LaGrange's water tower. He parked his car, turned off the engine, and pushed his seat back, waiting for Derek to arrive for their encounter. He was alone in his car.

Kyle had not been in many altercations growing up because he could always de-escalate tensions before they got out of hand. But no one had ever called him a coward before. *That can't stand,* he thought to himself as he leaned his head back against his headrest.

But what would Jesus do? He would turn the other cheek, of course. That's what Jesus would do. So... show me what to do, Jesus. Give me the words I need to say to this young man, Lord.

Soon, Kyle saw headlights slowly progressing up the twisty

road toward the water tank. After several minutes, Derek pulled his pickup truck behind Kyle's car, shut off the engine, and stepped onto the road. Kyle exited his car and walked up the road toward the water tower. He stopped and turned toward Derek, who was slowly walking up the gravel road with his eyes fixed on Kyle. As far as Kyle could see, Derek had come by himself.

"I see you came alone. I'm surprised." Kyle called out.

"I don't need no help for the likes of you," Derek snarled.

"If you say so," Kyle shrugged as he continued walking. "What's your name?"

"Derek. What's yours?"

"Kyle."

The two men finally came together, with Derek slightly on Kyle's upside. Derek sneered and snapped, "Okay, Kyle, are you ready to get this on?" Then, without waiting for an answer, Derek swung a crushing right fist into the left side of Kyle's head.

Kyle blinked but did not move or waver. He stood erect and looked intently into Derek's eyes. Then, with a cynical grin, he asked, "Is that it? That's your best punch?"

Derek was obviously surprised and confused. He felt a painful throb in his right hand, and he was astonished that Kyle had not gone down. Now, lacking the confidence to look Kyle in the eye, he gazed down at his feet, then down the road at his beat-up truck.

Finally, Kyle said, "Derek, my dude. If that's the hardest you can hit, I advise you to jump back in your truck and go to the house. Otherwise, this is going to be a long night for you."

Derek glanced again at Kyle but then returned his gaze to his truck.

Seizing the opportunity, Kyle said, "What are you trying to

prove, Derek? How tough you are? Where has that gotten you? Think about that, Derek. Where has being the tough guy ever gotten you?"

Derek continued to look away from Kyle. Finally, he said, "Why do you care?"

"Well, I guess because I'm a coach, Derek. I coach young men. Most men like you have no peace until they discover the one person who can help them. That person is Jesus. He can bring peace into your life and remove all your anger and hatred. Don't you think that would be a better way to go?"

Derek said nothing. He continued staring into the darkness. Finally, Kyle said, "Derek, I'm about to give you the best advice you will ever hear. So, listen up. You will always be a loser in this life unless you give up your hopeless lifestyle and turn your life over to Jesus. He can make a real man out of you and give you hope for the future. Otherwise, you will continue to live in your dark and screwed up world and never realize how great life can be, helping other people instead of playing the tough guy role and trying to hurt people all the time."

Derek looked at Kyle with anger in his eyes. "I ain't no loser!"

"Yeah, you are, Derek," Kyle said kindly. "We *all* are without Christ. You just don't realize it. But Jesus can change us. You live in a dark world now, but the light of Jesus can penetrate that darkness. He can change your life, Derek, if you let him. I can help you with that if you'd let me."

Derek scowled at Kyle and shook his head. "You're freaking me out, man!" With that, Derek walked downhill to his truck. He opened the door and glanced back up at his adversary, who was still watching him. He slid inside the truck and slammed the door. As he drove slowly down the road, he was overwhelmed with confusion. *I hit that guy as hard as I could. It was like hitting a brick wall. I'm glad I won't be running into that dude again. He's a Jesus freak... with a hard head.*

Derek stopped at the stop sign on the gravel road. He looked both ways and pulled out onto Last Chance Avenue. He muttered aloud, "He's crazy. I like my life the way it is." Derek stomped on the accelerator pedal as the engine's whine echoed across the empty countryside. "Jesus, God, whatever, stay out of my life! Okay? I'm doin' things my way. No help is needed. Besides, I don't even think you exist. So why am I even talking to you?"

When Derek's truck's tail lights disappeared, Kyle walked to his car and opened the door. He paused, looked up into the star-filled sky, and said a short prayer for Derek: "Lord, I pray for Derek. Please, God, put somebody in his life who will lead him to Jesus. Make him into the man you want him to be. Thanks, God, for what you are going to do for Derek. Amen."

Then he got into his car and drove down the hill.

CHAPTER 16

At the end of practice each night of the following week, Coach Patton and Coach Agular hung a special canvas net in the goal at the west end of the soccer pitch. The net had four webbed pockets, one in each corner. With Matt Arnold in goal, the rest of the team lined up and practiced taking penalty kicks, aiming their shots at any of the four corner pockets. This routine became a regular end-of-practice drill. Over time, the players became deadly at hitting their targets, the four pockets in the net.

When practice was over on one Thursday night, Coach Patton sat at the end of the team bench and watched Aaron gather up some personal items. When Aaron finished, he walked over to where Kyle was and sat down.

"I think the new net is a great idea, Coach," Aaron said. "It might make a difference someday. You never know."

"Yeah, sometimes, it's the little things that make big things happen," Kyle replied with a smile. "Are you ready to pull out?"

Instead of standing, Aaron went silent for a few seconds, then said, "Coach, do you mind if I ask you something?"

"Of course not," Kyle replied. "Ask away."

"Well, I've heard a rumor that you might be a candidate for the coaching job at Unity. Is there anything to that?"

Kyle was startled by Aaron's question. "You mean there's a rumor out about that? Where did you hear it?"

"I can't share that, Kyle," Aaron said. "But it's out there."

"Was it from anyone on the team?"

Aaron shook his head and quipped, "Sorry, I can't share that either."

"Man, I hate that that's out there." Kyle paused for a moment, then said. "Yes, I did interview for the job. I haven't heard anything since then."

"What do you think your chances are? It affects me, of course."

"Of course. I understand," Kyle said, tipping his ball cap to the back of his head. "I promise to keep you informed as things move forward, Aaron."

"That's all I can ask. Thanks, Coach."

Friday night's game that week was a quarter-final game in Jonesboro, a central Oregon community. Barrymore won that game handily by a score of five to two, giving them the right to move on to play Langford in a semi-final matchup the following week. Langford was the only team in their division to have beaten them. The players, coaches, and the city of Barrymore were excited to have the rematch.

Practice sessions that week were long and hard. Everyone understood the importance of this game. The entire season was on the line. The coaches had to have the players ready physically and mentally to beat Langford, an opponent they knew would be training just as hard as they were.

When Kyle came home from school Friday afternoon, he stopped, picked up the mail from his outside mailbox, and entered his house. It had been a hard week. Between game and lesson preparations, he had been unable to spend time with Kayla, which bothered him immensely. *I hope she understands. That's the life of a coach, I guess. She might need to get used to it.* That thought caused a slight smile to come across the coach's face.

Kyle threw the pile of mail down on a kitchen counter and went into his bedroom to change into his game clothes. *I don't have time for the mail now. I've got to get ready for the game, get something to eat, and get to the field. Whatever is there, can keep until I get back.*

***

The game against Langford went into instant high gear and grew more meteoric as time went on. Both teams were hawkish on offense and close to hostile when the other team had the ball. Langford's big center midfielder and their number 10 on the right wing continually put the Barrymore defense under pressure every time they had the ball at their feet. But it was no different when Barrymore had the ball. Michael Shepherd and Lorenzo Gonzales were flying down the touchlines, forcing the Langford defenders back on their heels every time they touched the ball. Jake Ledger dominated the midfield, mixing his distributions expertly to control the flow of the game. By the end of the first half, both teams had scored one hard-fought goal apiece.

At halftime, Coach Patton gathered his team together behind the west goal. The team sat on the ground, some members rubbing sore leg muscles and small bruises, but all listening to their coach with rapt attention.

"You're doing a good job pressuring them into making quick decisions," Coach Patton encouraged them. "Keep that up because it will force mistakes. There are also times when I see too much delay. Don't wait for a mistake. Force a mistake! When number 10 has the ball, notice he doesn't look around for someone to pass to.

He looks for an open shot. So don't be afraid to go after him, in pairs, if you see an opportunity. You are going to have to fight and scrap like never before. If you do that the way I know you can, we will walk away from here with a win and a date for the state championship. Are you with me on this?"

A loud, unanimous "YES, SIR" erupted from the sixteen young men as they jumped to their feet.

At an almost screaming pitch, Coach Patton finished with: "This is our game! We've worked hard for this moment, men! Let's finish the job!"

The second half started with the same fury as the first half. But at the seventieth minute, a huge break fell the home team's way. Jake stole the ball from the feet of an opposing midfielder and quickly knocked it left into open space, to where Michael was racing at full speed. The defending Langford player had the advantage at first, but Michael overtook him, collected the ball at his feet, and raced to the goal. Lorenzo Gonzales barreled up from his mid-field position, drawing immediate attention from Langford's right back, who was doing his best to contain Michael. Michael was open and barreling forward at full speed toward the Langford goalkeeper, who moved forward toward Michael but at the same time kept a cautious eye on Lorenzo coming in from the right.

Remembering his coach's words, "Force them to make a mistake," Michael gave Lorenzo a crucial head nod and faked a move in his direction. Then, instead of passing the ball to Lorenzo, he hit the ball with the outside of his left foot and banged it into the left corner of the net. "GOAL!" erupted from the home crowd.

Michael was ecstatic as he ran to the middle of the field to meet the rest of the team, who began to pound him on his head, back, and shoulders. Coach Patton and Coach Agular shared a high-five handshake and fist pump.

"What a shot," Agular said. "Where did that come from?"

"Not sure, Coach. We'll have to ask him," Coach Patton whooped.

The final fifteen minutes of play were chaotic. Langford pushed all its players forward while Barrymore put everyone on defense, making sure no Langford player was unmarked. Several shots were attempted, but none of them could sneak through Barrymore's iron-clad defense, and the game ended two to one in favor of Barrymore.

"Great game, men!" Coach Patton said to his team when they gathered for the coach's final comments. "You responded to the challenge with the fight and scrap I asked of you. Now, go home. Celebrate with your families, and I will see you all on Monday."

****

Physically and mentally tired, Coach Patton pushed open the door from his garage into his small utility room and walked into the kitchen. He went to his refrigerator, grabbed a bottle of water, entered the den, and plopped down in his favorite chair. He thought through the game his team had just played. He was proud of his boys and the support that the school and town of Barrymore had displayed. Then he bowed his head and gave thanks for the win and the great support he had known as a soccer coach at Barrymore High School.

"I don't know what you have for me going forward, Lord. I pray that I will hear from the university soon and that the news is good. I ask you, Father, and thank you that I will win the job and be named the new coach at Unity. Thank you, Lord. Amen."

Kyle stood and walked back into the kitchen. He then noticed the stack of mail he had received. He gathered it up and sat down at the kitchen table. Immediately, his attention went to an envelope from Unity University.

Okay, here it is. Let the good times roll!

Kyle carefully opened the envelope and pulled out a letter from the Athletic Department at Unity University. He read it aloud:

"Dear Kyle,

The purpose of this letter is to inform you that although your credentials are outstanding, we have decided on another candidate to fill the open position of Assistant Soccer Coach at Unity University. We appreciate your interest in our soccer program and wish you good luck in all your future endeavors.

Thanks again,

Andrew Sharpe, Director of Athletics, Unity University."

Kyle's mouth went dry. In addition to the sadness, he was stunned and strangely sickened. Kyle folded the letter and put it back into the envelope. He sat back in his chair and stared out the large kitchen window. His heart was broken, and he felt as if it had fallen into the pit of his stomach.

This isn't the way it was supposed to be. This was going to be my next step forward. I'm ready for college coaching! I was already putting a team together, including recruiting some of my current players. I can't believe it. And what about Kayla? We would have been able to have an open relationship. No more sneaking around, hoping not to be seen by Barrymore students or locals, for that matter. What's going on, God? Don't you get it? The coach remained in his chair and stared out his kitchen window for nearly an hour. Finally, he bowed his head and whispered, "Sorry, God. Of course, you get it. You're God. You have a purpose for my life. Thank you for this result, and I pray the new coach at Unity University will be a successful coach, a good leader, and a godly man. Amen."

***

Saturday morning, Michael Shepherd was not caddying, but he was in LaGrange. He had borrowed his dad's car and was on a mission to find "Strawberry Yogurt Girl." He parked in front of Frankie's Frozen Yogurt Shop, where he had first met her, and entered the building. Few people were buying frozen yogurt that time of day, which was no surprise to Michael. However, the prom event for Barrymore High School was that night, as was the part that included prom festivities in Olivia Cummings' hospital room. Michael was certain he would be the only attendee with no date.

"She's about your size," Michael explained to the young female teenager behind the cash register in the frozen yogurt shop. "She has brown hair and is cute. Something else that might trigger your memory: she had just had a terrible incident involving her dog that day."

"When was that?" the cashier asked.

"About two weeks ago," Michael replied.

"Do you know if she lives around here?"

"She must. She told me her folks brought her that night for a treat because of the deal with her dog."

The young lady thought for a few minutes and said, "No. I'm sorry. It doesn't ring a bell. Then she smiled and said, "But, you know, I might be available."

Michael's face flushed red. "Oh my gosh. Thank you. You're neat. I mean, I appreciate it. Um...." Lost for words, Michael stammered for a few seconds more, then said, "What's your name?"

"Hannah. What's yours?"

"Michael."

"Michael. I have a cousin named Michael. I like that name." she said with a slight blush and teasing smile.

Michael cleared his throat and said, "Well. Hannah. Let me have time to think about some things. Okay?"

"That's cool. I'll be here until closing time," Hannah replied.

"Great. Thanks, Hannah."

"We close at nine."

Michael vacated the shop at a near-sprint level.

* * *

Saturday afternoon, Coach Patton pulled his car up against the curb in front of Kayla's house and shut the engine down. This had become his regular Saturday routine for the past several weeks. Only this time, he sat for several minutes, thinking about how his whole world had changed since receiving the letter from Unity University.

Well, maybe not my whole world, but certainly my future. There was no way I wasn't going to get that job. I had such cool plans. I've got to get over this. I can't let it torpedo my career, especially getting ready to play for the state championship one week from today.

Coach Patton pushed open his car door, exited the car, and walked up the sidewalk to the front porch of Kayla's house.

* * *

At seven that evening, a large conference room in a wing at

University Hospital began filling up with young people from Barrymore High School. The boys were dressed in suits, the girls in beautiful gowns. Olivia Cummings, seated in a wheelchair, cautiously embraced everyone who entered the room. Olivia wore a beautiful pink gown with a white corsage Jake had bought for her. Her mom and dad were there, along with Jake Ledger and nurse Kelsey, who was accompanied by her boyfriend, Ryan Haas. Some musicians were also assembled: a violinist, a piano player, a guitarist, and a drummer.

Michael Shepherd and Matt Arnold were the only unaccompanied males at the party. Several teammates were there with dates. Everyone was happy, exchanging hugs and stories. Tables were decorated, and crepe paper hung from a large chandelier as the band played soft music from the back of the room. At seven-thirty, there was an abrupt drum roll. Michael stepped next to Olivia and Jake with a mic in his hand and said, "Hello, Barrymore High School. We're about ready to kick things off here. As we are honoring a special classmate tonight, I think it would be appropriate to start the dancing with our celebrant and her date, Jake Ledger, who will share the first dance. What do you think, Jake? Are you up to it? I know Olivia is."

That announcement caused a stir followed by a hush as Jake held out his arm to Olivia, who took it and slowly, with some help from Jake, stood to her feet. Then, ever so gradually, as the music began, the two of them embraced and began to dance. The crowd was stunned and slowly began to applaud as Jake and Olivia moved rhythmically in a small space near the wheelchair. There were no dry eyes in that assembly as couples slowly began to link up and dance. Romance was in the building and infused the participants, who displayed love and camaraderie then and throughout the evening. Jake sparingly shared Olivia with other dancers but was always standing nearby. It was a fairy-tale moment in everyone's eyes.

"How are you doing, girl?" Michael was swaying with Olivia when it was his turn to dance with her.

"I'm fine, Michael," Olivia chuckled. "It is so neat of you guys to do this. I will never forget this night."

"Well, you're special to all of us, Olivia. We will never forget it, either. Do you have any idea how much longer you will be here?"

"No. I'm hoping it won't be much longer. But I'm trusting God on that part," Olivia said with a smile.

Michael grinned. "Sounds like you've been talking to Jake."

"Imagine that."

****

Three hours later, Olivia and her parents, Jake, Michael, and Matt, were sitting in Olivia's hospital room. Still dressed in her formal attire, Olivia sat on the bed while the others mingled around the room. Everyone was giddy as they reveled in how special the evening had been.

"That was well done, Jake. Thank you for putting it together," Mr. Cummings said as he looked at Jake.

"Yes, that was so nice, Jake. We are so proud of you all," Brittany Cummings chimed in.

"Thank you," Jake replied. Looking at Olivia, he asked, "Did we wear you out?"

Olivia smiled and said, "No, not at all!"

Mrs. Cumings, looking at her daughter, said, "I think we need to let you get some rest anyway, dear. Maybe your friends can check back with you tomorrow or the next day."

Jake rose to his feet and counseled, "Moms are usually right. We should pay heed." Michael walked over to the bed and patted Olivia's covered leg. "Good night, Olivia. Thanks for showing that Husky toughness. We'll check back with you later."

"I'm so glad you were here, Michael. I hope you connect with Miss Strawberry Yogurt soon."

"Yeah, I do too. Thanks, Olivia," Michael smiled.

Jake reached a hand forward to Olivia, who grabbed it at once and looked Jake through bleary eyes. "Thank you, Jake. I will never forget this night." At that, her voice choked. She couldn't continue.

Jake leaned forward, and the two embraced. Then Jake turned and looked at Michael and Matt. "Are you ready, gents?"

Both boys nodded, edged up to the side of the bed, and carefully patted Olivia on her arm.

Jake moved over to Mr. and Mrs. Cummings. He hugged her and then shook hands with Mr. Cummings. Michael, Jake, and Matt then departed.

The boys were soon on the street, heading toward the hospital parking lot.

"Good job, bruh," Michael said, looking at Jake. "That little event was worth more than money could buy in counseling and preparation for her reentry into society."

"She has to feel encouraged," Matt added. Then he said, "By the way, are either of you going to the actual prom? It's probably still going on."

"Not me," Jake answered. "I'm out of gas. I'm going home."

Matt looked at Michael. "How about you, bruh?"

"No, I don't think so, Matt. But I've got a hot tip for you."

"Yeah, what's that?" Matt asked.

"Do you know the frozen yogurt shop that's just before you make the turn to Barrymore?" Michael asked.

"Yep, Frankie's."

"Well, a charming young lady is working there looking for male companionship. She wants a date and probably a boyfriend. If you're interested, you'd better hurry because they close at nine, and she'll be gone."

"Are you messing with me, Michael?" Matt asked, eyebrows raised.

"No, sir. Matt, I learned long ago never to mess with a goalkeeper. But, like I said, you better get moving, or you will miss her."

"Okay, thanks. I'll give it a shot."

"Cool. Tell her Michael sent you."

"I will," Matt hollered over his shoulder as he hurried to the parking garage.

CHAPTER 17

Earlier that afternoon, Kyle, Kayla, and Joshua had spent their time together doing their usual Saturday routine. There was plenty of soccer. Some of it was training. Some of it was relationship-building, and all of it was fun. They also had dinner together. This time, Kyle grilled chicken while Kayla made a salad and baked some potatoes.

After dinner, the adults relaxed on the sofa while Joshua amused himself by playing nearby with his set of Legos.

"You're quiet tonight, Coach," Kayla said. "Is everything okay?"

Kyle didn't answer immediately. He leaned back, stared at the ceiling momentarily, then sat up straight and turned to Kayla. "Well, now that you mention it, things have suddenly taken a surprising turn."

"Why? What happened?" Kayla asked.

"I received a letter yesterday from the university's athletic department," Kyle said.

"Oh, you did? That's what you've been waiting for. Was it about the job? Did you get an offer?"

"No, I didn't get an offer. I got a rejection."

"A rejection! What do you mean?" Kayla asked, surprised.

"What I mean is, they have given the job to someone else."

"Oh, no. How could they do that?"

"Well, I wasn't the only candidate, you know. Obviously, they found someone they liked better than they liked me." Kyle paused and smiled. Then, he surmised, "So, it looks like I am staying here, which is fine. Now, however, I wish that...."

"Wish what?" Kayla asked.

"I wish the opportunity had never come up. Everything was super. I was happy with the way things were going. There were no distractions." He paused momentarily, then lamented, "Now, I'm not so sure they will ever be that great again."

Kayla scooted over to Kyle, put her hand over his hand, and looked deeply into his eyes. "It'll be okay, Coach. You've done a great job here. Everybody loves you here."

Kyle grinned as he returned the intense gaze. "Everybody?" Kyle asked. "How about you?"

Kayla squeezed Kyle's hand. "Especially me, Coach."

The two embraced momentarily, but that special moment was short-lived because it was interrupted by Joshua. "Coach Kyle, I can't get these two legos apart."

Kyle released his hold on Kayla. "Okay, bud. Let's see what you've got here." He turned and took the Lego piece from Joshua's hand, quickly popping it apart. Joshua happily returned to his building project.

"Joshua, what do you say to Coach Kyle?" Kayla frowned at Joshua.

"Thank you, Coach Kyle. I'm sorry," Joshua said sheepishly.

"You're welcome, Joshua," Kyle said with a smile.

Then Kyle turned back to Kayla and asked, "Now, where were we?"

"We were talking about your future, remember?" Kayla laughed.

"Huh uh. We were talking about *our* future," Kyle smiled.

Kayla perked up. "We were? *Our* future? Are you saying our future as in our future together?"

"I am, dear girl. Our future together..." Kyle paused briefly. "I was planning a more elaborate setup to ask, but now seems as good a time as any. Will you marry me, Kayla?"

"Oh, yes!" Kayla exclaimed happily, almost jumping on Kyle in a hug. "Of course, I will marry you, Coach Kyle Patton!"

Once again, the couple shared a prolonged kiss. Then, Kayla pulled away from Kyle and asked, "So... *Coach* Kyle, how will we handle this?"

Kyle pushed back in his seat and thought for a few moments. Then he looked back at Kayla and said, "Well, I think we will still have to keep things under wraps until we're actually married. We need to avoid what has probably been obvious to everyone. It needs to be done right to present a good image to the kids. But Kayla, we'll need to share it soon. Let's give it some thought and prayer. Maybe we can have a plan by the time school is out for the summer. In the meantime, I've got a game to get ready for. That's where my mind needs to be for the next few days."

Kayla avoided being sidetracked. "You do realize that the end of the school year is only three weeks away, don't you?"

"Like I say, my mind is on the game," Kyle laughed. "That's big on my to-do list right now."

"I understand, coach."

"I hope so. Being a coach's wife is difficult, dear girl."

Kayla smiled. "With the Lord's help, we'll make it work."

Later that night, at home, Kyle sat in his favorite chair in front of his fireplace, rereading the letter he had received from Unity University's athletic director. Once again, this put him into a funky mood.

This could have been so perfect. The timing of our engagement, departing from Barrymore High School and taking a new coaching job at the university, recruiting opportunities, and no more secrecy about my love for Kayla. Most importantly, an opportunity to have more freedom to reach out more with the Gospel to older students. That's not easily done in high school. College would not be so restrictive.

But I know God's ways are not my ways. His thoughts are above my thoughts. So...

"Lord, help me put all this in perspective. Help me be pumped to come back to coach another year at Barrymore. I owe that to the kids. I owe that to you, Lord. Yes, and Lord, help me prepare the team for Saturday against Forest City for the state championship. Amen."

***

The setting for the state championship game was the soccer pitch at Unity University in La Grange. The stadium began filling early with a scheduled kick-off at 7:30 p.m. The Barrymore Huskies were on the field, gathered around Coach Patton and Coach Agular. Their opponent, the Forest City Loggers, was with their coaching staff across the field. A mild chill was in the air, with a slight northern breeze blowing across the field. Field lights were on, although not necessarily adding needed light as the sun was still on the horizon. It was an ideal evening for a soccer game.

Coach Patton addressed his team. Eighteen pairs of eyes and eighteen pairs of ears leaned into every word. He cleared his throat and began to speak. "Listen up, men. I have waited until now to address a rumor that has come up recently about my tenure as your coach. I want you to know that I have no plans to leave Barrymore for another coaching job. I will return as your coach next year, and that is that. Please put that rumor to bed right here and now, okay?"

Strong "YES, SIRS!" rang out across the field.

"Great. That's settled, once and for all. Now, let's talk about what we're here to do," Kyle continued. "We have emphasized all week that this team's strength is its strong defense. They guard their goal like no one we have played all year. They will plug up passing lanes and force turnovers with tremendous pass anticipation and pressure on the ball. Do not try to be cute when you have the ball. Just control it and play it quickly to space or an open man. Do not hold the ball! And do not force it into impossible situations. Our game will be to 'out-motor' them with speed, relentless pressure, and a withering defense. Can we do that?"

"Yes, Sir!"

"I DIDN'T HEAR YOU!"

"YES, SIR!"

"THEN GO DO IT!"

The tempo for the state championship game began with quick ball movement through mid-field and into the goal zone but slowed on each end because of the brutal defense played by both teams. There were few shots on goal, and the first half ended nothing to nothing.

Coach Patton's words to his team at halftime were brief and encouraging: "I'm proud of you men. All of you. Continue to pressure. Don't force anything. Opportunities will come. Just be ready when they do."

Midway through the second half, an opportunity came. At the

sixty-seventh minute, the ball was played into the Loggers defensive third of the field near the penalty box. With his back to the goal, Barrymore's striker, Ian Gregson, controlled the ball but was immediately stripped of it by the Forest City center-back, who hit it toward his right touchline. Speeding down his left touchline, Michael saw the opportunity and charged the ball at full speed. He and the defending right back were in a dead heat to reach the ball. The defender had the advantage of closeness, but Michael had the benefit of speed. He won the race, he had the ball, and he had the advantage.

Bypassing the slower defender, Michael charged the goal with the ball at his feet and took on the goalkeeper one-on-one. In a split second, the ball was in the back of the net, and Barrymore led, one to nothing, with twenty minutes left to play.

In the closing minutes, everything was going well for Barrymore until, with three minutes left, the ball was played out behind their goal line, calling for a corner kick for Forest City. With only a minute left and every player, including the goalkeeper from Forest City, in the penalty box, the corner kick swerved in toward the goal, and a tall Forest Hill defender out leaped everyone and headed the ball into the net to tie the game one to one.

This sent the game into overtime, which consisted of two ten-minute periods. The tempo of play during overtime remained furious as both teams moved up and down the field with grinding intensity. Despite the fervency of attacks on goal, no goals were scored. Penalty kicks would decide the game.

"This is it!" Coach Patton said to his team as they huddled together, awaiting the referee's signal to begin the penalty kick series, where five players from each team were selected to attempt to score by taking a single penalty kick against the opposing goalkeeper. "You know where the corners are. Choose your target, but don't reveal it. Just hit it!"

The players lined up. For Barrymore, Jake took the first kick, which he placed perfectly into the bottom left corner of the net. He was followed by the Forest City striker, who also found the back of the net, lofting a high ball into the upper right corner. The game score was tied.

Lorenzo Gonzales walked to the penalty spot, picked up the soccer ball, spun it in his hands, and put it on the ground. One minute later, it was in the back of the net. Barrymore led by a goal.

"You're the man, Lorenzo!" and, "Great shot, Lorenzo!" The rest of the kickers called out to Gonzales as he high-fived his way back to his team.

The next player for Forest City walked to the penalty spot. He put his right foot on the ball and rolled it around until it was exactly where he wanted it. He stepped back five steps, paused for a few seconds, then moved forward and struck the ball toward the right side of the goal. Goalkeeper Arnold dove to his left and smothered the ball with his body. The Barrymore fans erupted. Their team is led by one goal.

Ian Gregson was the next player up for Barrymore. He struck the ball perfectly into the left upper corner of the net, putting Barrymore up by one goal and holding the advantage. Excitement was high on the Barrymore side as Ian returned to his team and was met with high-fives and shoulder hugs.

Seth Stockton, Barrymore's next man up, met him halfway with a high-five followed by a bear hug. "Perfect shot, my man! Perfect shot!"

Forest City's next kicker tucked the ball under his arm, strode confidently to the penalty spot, spun the ball in the air, sneered at Matt, and placed the ball on the ground. He stepped back and locked eyes with Matt Arnold. Matt displayed total confidence as he positioned himself on the balls of his feet. "Bring it on, buddy. Bring it on," he mouthed. The intensity of the moment was heightened by the antics and arrogance displayed by both players.

The Forest City player was in no hurry. He waited patiently for the referee to blow his whistle, which finally came after several seconds of quiet tension bewitching the fans and players alike. At the sound of the whistle, the Forest City player stepped back, looked again at Matt, then to the left corner, then back to Matt. Then he struck the ball solidly into the right bottom corner of the goal. Unfortunately, Matt went to the opposite side, and the goal added another point for Forest City. The Forest City fans cheered wildly as their kicker returned to his team.

Seth Stockton was up next for Barrymore. He wasted no time. When the ball was placed down, he struck a perfect shot into the lower right corner of the net. However, Barrymore's one-point lead remained the same when the fourth man up for the Loggers put his shot up high into the left corner, out of Matt's reach.

The next man up for Barrymore was Michael Shepherd. Barrymore had a one-goal lead. If Michael scored, the game would be over. If he didn't score, Forest City would still have a chance to tie the game, a possibility Barrymore wanted no part of.

Michael walked to the soccer ball, picked it up, wiped it on his grass-stained jersey, and set it back down. Michael locked his eyes on the lower right corner of the net and took five steps back and to his left. He stopped, looked at the ball, and returned his eyes to the target. Then he moved forward and struck the ball, powering it into the right bottom corner of the net. The Forest City goalkeeper dove to the opposite side of the goal. Michael thrust his arms up in victory.

The dejected goalkeeper crumpled to a sitting position, leaned back on his arms, and watched Michael dance back to his team, pumping his arms in the air in a victory celebration. Barrymore had just won the Oregon state championship in soccer! Altogether, five Barrymore players kicked scoring goals.

As the Barrymore players began to celebrate their victory, they were joined by many of their fans who had faithfully cheered them throughout eighteen games and one hundred and ten minutes of state championship play.

"Great season, Coach!" Aaron said as he and Kyle shoulder-hugged in the middle of the players and fans pounding one another on the backs and shoulders. "I'm so glad we practiced with the net. That made the difference."

"Yeah, five for five. Not bad," Kyle replied.

"Right on, Coach," Aaron smiled. "Congratulations."

Then, in the bedlam of the celebration, Kyle shouted, "What have you decided about next year?"

"I'm not going anywhere, Coach."

"That's tremendous, Aaron. Thank you." Kyle replied with a grin.

The two coaches shook hands. Then, they turned their attention to the public announcer as the awards ceremony was about to begin.

"Have you decided to join me at Unity this fall, or are you still thinking about it?" Jake asked Michael as the two stood together in the crowd gathered for the closing ceremony.

"We're going to need each other to reach our goal, you know."

"So what's our goal, bruh?"

"You know, bruh. From good to great! We're going to need each other for that."

"Yeah, I guess I can't let you look to your left and not see me over there calling for the ball. There's no telling what you might do with it."

"Right on, brother. Right on," Jake laughed.

***

Spring fever was in the air the following Monday. Students and teachers were dealing with year-end tests and reports. Fun and social hijinks were hampered by constraints imposed by teachers who expected the students to be in the classroom and paying attention. This was not an easy assignment.

Kyle got home early that evening as there was no soccer practice. He and Kayla had crossed paths once or twice during the day but had done their best to camouflage their relationship in their continuing effort to curtail the rumor mill.

I'll call her tonight. I hate having to wait until Saturdays to spend time with her. I'm not going to live with that for another year. We'll make it happen this summer. The Bible says repeatedly, "Wait for the Lord. Blessed are those who wait for the Lord. And the psalmist answered, "How long, Lord? How long?" That's my question as well: "How long, Lord?"

Kyle opened his screen door and walked out to his patio with a glass of iced tea. He sat down and gazed out into his yard at the half-empty bird feeder, which several small sparrows and a couple of cardinals were attacking. A blue jay was enjoying a splash in the bird bath in the middle of his azalea bed. This scenery had a soothing and relaxing effect on the coach, who was suddenly disrupted by his cell phone with its doorbell ringtone.

Not recognizing the caller's number, Kyle hesitated momentarily, then answered.

"Hello?"

"Coach Patton, I'm glad I caught you. This is Andrew Sharpe, Unity Athletic Director. How are you doing today?"

"Doing fine, Andrew," Kyle replied, surprised. "How about you?"

"I'm fine. Thanks for asking," Andrew said. "I want to update you on our coaching situation."

"Okay. I'm all ears," Kyle replied.

"Well, as you know, we had another candidate to whom we offered the job, and he initially accepted. However, something came up for him personally, and he has withdrawn his name."

Kyle's heart began to speed up, prompted by a surge of adrenaline. "That's interesting," he said. "So...."

"So, President Hardy and I would like to know if you are still interested in joining our coaching staff as an assistant coach."

Kyle was shell-shocked and momentarily speechless. But then, recovering quickly, he managed to ask, "So, are you offering me the job?"

"Yes, sir. Both of us want you. You're our man, Coach. Will you join us?" Andrew asked.

Kyle was ecstatic—but only for a moment. His mind began to flood with negatives. He was ready to turn in his new contract with Barrymore High School, which he had already signed. He had told everyone he was returning, including his players, which was significant. Kayla knew and, therefore, had decided not to sign a contract to teach full-time next year even though one had been offered.

"Coach, are you there?" Andrew asked.

"Yes, I'm sorry, Andrew. This is quite a problem. I want to accept your offer, believe me. But I'm sorry. I can't. I would have to break too many promises and commitments I've made since I received your letter. I can't do that. Again, I'm sorry. You will never know how sorry I am, but I just can't."

"I understand your dilemma, Coach," Andrew sighed. "We are up against some time constraints, of course, but we can give you a couple of days if you want to think about it."

"No, thank you," Kyle replied. "I appreciate that, but I don't see how I could change my mind. I'm grateful for the offer. Please believe me."

"Okay, I understand, Coach. I'm sorry we couldn't make it work. Please stay in touch, and we hope you have a successful season again next year," Andrew said.

"Thanks, Andrew."

Kyle let out a deep sigh as he clicked off his phone. *I can't believe it*, he thought. In heart-filled sadness, his eyes lifted to the late afternoon sky. *"Thank you, God. I know that you cause all things to work together for good to those who love you, to those who are called according to your purpose. I claim that verse for myself right now. Amen."*

* * *

Tuesday morning, excitement filled the air at Barrymore High School outside of Coach Kyle Patton's history classroom. As the class members lined up to enter the room, they all turned to a young lady seated in a wheelchair steered through the door by Jake

Ledger.

Coach Patton reached his hand out to Olivia Cummings when she reached the room.

"Welcome back, Olivia," he said, grinning widely.

"Thank you, Coach. I hope I'm not going to be a big distraction," Olivia replied. "It's so good to be back."

All the students crowded around Olivia as Jake parked her in the front row. Coach Patton allowed everyone to personally welcome Olivia before he moved to the front of the class. When all were seated and roll taken, Coach Patton came to the front of the room and began to speak.

"This is truly an exciting moment and a very fitting way to close out our study of American history for the year," Coach Patton said with a smile. "We all have learned a lot about our country this year. For those of you graduating and moving on to your next set of challenges, I ask you to consider at least two takeaways from our year together. There are many more, of course, but I would like to emphasize these two."

"Number one, we are privileged to have lived in a country where freedom reigns. We are free to come and go as we please. We are free to believe in a higher power or not to believe in a higher power. We are free to say what we want, think what we want, and do what we want so long as we abide by the laws of the land. If we don't like what we see our leaders do, we can vote them out of office. We can even run for political office ourselves. We live in a country where these freedoms were paid for by the blood of many great Americans who went to war when they were called to fight for their nation. Many of them did not come home. You will be responsible for protecting these freedoms for the young people behind you. If you don't, who will?" Patton asked.

"Don't be surprised when someone accuses you of being a bigot for feeling this way," he continued. "It's going to happen. So, please expect it, and as we have learned, others have every right to say that. We can't change that, nor do we want to. We can argue the point, however, and we should. We need not be afraid to stand up for what we know is right, honorable, and true. This country's direction will be in your hands in a few years. Be worthy of the responsibility. As I said, the blood of many patriots bought us that privilege."

Coach Patton paused and smiled at Olivia. "The second lesson is what we have just seen demonstrated before us this morning. We are a family. If one of us is hurting, we all hurt. And we are free to react to that person's needs in any way we want, whether by prayer, personal service, or just plain love. The measure of a good friend is how they react to someone's needs. You all passed this test with flying colors. Congratulations, class. I couldn't be prouder of you."

Coach Patton paused and swept the room with his eyes. Every student was quiet, their eyes fixed on the coach—that is, until he said, "Please get out your pencil and paper."

There was instant silence as all eyes diverted from Coach Patton. Immediately, the grumbling started.

"Aw, come on, Coach," Matt muttered. "That's not fair."

"Yeah, come on, Coach, school is over," someone whined from the back of the room.

"Now listen up," Coach Patton chided. "This is your chance to speak. I want you to write down one takeaway from this class on one page. You have the freedom to say what you want to say however you want to say it. Your grade has already been determined, so this will not affect your grade. When you are done, you are free to go. Just don't disrupt any class that is still in session. Please drop your paper off at my desk. As for you seniors, I will miss you more than you can imagine. Have a great summer, everybody."

CHAPTER 18

Tom Boswell had been the principal at Barrymore High School for twenty-two years. The end of the school year was always a busy time for him. His challenge for the past several days had been to execute new contracts for his current staff of teachers for the upcoming year. He only had a few appointments over a two-day period in early May and was looking forward to getting them done so he could move on to other tasks, begging for his attention. Looking at his schedule of remaining interviews brought a smile to his face.

These should not be complicated.

He was wrong.

His aide, Jennifer Mayfield, in her late forties, occupied a desk just outside Mr. Boswell's office. She beeped into his office speaker and announced, "Miss Leanard is here."

"Good, send her in," he replied.

He stood and greeted Kayla Leanard as she walked into his office. "Hello, Kayla. Please have a seat." He motioned to a side chair next to his desk. "How are you today?"

"I'm fine, Mr. Boswell. Thank you."

Mr. Boswell sat back in his chair and picked up a folder from his desk. "So, Kayla. I am pleased to have you back next fall as a full-timer. Congratulations."

Kayla looked down momentarily, then into Mr. Boswell's eyes. "I'm sorry, Mr. Boswell, but something unexpected has happened, and I cannot sign a contract for next year."

Boswell was surprised and noticeably disappointed. "Well, that is a surprise, Kayla. I thought you were happy here."

"Oh, I am," Kayla replied. "Very happy."

"So, what happened?" Boswell asked, confused.

Kayla's eyes began to tear up. "It's personal, Mr. Boswell. It's nothing about the school or you or anyone else, for that matter. It's just... complicated."

"So, please tell me. Maybe I can help," Mr. Boswell said sympathetically.

"I can't, sir. I'm sorry."

Kayla grabbed her purse and hurried out of Principal Boswell's office.

In less than a minute, Mrs. Mayfield entered the office.

She closed the door and said, "Kayla was in tears. Is everything alright?"

"Why, I don't know. She said she couldn't sign the contract, teared up, and left. Something's going on with her. She's very emotional. I'm not sure what to think. Do you know what's going on?"

Mrs. Mayfield paused, then said, "I think I do, sir." She pointed at the empty chair. "May I?"

"Yes, please."

Mrs. Mayfield sat down, gazed at the principal, and said, "She's in love."

"In love? With whom?"

"Coach Patton," Mrs. Mayfield revealed.

"Really! I didn't know they were dating."

"Well, you're not the only one. They have been very discreet about it."

"How do you know about it?"

"Kayla and I are friends. She shared that information with me in confidence, so I am sharing it with you in confidence as well," Mrs. Mayfield replied, eyebrows raised.

"So, what can you tell me, if anything?"

"It's complicated."

"Yeah, that's what she said," Mr. Boswell sighed. "I get that."

"Kayla and Coach Patton are getting married this summer. Kayla very badly wants to teach full time, but they don't feel it would be a good idea to attend the same school as newlyweds."

"Well, they could still...." Mr. Boswell said.

"Wait, hold on," Jennifer interrupted. "You need to know something else. I'm endangering a confidence in telling you this, but it's important. Very important."

Mr. Boswell sat back in his chair and linked his fingers under his chin. "I'm listening," he said.

"Coach Patton plans to sign his contract tomorrow afternoon," Mrs. Mayfield explained. She hesitated before continuing, "But he doesn't want to."

"He doesn't want to sign his contract? Why not?"

"That, too, is complicated."

The principal sighed. "Why am I not surprised?"

"A few months ago, Coach Patton was interviewed for an assistant coaching job at Unity University. Were you aware of that?"

Mr. Boswell shook his head. "No, I was not."

"Well, Coach Patton saw an opportunity to take a step up, career-wise. But unfortunately, they offered the job to another candidate. The coach was disappointed but put it behind him and moved ahead for another year at Barrymore High. To quell the rumors that he might be leaving Barrymore, he assured his kids, right before they took the field for the championship game, that he would be back next year. Then, yesterday, he got a call from the University that the other candidate couldn't take the job after all and that the job was his if he still wanted it. As badly as he wanted to say yes, his high sense of integrity wouldn't let him. So, he told them no. He's bummed out about it, of course, and Kayla is broken-hearted as well, which doesn't make for good relationships on several fronts if you want my opinion."

Mr. Boswell went silent. Mrs. Mayfield sat tight for a minute, then stood and stepped away from her chair.

"I'm assuming Kayla shared this information with you as well?" Mr. Boswell asked.

Mrs. Mayfield nodded.

"Well, thank you, Jennifer. I appreciate your candor."

"You're welcome, sir." Mrs. Mayfield turned and left the school principal, still deep in thought.

Fifteen minutes later, Jennifer Mayfield's intercom beeped, followed by Mr. Boswell's voice, "Please see if you can get the president of Unity on the phone. His name is Hardy—Preston Hardy, I believe."

"Yes, sir. Right away, sir."

* * *

The following day seemed unending to Coach Patton. It was

the final day of school for the kids. Some were unloading their lockers, while others wandered around the hallways, saying their goodbyes. Kyle walked into Aaron Agular's office and sat as Aaron packed some transfer boxes with files and personal items.

Kyle felt a deep admiration for his assistant coach and long-time friend. He asked, "How does an English teacher's mind comport with a soccer coach's mind? That's always been a mystery to me."

"Simple, Coach. Go to college on a soccer scholarship and graduate with a degree in English," Aaron laughed.

"Plus, love what you do, right?" Kyle replied.

"Right on, Coach."

"Well, you are great at both, Aaron," Kyle said with a smile. "I'm glad we'll have another year together. Have you signed your contract yet?"

"Nope. Tomorrow afternoon, right after you sign yours. You are going to sign your contract, aren't you?"

"Yes, I am Aaron," Kyle said. "Guaranteed!"

"Good. The rumors, you know. They were flying around."

"I know they were. I'm sorry in a way. It would have been a good chance for you."

"Yeah, maybe. But I'm only twenty-six. I'll get my chance someday. In the meantime, I'm glad you're staying. I've learned a lot working under your leadership."

Kyle stood, walked over to Aaron, and gave him a bear hug. "Thanks, Aaron. Love you, brother."

"Love you too, Coach."

The next day, Coach Patton arrived at the school early. He

wanted to have some time to help Kayla, knowing she might be feeling emotional as she cleaned her office on her final day at Barrymore High School.

Kayla was already hard at it when she heard Kyle's greeting as he entered her room.

"If you aren't the most gorgeous girl in the whole school today, I don't know who is," he proclaimed as he entered the room.

"That's because there are no other girls here right now," she quipped. "What are you doing here anyway? I thought you had all your stuff packed up."

"I thought you might need some help. Are you okay?" Kyle asked.

"Yeah, I'm okay, Coach," Kayla smiled. "Do you know why I'm okay?"

"No, please tell me."

Kayla turned and quietly mouthed, "Because I'm getting married soon."

"You are? "Who's the lucky guy?"

"His name is Kyle. He is a very nice guy. You wouldn't know him."

"Maybe you could introduce me to him sometime. I want to meet him."

"I might do that. In the meantime, would you mind helping me finish packing this box?"

"No way. Get Kyle to do it," Kyle laughed.

"I can't."

"Why not?"

"He's goofing off somewhere. Probably killing it with some

cute teacher somewhere," Kayla said with a chuckle as she handed Kyle a roll of packing tape.

"Okay, show me what you want me to do," Kyle grumbled with a smile.

***

Two hours later, Kyle Patton stood in front of Jennifer Mayfield's desk. She pushed the intercom on her phone and said, "Coach Patton is here for his appointment."

"Please ask him to come in," Mr. Boswell's voice crackled across the speaker.

Jennifer motioned to Kyle, "He's all yours, Coach."

"Thanks, Mrs. Mayfield."

Kyle stepped around Jennifer's desk, pushed open the door, and walked into Mr. Boswell's office.

Mr. Boswell stood and extended his hand to Kyle, who gave him a hearty handshake.

"Sit down, Kyle. It's good to see you."

"Thank you."

Mr. Boswell rocked back in his chair, again lacing his fingers together as he locked his eyes into Kyle's eyes. "You had a great season, Kyle. I am very proud of you. Winning the state championship. What a way to go out!"

What a way to go out! What does he mean by that?

Kyle blinked, then stammered, "Out, Sir?"

Mr. Boswell's countenance didn't change. "I'm afraid so. We aren't renewing your contract, Kyle."

Kyle felt a sharp surge of unbelief sink deep into his gut. "You, uh. You're not renewing my contract? You're kidding, right?"

"No, I'm not, Coach," Mr. Boswell replied.

Kyle was shocked. "Why not?"

"We have good reason, Coach."

"Please elaborate. With all due respect, I'm flabbergasted!" Kyle exclaimed, trying to keep his emotions under control.

Mr. Boswell scooted forward and looked deeply into Kyle's eyes. "Because we have reason to think you don't want this job."

Kyle paused thoughtfully and then asked, "Why do you say that? I've never given you any reason to think that about me."

"Of course, you haven't. But this year, well, there are two elephants in the room. One of those elephants is a job opportunity at Unity University you badly wanted but passed on due to loyalty to your kids here. It's my understanding you were passed over for the job, and when it was later re-offered, you turned it down. Am I right about that?" Mr. Boswell asked.

"Yes, that's about it," Kyle conceded. "No disloyalty intended. I looked at it as a step up, so to speak. But once the rumors heated up, I felt I should address the issue with the players."

"You are a man of integrity, Kyle, which is so important. But no one here wants to stand in the way of your great opportunity to take a coaching job at the university. As much as we hate to lose you, we feel it's a job opportunity you shouldn't turn down."

Kyle was momentarily speechless. He sat back in his chair. One of his favorite Bible verses flashed through his mind. *"Be quick to listen, slow to speak, slow to anger."*

"I don't know whether to laugh or cry," he said. "But I'm not sure the college job is still open. They were about out of time to make the hire."

Mr. Boswell responded quickly. "Oh, it's still open. I already called."

Kyle smiled, obviously relieved. Then he hesitated and said, "I have one concern. What about Aaron Agular? I strongly recommend him for my job."

"Do you think he has the maturity to be our head coach?" Mr. Boswell asked.

"Absolutely! No question. He is by far your best bet," Kyle said emphatically.

"Thank you, Coach. Your endorsement means a lot. Now, I would advise you to make a phone call to the university."

"Yes, sir. I will do that as soon as I am out of your office."

"Good deal, Kyle. Oh, one more thing..." Mr. Boswell trailed off.

"What's that?"

"Please ask Kayla to call me."

"Is that the second elephant?" Kyle asked with a chuckle.

"You're quite perceptive," Mr. Boswell replied.

Kyle stood and grinned. "I'll do that. Thank you, sir."

The two men shook hands, and Kyle departed.

CHAPTER 19

THREE MONTHS LATER

Recently hired Unity soccer coach Kyle Patton had just returned from a recruiting trip intended to confirm commitments received from soccer players in the Northwest, including California and Washington, where the hotbed communities of soccer were most prevalent. The Unity soccer players had been working out on their own for the last two weeks in July. According to NCAA rules, no coaches could be present during these preseason workouts.

August would be a busy month for the new coach. He would meet his coaching associates and many of his players for the first time. Unity had lost a total of thirteen players through graduation and non-returning undergraduates. Twelve players returned, six of whom were starters from the previous year. Unity's soccer team had not been very good over the past few years. This was no surprise to Coach Patton, as he had casually kept up with the team, a normal expectation for a local soccer coach. As a new coach, Kyle hoped he could be a difference-maker in advancing the soccer program at Unity.

Classes were scheduled to begin on September 23. Soccer season would start on September 7, with the players to be ready for twice-daily practices until the season opener against Fremont College on September 27. As he filled in his daily planner, Kyle Patton had plenty to consider.

"I feel good about how this is coming together," Kyle said to Kayla. They were enjoying an afternoon together in Kayla's backyard. "Want to hear what I've got here?"

"Sure, I would like that," Kayla replied.

"Our first practice is on September 7. We will have two practices a day until our first game against Fremont on September 28."

"When will you meet the other coaches?" Kayla asked.

"As far as I know, September 7," Kyle said.

"Hmm. It seems like Coach Cathey would want to get you together before that just to get acquainted."

"Well, he could still do that. We'll see."

Kayla leaned forward and looked Kyle in the eyes. "Do me a favor, okay, Coach?"

"What's that?" Kyle asked.

"Please try to keep August 17 open, okay?"

Kyle leaned back and smiled. "Why is that?"

"We're getting married that day."

"Oh, yes. That's right. I guess I'm going to have to write that down. August 15, you say?"

"Very funny, Coach," Kayla rolled her eyes. "And no soccer for the next ten days after that, okay?"

"Why not?"

"Because you will be in Hawaii with your new bride."

"Oh, bummer. That's right. Almost forgot."

"Funny!"

Kyle leaned back in his chair, looked at the shimmering elm leaves, and said, "I'm a happy man, Kayla. I'm happier than I've been for a long time. We are both beginning new careers, getting married in a few weeks, and I'm getting a son to raise. God is good."

"Yes. He is. All the time," Kayla replied with a smile.

＊

Michael Shepherd's dad, George, returning from a day at the office, pulled his car up a few feet into his driveway, got out, and walked to the mailbox. It was stuffed full. Most of it was junk mail, a few bills, and an envelope addressed to the Shepherd Family in Barrymore. The letter bore a return address in British Columbia, Canada. The name on the return address was Mr. and Mrs. James Reynolds.

George got back into his car, drove up the driveway into his garage, and parked his car, all the time wondering who in the world the Reynolds were. George entered his office inside the house, placed the mail on his desk, and pulled out the mystery letter. He slowly read the letter through, word by word. His hands were trembling by the time he got to: "Sincerely Yours, Lauren Reynolds."

"I can't believe this," he whispered aloud.

George did not move for the next twenty minutes until he heard Abigail's car pull into the garage. He returned the letter to its envelope. Then he knocked on Michael's bedroom door and yelled loud enough to overcome the radio blather, "Hey, Michael. I need you for a few minutes."

Michael popped the door open a few inches and said, "Hey,

Dad. What's up?"

"Short meeting. Shouldn't take long."

"Okay. I'll be out in a minute."

George then walked to the door leading to the garage. "Need any help?" he asked as he opened the door for his wife.

"Nope, I'm good," Abigail replied. "Did you get the mail?"

"I did. Here, let me take that bag."

George took a heavy bag of groceries away from Abigail, turned back toward the kitchen, and set it on the counter.

As Abigail began to put the groceries away, George entered his office and retrieved the letter from Canada.

Coming back into the kitchen, he put the letter on the counter in front of Abigail and Michael, who were now standing by. "Here, let me finish doing that while you two read this letter. But you'd better sit down first." He slid the letter across the counter to Abigail.

"What's this?" Abigail sighed as she picked up the letter. "James and Lauren Reynolds? Who are they?"

"Read it out loud," George said.

Abigail began to read. "Dear Mr. and Mrs. Shepherd. My name is Lauren Reynolds. I know this will come as a shock to you, and for that, I deeply apologize. However, I want you to know that my intentions are pure, and the information I reveal in this letter is only intended to initiate contact. Please believe me. I have no ulterior motives. Here is my story."

"On March 20, 2005, I gave birth to a beautiful baby boy. My baby was the product of an unfortunate relationship I had as a sixteen-year-old girl on the run who had no sense and little parental guidance. I was not able to keep this child, so I put him up for adoption. In the years that followed, I was able to turn my life around and become a responsible adult. I married a good man. We have a solid marriage but have been unable to have our own children."

"Over all these years, I have wanted to know about my son, who he was, how he was doing, and what kind of a young man he was growing up to be. I'm sure you can understand this desire. I held back, however, because I did not want to interfere in his young life. About a year ago, I went to an agency that specializes in this business, and that's how I located you. I still don't want to interfere, and I understand Oregon law says that he must be twenty-one years old before I can legally contact him. However, I have recently learned that due to a terminal medical condition, I won't be around by the time he is twenty-one years old."

"Mr. and Mrs. Shepherd, this may be a request you consider inappropriate, and it may very well be. But I am asking you if I could meet our son, spend some time with him, and tell him I love him and have thought about him every day over the past eighteen years. Would you allow me to do that? If you feel this is something you cannot do, may I ask you to take a few minutes and give me some takeaways about his life, like what he wants to do with his life? Is he musically inclined? Or is he more interested in sports? Is he going to college? Please tell me how I can pray for him in the time I have left. Also for you, for that matter."

"If you wouldn't mind filling in some of these blank spots and perhaps sending some pictures, I would be most grateful."

The letter ended with, "Sincerely yours, Lauren Reynolds." She included her contact information. With teary eyes, Abigail looked at George and pushed the letter over to Michael. Then she looked at her husband and sputtered, "That poor woman. Of course, she can see her son—our son. There's no way we can deny her that privilege. Do you agree, George? Michael?"

"I certainly do," George concurred. "Michael, what about you? Do you have any objections?"

"Not really," Michael murmured, his eyes skimming the letter.

George continued. "I think we should run it all by Carson Trotter before we do anything to ensure we aren't opening the door to possible legal issues. It's probably okay, but let's ensure we're not overlooking something that could come back and bite us later."

Abigail turned to Michael. "Are you sure you are okay with this, Michael?"

"I guess. It's weird, but it would be cool to meet her," he replied. "Will you write her back, Dad?"

"Yes, I will, son."

***

After graduation from Barrymore High School, Michael Shepherd and Jake Ledger had agreed to room together in college and were assigned to French Hall, a large dormitory for men on the Unity campus. The two boys, along with Matt Arnold and Ian Gregson, had been accepted as walk-ons for the university's soccer team. Several freshman athletes were housed in the same dorm. Matt Arnold and Ian Gregson shared a room across the hall from theirs. They had all moved into the dorm the same day, the first Saturday in August.

All four were hanging out in Matt and Ian's room at four-thirty that afternoon.

"Okay, dudes," Jake pronounced. "The football game starts at seven o'clock. I'm meeting Olivia at the cafeteria and walking her to the stadium after dinner. You are welcome to join us for dinner, or we can catch you at the game. Your choice."

"Will she be able to sit through the whole game?" Ian asked.

"I hope so. If not, we'll leave early. It's no biggie," Jake replied.

"I'll do dinner with you," Michael said.

Matt and Ian looked at one another. Then both said, "Cool."

Jake held his hand up and said, "Also, I'm going to church tomorrow. You all are welcome to join me. Sunday School starts at 9:30, so if you want to go with me, please be ready to leave here no later than 9:00. Are there any takers?"

"I'll go," Ian uttered.

Michael's eyes circled around each boy, then back to Jake. Finally, he mumbled, "I'll go."

Jake smiled. "Great!" He looked at Matt. "No pressure, bruh. Do what lights your fire."

All eyes turned to Matt. With a sheepish grin, he said, "I should stay here and study."

The guys all snorted, "Study what? You don't even have any books yet."

"I'm studying the mating characteristics of the Australian cockroach. In fact, I might write a thesis on it. So, what's wrong with getting an early start?"

Jake chuckled and closed the conversation with, "That sounds interesting, Matt. But if you change your mind, we'll leave at nine o'clock."

***

Redeemer Bible Church was a popular place of worship for

many students who attended Unity. It was only five blocks from the college campus, within easy walking distance for the three new freshman enrollees. It was a warm Sunday morning, and several students walked along Gloucester Street to the large white pillared building with a wide porch. As the students climbed the steps to an open front door, they had to close ranks to make it through the door into the lobby area.

Michael felt uneasy. He had only been inside a church on one occasion. That was when his oldest sister got married ten years earlier in a Catholic church.

The boys, led by Jake, joined a line headed toward another set of doors. Michael noticed that this new set of doors was one of three leading into a huge auditorium. He stepped up close to Jake as they drew near to the doors.

I'm not sure what I'm doing here, but I know one thing: I won't be back. Jake's a good friend, but this is way out of my comfort zone.

The boys reached the doors leading into the sanctuary. A split second later, Michael glanced to his right. His heart jumped into his throat when he suddenly spotted "Strawberry Yogurt Girl" just as she entered the sanctuary.

Oh my gosh! That's her. That's her!

Michael immediately pushed past Jake and barged into the sanctuary, looking to his right as he got inside. The force of this distraction caused him to barrel into an usher, causing him to drop a handful of bulletins onto the floor.

"Oh, man, I'm sorry," Michael groaned as he looked at the mess on the floor. Then he quickly stole a glance to his right, but Strawberry Yogurt Girl was nowhere in sight. Michael then bent down and started to help the usher gather up the bulletins.

"I am so sorry, sir," Michael repeated.

"You must have been in a hurry to worship this morning, young man," the sixty-something usher jested as he rose from his squatting position and began to hand out bulletins again.

"I'm sorry," Michael repeated while simultaneously cranking his neck to the right, hoping to catch another glimpse of the girl.

"It looks like you're off to a roaring start," Jake chuckled as he looked at Michael. "Let's go find a place to sit."

"Yeah, let's sit over to the right," Michael said distractedly.

"Whatever you say, bruh," Jake laughed.

The boys moved down the center aisle until they saw three empty seats together. Once seated, Michael tried to fixate on the individuals he could see, but he didn't spot Strawberry Yogurt Girl anywhere in the mix. It wasn't long before the music began, coming from the platform at the front of the church. At the request of the music leader, the crowd, which had become large by then, stood and began to sing. Michael was happy to stand because it gave him a chance to get a better look at the people.

Jake and Ian joined the singing, reading from the words on two large screens high on the wall behind the musicians. Frustrated, Michael's attention flitted back and forth between the crowd, the musicians, and the people on stage. Jake glanced at Michael several times until it became clear to Michael that he was distracting his friend and he needed to forget about the girl and pay attention to the service, which he reluctantly did. The music lasted for several minutes until a man who looked to be in his early forties came to the pulpit and began to preach.

"Hello, Redeemers," he said. "Wow! Look at all the young people here this morning. School must be in session. Welcome to all of you, young and not so young. We're glad you're here. Guess what we're going to talk about this morning?"

"Jesus," several shouted in unison from the audience.

"Right on," the young pastor concurred. "We're going to talk about Jesus, who He is, what He did, and how you can have a relationship with Him."

That statement resonated with many in the audience that morning, evidenced by the hush invading the auditorium, but not with Michael. Michael was not interested in anything but finding the girl he had met in Frankie's Frozen Yogurt Shop.

Where did she go? There are so many people here. How am I going to find her in all this crowd? Maybe if I leave early, I can stand by the door and catch her when she comes out of the church. Michael clenched his teeth as he looked at the crowd in front and to his right. *THIS IS SO FRUSTRATING!*

"So, what's frustrating you today, young man, young woman?" That question boomed through every speaker in the auditorium.

Michael froze. His eyes darted quickly at the on-stage pulpit in front of the church. The man behind the pulpit seemed to be looking right at him. "There is no need to be frustrated. Don't you know that God causes all things to work together for good to those who love God and are called according to His purpose?"

Why is this guy looking at me?

"In His providence, young friends, God orchestrates every event in your life. Every event, no matter how small or how big. Are you here today because you love God? You will be okay if that's your purpose for being here. If you are here for any reason other than that, you should take steps to find out where you are spiritually. We have folks posted at the back of the church who can help you with that. Seek out one of them after the service concludes. I will be glad to meet with you as well. Just call my office, and we can set something up."

"Now, let's pray together. Then you may be seated."

Seventy minutes later, the three boys were outside on the church's front porch. Michael tugged on Jake's shirt sleeve. "Let's wait a few minutes," he said as he surveyed the folks streaming through the doors.

"Why, who are you looking for?" Jake asked.

"I'm pretty sure I saw her," Michael responded as he craned his neck, trying to get a look at everyone before they descended the steps and away from the church.

"You mean Strawberry Yogurt Girl? You saw her in the church?"

"Yes! That's what I've been trying to tell you!"

As the crowd slowly began to disperse, Michael's countenance darkened. Finally, he said, "She's not here. Let's go."

A few minutes later, the three boys were seated in Wixx Café, a small restaurant on Gloucester Avenue, enjoying some hotcakes and coffee. Jake looked at his two friends and said, "I'm curious. What did you all think of the service this morning?"

"I liked it," Ian said. "I'm glad we went."

Looking at Michael, Jake asked, "What about you?"

"I thought it was interesting," Michael replied vaguely.

Jake grinned, "What, the message or the possibility of spotting Strawberry Yogurt Girl?"

"I heard the message," Michael said. "Part of it anyway."

Jake smiled. "Really? What part caught your attention?"

Michael paused for a few seconds, then said, "I don't know. The part where God says, 'All things happen for good,' maybe. That's what you said about Olivia when we were in the hospital."

"Yeah, that's right. According to Romans 8:28, all things happen for good for those who love God. Good job, Michael. But there's a condition, isn't there?"

"Yeah, I guess," Michael admitted. "The part about loving God."

There was an uncomfortable silence for several seconds as the boys seemed to be searching Michael's heart. Then, nervously, his hands encircled his water glass, and he looked at Jake. "How do I know if God loves me? I've had some bad things happen to me. Maybe He doesn't."

Jake scooted back in his seat. "God loves you, Michael. John 3:16 says, 'For God so loved the world, that he gave his only begotten son that we might have eternal life.'"

"So that's it? We are all going to heaven because He loves all of us?" Michael asked.

"No. There's a condition in that verse as well. The entire verse says, 'For God so loved the world that whosoever believes in him shall not perish, but have eternal life.' So you see, only the people who believe in Jesus go to heaven."

"That's a lot there to think about," Michael responded.

Jake turned to Ian. "Ian, you're pretty quiet. How are you doing? Or maybe I should ask this: what's your relationship with the Lord like?"

"I'm good," Ian replied casually.

"That's cool," Jake continued. "There are some Christian organizations on campus. Maybe we could all get into one. Would you like me to check it out?"

Michael sipped his coffee and said, "Hmm, I'm not sure about that, Jake. We have a lot going on between classroom work and making the soccer team. We need to concentrate on those two things and forget everything else for now. What do you think, Ian?"

"You guys do what you want," Ian replied. "My focus is going to be on making the soccer team."

"I hear you," Jake asserted. "But I'm going to check it out anyway. I'll let you know what I find out."

CHAPTER 20

Saturday, August 17, was a cloudless day in LaGrange, Oregon. Kayla, her father, Marshall Leanard, his wife, Barbara, and her step-sister Nicole exited a parked car in front of Central Church with armloads of hanging clothes, including a wedding dress. Together, they walked up eight steps across the broad porch and pulled open the heavy door leading into the sanctuary.

Inside the door, they were immediately greeted by Julie Wicks, the church wedding coordinator with whom Kayla had been working.

"This is the day the Lord has made!" Julie asserted as she offered her hand to greet Kayla's family.

Kayla said, "Dad, Barbara, Amber, meet Julie Wicks. She has been a big help to me. I don't know how I could have done any of this without her."

"We are excited to meet you," Barbara said. "Thank you so much for all your help!"

"Let me lead you to the bride's room, where you can get ready," Julie said with a smile as she led the family through the church.

Two hours later, at 1:45 p.m., Barbara Leanard followed a young tuxedoed usher, Joshua Leanard, down the main aisle of Central Church. Joshua stood as Mrs. Leanard entered the front pew on the right side of the aisle. When she was seated, he double-timed it back up the aisle and reappeared immediately, escorting Kyle's mother, Donna Patton, to the front seat on the left of the aisle.

At 1:55 p.m., Kyle Patton and his best man, Aaron Agular, entered the sanctuary from a side door at the front of the church, followed by Reverend Patrick Ward, Senior Pastor of Central Church. Kyle quickly scanned the audience and smiled as he spotted his mother and then Joshua, now seated beside the Leanards in the front row. As Kyle waited for his bride, he noticed the auditorium was populated with many students from Barrymore High School, including Barrymore's entire soccer team, fellow teachers, and staff members.

Filled with anticipation, Kyle fixed his gaze on the open entry door to the sanctuary, knowing that his bride would appear in just minutes and that his life would change forever.

This is it. I thank you, Lord, for this moment. I pray our marriage will honor You and that You will never let me forget this moment. I pray I will always love my wife as much as I love her right now.

Soft, spiritual music continued as some late arrivals entered the church and found places to sit. Finally, bridesmaid Amber Leanard entered the sanctuary and slowly proceeded down the aisle. She was greeted with warm smiles by the three men standing at the front of the church.

After a moment of silence, the well-known bridal march rang throughout the sanctuary. Everyone stood. Kayla and her father stepped into view and started their slow descent down the center aisle.

Kyle Patton's smile was ear to ear as he watched his bride approach. *Oh, man. She is so gorgeous. How can this be happening to me? Thank You, God. Thank You for giving me this beautiful woman to be my wife. Amen, and amen.*

***

On the morning of September 7th, the Unity Defenders soccer team gathered on one of the practice fields next to Murray Stadium, Unity University's large football complex. The players were scattered about the field, working in twos and threes on ball skills such as juggling and ball passing. Some of the players were shooting on goal. Some were stretching. Others were engaged in small conversations, getting acquainted along the touchlines. There were no coaches present. The coaches were still in the dressing room, where Coach Jason Cathey stood before his three assistant coaches.

"Gentlemen, by now, you have all met Coach Kyle Patton. Kyle has had a very successful coaching career at Barrymore High School for the past seven years and is now moving to college-level coaching. His primary responsibility will be working with our defenders, but he has the moxie to take on other responsibilities as needed."

The coaches, all seated, smiled and signaled greetings to Kyle. Kyle acknowledged by waving his hand as Coach Cathey continued.

"Kyle is recently married, so go easy on him. He's breaking in two new bosses."

Everyone chuckled at that. Coach Cathey finished his remarks by saying, "We have eighteen new players this year, giving us thirty-eight young men who want to make the team. We must cut that number to thirty by September 27th when we go to Fremont."

"How many will travel?" Fletcher Hoxsey, one of the assistant coaches, asked.

"No more than eighteen," Cathey announced. He then paused and studied the faces of his coaches. "Any other questions?"

This inquiry was met with silence. With that, Coach Cathey stood. "Gentlemen, let's go meet our team."

Outside, as the four coaches approached the practice field, the players stopped what they were doing and turned toward them. Coach Cathey blew his whistle and motioned for the team to come forward, which they did with much enthusiasm.

For the next thirty minutes, Coach Cathey introduced the coaches to the new players and explained his coaching philosophy and what he expected from the team. After that, he broke the players into small units according to their positions and assigned coaches to each group. Coach Patton went with the defenders. Michael and Ian lined up with the forwards, Jake with the midfielders, and Matt Arnold with the goalkeepers.

Two hours and fifteen minutes later, thirty-five young men coerced their bodies across Patriot Avenue and into the training facility for showers and liquid refreshments. The coaches gathered in Coach Cathey's office for their practice critique.

Seated at his desk as the three assistant coaches stood by, Cathey looked around at his tired staff. He said, "Gentlemen, today is Saturday, and I know you would like to get home to your families. We are going to dispense with our usual post-practice critique. Instead, I would like you to give me a short write-up on your first impressions of each player in your group today. It doesn't have to be long. What I want is your initial gut feeling. Please drop your reports by my office Monday when you get here. That way, I will have a chance to read them before Monday's practice. Are there any questions?"

No one spoke. Coach Cathey quickly followed up with, "Okay, you're dismissed. Go home. Enjoy the rest of your day."

The coaches all looked at one another and, without a word,

turned and left Cathey's office.

* * *

"How did it go, Coach?" Kayla asked as she greeted her husband with a kiss at the door as he entered her house on Hickory Lane.

"It was okay," Kyle replied. "A little strange, maybe. But it was fine."

"What was strange?" Kayla asked.

"Just not being in control, I guess," Kyle shrugged. "It will be fine once I get used to it. How was your day?"

"It was good. I got some cleaning done and was able to work up some lesson plans for Monday. I don't know what to expect, but I'm looking forward to getting back in the classroom."

"Wonderful," Kyle responded. "Where's my boy?"

"He's with his buddies somewhere in the neighborhood. I told him to be home by lunchtime," Kayla replied.

"Good," Kyle said, "because I want to get some soccer practice in with my favorite player."

* * *

Unity's game at Fremont did not go well. Neither did the next game or the six that followed. By mid-season, the team's record was one and eight. Morale was in the tank. No one was happy. Rumors that the coaching staff were all going to quit or soon be fired were rampant. Home games were not well attended.

"It's a mess," Kyle complained to Kayla one night after a homecoming loss to Granite College. "The kids aren't motivated. Coach Cathey doesn't seem to know what to do to fix the problem."

"What *is* the problem?" Kayla asked.

"Well, we have five or six 'glory guys' out there who seem to be–well, not *seem* to be, *are*–playing for themselves, showcasing their own skills, and not giving a flip about the team. Our name is Unity. That's crazy. That's the last thing we are!"

"So, what would you do, Coach?"

"Bench half the team," Kyle replied. "Let the kids play who want to play together."

"Have you talked to Coach Cathey?" Kayla asked.

"I've tried to, but he won't listen to me. He doesn't have any answers, but I can tell he certainly doesn't want any suggestions from this rookie coach." Kyle paused, then added, "I tell you, Kayla, I'm sorry to say this, but this might be 'one and done' for me."

"How come we haven't been praying about this?" Kayla asked, hands on her hips.

"I have been. I just haven't wanted to worry you about it," Kyle sighed.

"That shouldn't be, Kyle. We are to pray for one another, remember?"

"You're right." Kyle bowed his head, reached out, and took Kayla's hand.

*****

Michael and Jake were in their dorm room. Jake was sitting on his bed, propped up by pillows and reading from his "Survey of English Literature" tome. Michael was sitting at the lone desk in the room, hurriedly writing in a notebook.

Jake looked at his watch, put his book aside, and said, "Are you about ready?"

"Ready for what?" Michael answered without looking up.

"Ready for Exchange. The Christian group. You know, we talked about that."

"Is that tonight?" Michael asked.

"Yep. And if we're going, we need to be leaving in the next five minutes."

Michael put his pen down, turned in his chair, and frowned. "I'm not sure, Jake. I've got a ton of homework to do. Why don't you go ahead without me? Okay?"

"Cool. You stay here and study. I'll go and meet some great people. Have fun. Learn some Bible facts. Eat some scrumptious desserts, like strawberry shortcake. You stay here and enjoy your calculus pudding."

Jake swung his legs down and stood by his bed. "I'll see you about ten o'clock. Don't wait up for me, roomie."

"They have dessert?" Michael asked plaintively.

"That's what I'm told. They also have girls. But don't let that distract you. You have a lot of calculus to eat. See you later."

Jake headed for the door, followed in step by his now compliant roommate.

"You're coming after all?" Jake chuckled as he held the door open for Michael.

"You got me with the 'learn some Bible facts.' Let's go, Dumbo."

"Yeah, right," Jake laughed. The boys stepped out into the hallway and closed the door behind themselves.

***

Cody Freidman moved about the Satellite Room in the Student's Lounge at Unity University, ensuring that plenty of chairs were set up for what was expected to be an above-average turnout for the Exchange ministry meeting. Cody was the leader of the Christian group, a role he held for the previous two years. Cody, a Senior, was a transfer student from Montana State University in Bozeman, Montana. At six feet four inches, Cody had been an all-conference forward on the university basketball team and an honor roll student.

"How are we looking, Emily?" Cody called out to Emily Cross as she filled up water glasses on a large table full of platters of food, including salads, meat and vegetable dishes, and plenteous desserts arrayed in every manner imaginable.

Blue-eyed and auburn-headed Emily paused her glass-filling routine, smiled, and said, "We're looking good, Cody. I think we're ready."

"Good. Folks should start showing up any minute now. It's going to be a great night," Cody beamed.

Thirty minutes later, the room was full of young college students. They were gathered in groups of three to five, exchanging greetings and engaging in small talk. Some were hanging out at the food table, enjoying the taste of small finger food offerings. Michael, Jake, and Ian Gregson were there. Olivia Cummings was also there, in the company of several young ladies. Most of the students were engaged with one another, sharing stories and hugs. Uncomfortable, Michael isolated himself near the food table.

Cody Friedman walked up to a podium at the front of the room, unhooked a microphone from its base, and stepped in front of it.

"Good evening, and welcome to the Unity University Exchange. Please remain standing for a minute as we open our meeting with a prayer. Please bow your head and close your eyes." Everyone's head went down.

The noise abated as Cody lowered his head. He paused until there was complete silence. Michael's heart started to beat rapidly. He didn't like the silence and felt intimidated by the atmosphere.

Here I am again. In a place I do not want to be. When will I ever learn to say no to Jake?

"Father God," Cody began his prayer. "Thank you for the start of a new school year and this first day of a new season for our Exchange ministry. We look forward to this opportunity to learn more about you this year, how to serve you, and how to serve our fellow students. We pray you will help us find new friends, special people we will grow to love."

Michael thought to himself. *Not me, God. The first thing I want to find is an exit door out of this place. These clingers are freaking me out.*

"Please bless and be pleased with what you see here today, Lord. In your great name, we pray. Amen."

When Michael opened his eyes and looked up, he was instantly awestruck. What filled his vision and overwhelmed his senses was none other than Strawberry Yogurt Girl. She was standing amid some other girls and a couple of guys. She was wearing a light blue sweater and crisp looking blue jeans. She was stunning. Everything immediately changed in Michael's mind. He couldn't believe his good fortune.

His eyes locked into her eyes as he made a quick move to get to her before she disappeared on him a second time.

"Well, hello," Michael said as he extended his hand to the girl.

Annie smiled and said, "Oh, hello. I remember you. The frozen yogurt shop, right?"

"That's right," Michael replied. "Please tell me your name."

"My name is Annie," she replied. "Annie Smith."

Still holding her hand, Michael said, "I'm glad to know that. I've been back to the frozen yogurt shop hoping to see you again, but, of course, I never did."

By now, a young man stepped forward to join the conversation. Michael released Annie's hand, smiled, and offered his hand to the stranger. "Hello," he said. "I'm Michael. Michael Shepherd."

Annie said, "Michael, this is Tyler. He's a senior, believe it or not. Here, let me introduce you to the rest of these folks."

"Cool,"Michael replied.

Michael began shaking hands with Annie's friends. He was impressed by their friendliness.

"Nice to meet you, Michael."

"Welcome to Exchange, Michael. Where are you from?"

"What's your major, Michael?"

"Hey, I think we're in the same Chemistry Lab. It's good to meet you, Michael."

"Aren't you the soccer player from Barrymore?"

He had gotten halfway through the group when Cody Friedman's voice boomed through the satellite room speakers.

"Ladies and gentlemen, to get to know one another better, we are going to play a little game. Please break into groups of five or six and sit in a circle facing one another. There are roughly fifty students here tonight, which will give us about ten small groups."

Michael moved next to Annie. He was no longer interested in looking for an exit door. He was all in for the evening's program, no matter where it took him.

Two girls and a boy joined Annie, Tyler, and Michael in their circle. They took their seats as Cody began to issue further instructions.

"We are going to play a game called Two Truths and One Lie. I want you to think of three things about yourself. Two of them are true, and one is a lie. So, one of you starts in your small group by telling everyone your name and where you're from."

The room was immediately filled with noisy chatter from every quarter.

The six in Michael's group got comfortable. There was an awkward silence until Tyler piped up.

"I'll start," he announced. Tyler looked around the group and spoke with an air of great confidence. "My name is Tyler Weatherford. I was born in Waco, Texas. My family moved to Seattle when I was ten years old. My dad was a machinery salesman. He did so well that we could afford to own a sailboat, which I learned to sail when I was fifteen. I also used to ski on Mt. Rainier and began giving skiing lessons by the time I graduated from high school." Tyler smiled and relaxed back in his chair. "That's it," he said.

The participants hashed through Tyler's story, and after several minutes, Tyler confirmed he had never been on a sailboat his entire life.

"How about you?" Michael asked, looking at Annie. "What's your story?"

Annie pushed forward in her chair. Her confidence level was not on par with Tyler's. She was nervous but responsive, and her voice grew stronger the more she got into her story. "My name is Annie Smith. I was born in LaGrange, Oregon. My dad is a salesman. My mom is a teacher. I own a horse. His name is Blue Boy. I took ballerina lessons when I was a kid." Then she laughed out loud and continued. "I still have a tutu I wore in those days. It doesn't fit anymore." The whole group laughed at that.

"Well, we know that's not the lie." Tyler quipped. Annie smiled and sat back in her chair.

The group discussed Annie's story for several minutes. They rightly decided the lie was the horse named Blue Boy.

"Okay, who's next?" Tyler asked. "What about you, Michael?"

Michael didn't hesitate to respond. "My name is Michael Shepherd. I was born in Portland to parents whom I have never met. I came to Unity as a walk-on for the soccer team. I am also a scratch golfer. My parents belong to the LaGrange Country Club, and I play every weekend."

"That's four things, Michael," Tyler observed.

"Yeah, but not if you combine the last two," Michael replied.

"Okay. Got it. Sorry," Tyler said with his hand up.

"No problem, bruh," Michael responded.

Aiden, a tall, slim, girl said, "I think the lie is that you didn't meet your parents. How could that be?"

"Well, he could have been adopted," Tyler said.

"Were you adopted, Michael?" Annie asked.

"Yes, I was."

"I believe the lie was that you are a scratch golfer," Kip Householder said.

Michael smiled, "Nor do I play golf every weekend."

Once again, Tyler countered. "Uhm, that's two lies. You only need one."

Tyler's comment caused Michael to frown and think to himself. *What a jerk this guy is.* He wisely made no follow-up comment.

Aiden was just getting started on her story when Cody Friedman's voice again echoed through the speakers.

"Sorry, folks. We need to keep moving along here. Hopefully, you all know a little more about someone you may have already known coming into today's get-together and maybe a great deal about someone you may have just met. That is what we want to accomplish, of course. That's one of the reasons we call ourselves 'Exchange.' You have just exchanged a great deal of information among yourselves. As you begin your new year at Unity, the staff wants to encourage you to continue to exchange with one another, whether it is helping someone get acquainted, finding a classroom, or finding counseling if needed."

"But, is that the major reason we call ourselves Exchange? To answer that question, I am going to ask Emily Cross to come to the mic. Emily, come on up."

Emily stepped up, took Cody's mic, and, with the aplomb of an insurance salesman, took control of the mic and, for the next several minutes, the entire meeting.

"When I came to Unity three years ago, I was about as naive as an undecorated Christmas tree. I was unchurched and living for whatever the world could give me. I did not have a relationship with Jesus Christ. I didn't even know if He existed. I was struggling with my classes, a broken relationship, and pressure from my parents to do better or move back home. I was at a crossroads when someone invited me to an Exchange meeting. What a difference there was in my life after that. We played the Two Truths and One Lie game that first night, and, as designed, a lot of personal information was exchanged among the participants."

"But I'm here to tell you there is a vastly more important exchange in Exchange than you've witnessed tonight. The exchange I'm talking about is a life exchange. The exchange I'm talking about is between you and Jesus. You exchange your death for His life. Yes, you heard me right—your death for His life. The Bible says in Romans chapter six, verse six, that we are all sinners. It says, 'All have sinned and fall short of the glory of God.' Later in the same chapter, verse twenty-three says, 'For the wages of sin is death, but the free gift of God is eternal life through Jesus Christ our Lord.' The Bible also tells us that 'anyone who is in Christ is a new creature; the old things passed away. All things have become new.'"

Emily paused for a minute to snatch a drink from her water bottle. Then she held the mic close to her mouth and continued. "The very minute I believed, Jesus handed me His goodness, purity, and innocence. At the same time, I handed–or rather, He took–my sinfulness, shame, and guilt onto Himself." Her eyes moved around the room. No one looked away from her. No one moved. Then she said, "If you don't mind, I would like to ask you for complete silence while you think about that. So right now, please bow your heads and think about the magnitude of that exchange... His goodness for our shame."

For the next two minutes, the room was completely silent. No one said a word until Emily spoke again. She then spoke softly, "Second Corinthians, chapter five, verse twenty-one says, 'He made him who knew no sin to be sin on our behalf so that we might become the righteousness of God in him.'" She paused and said, "Did you get that? God made Him, Jesus, who knew no sin, to be sin on our behalf so that we, you and I, might become the righteousness of God in Him." Emily was visibly excited, smiling broadly and moving about the front of the room. She extended the mic in the air and held it high until she began to wind down to her conclusion.

"Ladies and gentlemen, that is it—the entire Gospel of Jesus Christ in one verse. That's all you need to know. We are given eternal life because of Christ's death on the cross. That is the Great Exchange. It defines who we are as Christians. Put your life in His hands, brothers and sisters. Give Him the keys to your heart, and He will give you the key to eternal life. I guarantee you will never regret what you did. Never!"

Receiving a rousing ovation, Emily smiled broadly and handed the mic back to Cody.

Awestruck and overwhelmed by Emily's expression of her deep-seated faith, Michael could only utter one word. "Wow!"

His eyes followed Emily as she moved back to the food table to help serve. The sensation remained until he felt a hand on his shoulder from behind.

"How did you like that?" Jake grinned as he gave Michael's shoulder a not-so-gentle shake.

"That was amazing," Michael replied. He turned and faced Jake and Olivia, standing together and holding hands. "I've never heard anything like it. Do you know her?"

"Of course not. I'm new here, too, bruh," Jake laughed. "By the way, why don't you introduce us to your Strawberry Yogurt Girl?"

Annie was engaged in a conversation with Tyler and others in their small group. Michael caught her eye and motioned for her to join his friends. She smiled, excused herself from Tyler, and stepped toward Michael. Michael didn't miss the sudden frown from Tyler as Annie stepped away from him.

"Annie, I'd like you to meet some of my friends, Jake Ledger and Olivia Cummings."

The three exchanged handshakes as Cody Freidman's voice again boomed through the speaker system.

"Ladies and gentlemen, there is plenty of food left. Please continue fellowshipping. This afternoon's guest speaker is Francis Miller, Pastor of Student Ministries at Redeemer Bible Church. He will begin his remarks in about fifteen minutes. So, load up on the food, and I'll be back in fifteen to get us rollin'."

As the four new students conversed, Michael seized the opportunity. He gently put his hand on Annie's elbow and asked, "Annie, can I walk you back to your dorm when this is over?"

Annie smiled and said, "I'm sorry, Michael. A few of us are going to Tyler's for some afternoon barbeque and a movie."

Michael tried to disguise his disappointment. "Oh, okay. Another time, maybe?"

"Yes, I'd like that, Michael," Annie smiled.

"Cool. How about a phone number?"

"Sure. No problem."

"Hold on," Michael said as he pulled his phone out from his back pocket.

Doing his best to disguise his excitement, Michael keyed in Annie's phone number as she recited it to him.

CHAPTER 21

Later that evening, Michael sat on his bed, his body propped up by pillows. He was alone, staring at the wall as his mind tumbled through the events that had taken place earlier in the day. He thought about Annie and how beautiful she was. What would he say when he called her, and where might they go on their first date? *Will I be able to kiss her? No, better not try that. Well, it depends on the setting, and the setting is up to me, isn't it? Yeah, but nah, I'd better forget that. That might really turn her off, like what happened with Ashley. And what about Tyler? Is he her bodyguard or something? I don't like that guy, and he clearly does not like me. Where does he fit in this picture, anyway?*

Michael swung his feet around and started to stand up just as Jake entered the room.

"Hey man," Jake said as he sat in the desk chair. "What's up?"

"I don't know, man," Michael replied with a sigh. "Just thinking."

"About what? Let me guess. Your upcoming calculus exam. No? Our game this week with Findlay. No?"

"Shut up, man. You're not helping," Michael laughed wryly.

"I'm just messing with you, bruh. Have you called Annie yet?"

"No. She's probably not home yet."

"Yeah. Probably having a good lip-syncing time with Tyler

about now."

"You're not helping...." Michael groaned.

"What did you think of Emily?" Jake asked.

"I liked her."

"Michael, what she said. Did that make sense to you?"

"Yes, it did," Michael replied.

"Would you like to talk about it?" Jake asked.

"Yeah, sometime. Not right now, though. I need to think about it for a while."

"Let me know when you're ready."

"I will."

"Maybe we can talk about it on the way back from Findlay tomorrow," Jake said, referring to their upcoming game.

"Yeah, maybe. Or maybe during the game. We can sit together on the bench," Michael said, rolling his eyes.

"Come on, man," Jake protested. "At least we made the travel team."

"You're right, Jake. All things happen for good, right? That's what you keep saying anyway. Yet, we're one and eight."

"I know, bruh. But we're the best one and eight team in the league. Don't you think?"

Michael smiled. "Whatever you say, bruh. That's what I love about you, man. You never get down. How do you do that?"

"Easy. The Bible says we should not be anxious about anything and trust God in everything. That's what I try to do, Mike," Jake explained. "I have my down days occasionally, but I know God is always there for me and is there for you, too, if you want him to be."

Michael leaned forward, put his head down, and his arms on his knees. "I don't know, Jake. This is all so weird."

"Of course it is, Michael. But it doesn't have to be." Jake paused for a few seconds and said, "The folks we were with today. What did you think of them?"

Michael turned his head to Jake. "They were pretty cool."

"Cool? What do you mean by that? Like special, maybe?"

"Yeah, I'd say that," Michael replied.

"How were they special?" Jake prodded.

"Well, they all love one another. That was obvious."

"Anything else?"

"Yeah. They all believe the same thing."

"Like what?" Jake asked.

"Well, that Jesus is their God, and they are all going to go to heaven when they die..."

"Bingo! Isn't that something you would like to be a part of?" Jake asked.

"Well, I guess...." Michael said slowly.

"There is no guessing involved," Jake advised. "However, there is a choice to make. One option is to believe Jesus died on the cross to pay for your sins, and the other is to believe that somehow you are going to get to heaven because your goodness outweighs your badness. Therefore, God will be forced to take you into heaven if you score enough points. Which one makes the most sense to you, Michael?"

"I don't know, Jake. Let's talk about something else," Michael replied, slightly annoyed.

"Hmm. That's a good idea. How about we discuss how to find

the size of a right triangle so that the radius of the circle inscribed is maximum for a constant hypotenuse?"

"You're a scumbag. Do you know that?" Michael grinned and moved from the bed to the floor, where he leaned back against the bed.

"Okay. You don't want to talk about calculus?"

"No way," Michael laughed.

"All right. How about current events?"

"Current events sound acceptable."

"Okay, good. So, I read on my phone on the way over here where a cement truck ran into a school bus full of kids on a field trip. Several kids were hurt. The bus driver was killed."

"That's terrible."

"We are going to be on a bus tomorrow. What if we were in an accident, and you were killed as a result?" Jake asked. Michael remained silent. "So you are standing at heaven's door, and God says to you, 'Tell me, Michael Shepherd. Why should I let you into my heaven?' What would you say?"

Michael said, "Well, I'd probably say I hadn't done anything really bad like kill someone or rob anyone. I don't' cuss... much. Of course, I haven't joined a church, but I don't think that's a requirement, is it?"

"No, you're right. It's not a requirement," Jake agreed.

"So, why wouldn't God let me in?" Michael asked.

"Because admission to my heaven is not dependent on what you do or don't do, Michael. It's about what God did for you. Do you remember the banner that we sometimes see at football games that reads, 'John 3:16?'"

"Yep," Michael replied.

"Do you know what John 3:16 says?" Jake asked.

"No, but I'm sure you're going to tell me, right?"

"John 3:16 says basically that God so loved the world that he gave his only son that whosoever believes in him, has eternal life. So what should you say to God when He asks you why He should let you in is…"

"Because I believe in your son, Jesus Christ?" Michael asked.

"Bingo!" Jake exclaimed.

"Yeah, Jake, but there's only one problem. How can I say I believe in Jesus when I don't know anything about Him?"

"That is an excellent question, Mike. The answer is simple. How are you learning about calculus? By studying calculus. Right? It's the same, but a lot more important. You need to study the Bible. The best way to do that is to join a local Bible study group. But first, let's go back to the urgency of the matter. Suppose there was an accident, and your life was taken from you. Prayerfully, that won't happen, but you need to be prepared if it were to happen.

My point is we need to settle this question of where you are going to spend eternity tonight. Right now, in fact. Do you not agree?" Jake asked.

"Yes, I agree, but–"

"But what?"

"There is just so much I don't understand. I feel overwhelmed and stupid about this stuff, but I'm being pressured to buy into it."

Jake paused for a minute and said, "Do you know where that pressure is coming from, Michael?"

"Yeah, from you!" Michael retorted with a grin.

"No, you are wrong about that, bruh, Jake said. "The pressure is coming from someone way above my pay grade. The pressure you are feeling is coming from God. He is ready to move into your life, Michael. You need to let him in. A verse in Revelation says, 'Behold, I stand at the door and knock. If anyone hears my voice and opens the door, I will come into him and dine with him, and him with me.'"

"Jake, you don't know how little I know about the Bible," Michael said.

"We can handle that, bruh. "Don't you want to get this thing taken care of now? Coming to Christ can change your life just like it changed Emily's life."

After a short pause, Michael looked into Jake's eyes and whispered, "Yeah, I'm ready."

Jake grinned. "I'm going to lead you in a short little prayer in which you will tell Jesus you have sinned, that you are sorry for your sins, and that you believe His death on the cross paid the price for your sins. Then, you will ask Him to come into your heart and be your guide for the rest of your life. After that, we will thank Him for saving you and allowing you to live in Him and for Him in everything you do."

Michael closed his eyes and lowered his head. Jake spoke the words he had just given to Michael, and Michael repeated them word for word. As they closed the prayer, Michael felt overwhelmed and relieved. The boys stood and shared a strong bear hug and many pats on the back.

Jake finally closed the conversation by whispering, "Good job, bruh. I love you, man."

"Thanks, Jake. Love you too," Michael replied.

"Now you need to tell some folks what you've done."

"I do? Why?" Michael asked, confused.

"People are going to see a change in you, man, and they will want to know why. They need to know on the front end, and you want them to know. The Bible says, 'When anyone comes to Christ, he is a new creature; the old things are gone; all things have become new.'"

"Well, okay, I can do that," Michael replied.

"Good. I'd recommend you include Coach Patton on your list. As well as your folks."

"That's what I was thinking, but first...."

"I know. I think Strawberry Girl will be excited," Jake laughed.

"I hope you're right, bruh," Michael said with a smile.

"I am, man!"

"Hey Jake."

"What?"

"Do you think it would be okay to pray about our game against Findlay?"

"Absolutely. The Bible says we can pray about all things. Why don't you take it to the Lord right now?"

"Me? I'm not sure what to say," Michael said hesitantly.

Jake closed his eyes and said, "God will give you the words. Just wait on Him."

Michael and Jake sat quietly for several minutes with their heads bowed. Finally, Michael began to speak. "God, you know our team, uh, Unity. We're not doing very well. We need to come together, God. We're so divided. Please help us play better tomorrow. I'm not asking for a win, God. Just help us do better as a team, I pray—and God, Jake, and me could help the team, God, if Coach Cathey would just put us in the game... which would be a miracle if he did. Thanks, God. Amen."

CHAPTER 22

The Saturday afternoon game against Findlay proved to be a harbinger that things were not going to get any easier for the Defenders of Unity University. Findlay took control from the start, dominating every aspect of the game. Unity could not get out of their defensive end of the field, and by halftime, Findlay was up four to one. Coach Cathey was frustrated. He began experimenting with different player combinations, including position changes, but nothing worked. Finally, with forty minutes to play, the coach walked down the Unity bench line and looked at Jake and Michael sitting side by side on the bench.

"You two. Warm-up. You're going in."

The two men immediately jumped up, retreated behind the player's bench, and began to run short distances up and down the touchlines. Both players were excited as they ran, anticipating their eventual call to enter the game. It happened when a throw-in opportunity came to Unity. Jake replaced Gunther Rigsby, a long-time mainstay at Unity's center midfield position.

Michael replaced another stalwart player, Troy Cobb, on the left wing. Gunther and Troy frowned at Coach Cathey as they trotted off the field. Their expressions remained fixed as they traded fist bumps with some players on the touchline and then took seats on the player bench.

When play resumed, Jake immediately intercepted a pass from

a Findlay defender. He pounded the ball forward to space in front of Michael, who, with speed the Findlay defenders had not seen up to then, charged down the field and into the left corner of the box, collecting Jake's pass along the way. Michael brought the ball under control and immediately blasted it into the top right corner of the goal. In less than one minute since the substitution, the score became four to two. With the sudden change, there was a faint whisper of a possible momentum drift. The Findlay coaches moved to the touchline and showed a renewed interest in the game.

As the ball was being retrieved by one of the game officials, Jake began to rally his teammates. "Let's go, Unity. Let's go!" Jake bellowed as he ran among the Unity players as they positioned themselves for the game restart. "We can do this!"

Many Findlay players were amused and chuckled as they watched Jake interact with his teammates as if thinking, "Where did this goofball come from?"

Jake didn't care. For the first time all season, he showed the juice of being in a soccer game. Michael joined in as well. "Let's go, Unity!" Michael shouted. "Here we go! Win the ball!"

"Let's go, guys! We're going to win this!" Jake continued.

The Findlay players, who were up by two goals, seemed unconcerned. However, their coaches remained on their feet, watching and coaching their players on the field as the play went back and forth. Findlay was able to penetrate Unity's defense on several occasions, but Unity repelled every attack with a ferocity not seen earlier in the game. At the sixty-minute mark, Unity's senior goalkeeper, Dexter Stanley, made a long throw up field to his right midfielder, who controlled the ball and, after a quick give-and-go exchange with Jake, burst into the box and played the ball to his right, over to the feet of striker Riley Bazemore. Bazemore one-touched the ball into the net for goal number three for Unity. The crowd suddenly realized they had a close game at hand and began to raise the cheering level in the stadium.

With great enthusiasm, Jake Ledger revved up his chatter. Jake's arms were flapping up and down like eagle wings. Almost screaming, he hollered, "Here we go, guys! I'm telling you, we're going to win this game!" Michael and goalkeeper J. D. Stanley joined in with their own boisterous chatter. In seconds, the rest of Unity's team began to stand and root for their team. Play in the final few minutes was at an intensity level Unity had not played at all season.

The game entered into stoppage time, the time lost due to interrupted play during the course of the game. Only the referee knew how much of that time was left. A throw-in for Unity at midfield on the left side produced a ball for Michael to control and bring down to his outside foot. He played the ball inside to Jake, who took it forward until a Findlay defender picked him up and forced him to release the ball to the right side, where right-wing Nick Carrol controlled it and took it deep toward the corner, and, with no change in motion, he crossed the ball toward the left side of the net, where two men waited for the crossed ball to descend. One was a defender for Findlay; the other was Michael, the taller of the two. He had the advantage. He jumped high and, with a violent head twist, using the crown of his forehead, knocked the ball into the back of the net. The clock ran out with the score tied at four goals.

Both teams were on their feet as the first overtime period began. The play was furious. Findlay was playing to avoid the embarrassment of losing to the worst team in the league, while Unity was fighting for its second win of the season and a smidge of self-respect. Emotions were sky-high. Body contact was frequent and brutal. The game's outcome could come down to who made the first critical mistake.

Midway through the second overtime period, Unity's John Carrol controlled the ball and charged into scoring position. John was short but powerfully built, and as he came into scoring position, one of the Findlay defenders brought him down from behind. John went to the ground in agony, holding his right knee and screaming out in pain.

Immediately, the referee blew his whistle and pointed at the penalty marker. After helping John off the field, both teams lined up for the penalty kick, which Unity's senior right midfielder Cal Owens would take.

Cal placed the ball on the penalty spot, took three steps back, and wasted no time in driving the ball into the lower right corner of the net. Unity players began to celebrate. They had just won their second game of the season.

The ninety-minute bus ride back to the Unity campus was not quiet—except for two players, Troy Cobb and Gunther Rigsby, and two coaches, Jason Cathey and assistant coach Fletcher Hoxsey. Everyone else was pumped. After multiple losses, they had won a game. Their elation was understandable.

"I tell you what, Coach. I'm not happy," Troy complained to Coach Cathey. "We were just about to turn the game around when you jerked me and Gunther out. Findlay was out of steam. I could tell. Me and Gunther agree on that. Those two guys you put in for us were pickin' up the goodies we set up. It's not fair, Coach. Gunther told me he might leave the team over this. And I might too. That's how bad it is, Coach."

Coach Cathey shook his head. He said, "Come on, Troy. We were losing the game. Badly! You know that. Then, when Jake and

Michael go in, they get everybody fired up, and we turn the game around. It's as simple as that. You need to be excited about the win."

"So, does that mean me and Gunther are not going to start next week? Because if that's the case... Well, it's adios for me, and probably Gunther too. We're gone," Troy threatened.

"No, I'm not saying that, Troy. Not at all. But you need to see it as a challenge to up your game. To assume more of a leadership role. The guys look up to you. The team needs you, Troy. I need you to go out there and pull this team together. Do you know what I mean, son?"

After a pause, Troy looked at his coach and said, "Yeah, I do, Coach. I can do that. But, can I tell you something?"

"Of course," Coach Cathey replied.

In a muffled voice, Troy leaned into Coach Cathey and said, "Coach, I have a problem with Coach Patton, and I'm not alone."

"Oh? Well, that's too bad. But this is not the place for that discussion. We'll have to hold off on that where we have some privacy. Do you understand what I mean, Troy?"

"Yes, sir. I'll get with you later on that."

"Okay, Troy. Stop by my office sometime next week. We'll talk about it. In the meantime, don't worry about your place on the team. Just up your enthusiasm for the team. Be the leader we need. We'll pull this team out of the mud together. Okay, Troy?"

"Sounds good, Coach. Sounds good."

***

It was a cool October evening. Michael Shepherd stood at the bottom of the steps outside Queen Esther Hall, the living quarters for all female Unity first-year students. Michael was excited and had a lot going through his mind as he waited for Annie to emerge through the building's large and commanding front doors. Anticipating what they would talk about was foremost in his mind.

I need to let her know I made a confession of faith—or was it a profession of faith? I'm not sure. Anyway, I prayed to receive Jesus. She needs to know that, for sure, and I'm going to need her help with that. Jake challenged me to grow in faith. Annie is a lot further down that road than I am.

Where is she? Did she forget our date? Oh, man. I hope not… Should I hold her hand while we walk across the campus? Oh, don't be stupid, Michael. Of course not. You dummy! Let's see, we can talk about the Exchange Club meeting… wait a minute. Here she comes through the door. Oh, man. Look at her. She's so beautiful!

Annie stood for a few seconds until she spotted Michael in the large number of students. He had begun to walk up the five steps leading to the large porch at the front of the building. Annie was dressed in a blue sweater and light blue jeans.

"Hey, Annie," Michael spoke as he stuck his hand forward to help her down the steps. "You look very nice."

"Thank you, Mike." Annie smiled and said, "I hear we won the game."

"Yes. As a matter of fact, we did. It was somewhat of a miracle," Michael laughed,

They started walking together on a curving sidewalk past a large fountain filled with water lilies and narrow-leafed greenery.

"Where are we going?" Annie asked.

"That is an excellent question, Annie. So, assuming you stuck to our agreement and had no dessert after dinner, we are headed to a place where we can get a great dessert. How does that sound?" Michael asked.

"Very cool," Annie said with a smile. What's the name of it?"

"Wixx Café. It's just a few blocks up Gloucester Avenue. We had breakfast there Sunday after church. It was good," Michael said.

"Were you at Redeemer on Sunday?" Annie asked.

"Yep."

"So was I."

"Yeah, I know. I saw you go in but didn't see where you were sitting. Where were you?"

"In a classroom. I teach a class of six-year-old girls every Sunday."

"That's pretty cool, " Michael said as they began their stroll across the campus.

No words passed between them for the first few steps of the walk. The silence bothered Michael, so he blurted out what had been on his mind since they had made the date.

"I have something to tell you, Annie."

"You have? What's that?" Annie asked.

"I prayed to receive Christ," Michael said with a broad smile.

Annie stopped and turned toward Michael. "You did? Wow, Michael. That's wonderful. I am so happy for you! Tell me how it happened."

"Well, my friend Jake," Michael began with a laugh. "He's been harassing me forever. But I wasn't ready until I heard Cody Friedman and Emily at the Exchange meeting. When I heard Emily's testimony, something happened to me. I felt Jesus was tapping me on the shoulder. It was amazing. So, Jake and I prayed together. And that was it."

"That's so exciting, Michael. You're a brother now."

"Yeah, I guess so. I'll try to live up to that honor," Michael replied.

Annie blushed. "That's sweet, Michael. Thank you."

When the two arrived at Wixx Café, Michael held the door open for Annie and another couple who had arrived at the same time.

Michael and Annie were led to an open booth and sat across the table from each other as the waitress dropped off two menus and two glasses of water.

"We're just having dessert," Michael said.

The waitress, a college-aged girl, looked at Michael and said, "Well, you've come to the right place. We are world-famous for our desserts, especially our pies."

"Really?" Michael asked. "I bet you don't have huckleberry pie."

"Oh, but we do have fresh huckleberry pie."

"That's what I'll have, with a scoop of ice cream."

"And you?" She asked, looking at Annie.

"I guess I'll have the same," Annie answered. Annie picked up Michael's menu, smiled, and handed both menus back to the waitress.

As the waitress stepped away from their booth, Michael looked at Annie, cleared his throat, and nervously queried, "May I ask you a question that is clearly none of my business but one that has been nagging me since we met at the Exchange meeting?"

"Of course," Annie said. "What's your question?"

"I'm wondering about you and Tyler..." Michael began. "Are you, you know, an item? Like I said, I know it is none of my business, but I'm curious."

With a slight smile, Annie answered, "Well, I guess we might be. Why are you interested in knowing that?"

"Because I need to. I'm interested in you... In your welfare." He grinned at Annie. "I'm your brother now. You said so yourself."

At that moment, the waitress brought two pieces of huckleberry pie a la mode and placed them on the table.

"There you are. Enjoy," she said. "Is there anything else I can bring you?"

"No thanks," Michael answered. "We're good. Thank you."

As the waitress disappeared, Annie looked at Michael and asked, "So you want to protect me?"

Michael smiled. "Well, yes. Like I say, I'm your brother now."

"And you think Tyler might be a problem?"

"Sort of," Michael said. "Yes. Not to be mean, but he acts like he owns you."

Annie smiled, took a drink from her water glass, and said, "It's possible, I guess. I love Tyler."

Uh oh... "You do?" Michael stammered, trying to keep the shock out of his voice.

"Yes, he's my brother, you see," Annie said with a smile.

"Tyler's your brother? You mean like I'm your brother?"

"Well, yes. That too, but he's also my brother, brother. Tyler Weatherford is my brother from another mother." Annie giggled. She paused, then dropped her smile. "Seriously, my dad lost his first wife to cancer. Tyler was about a year old when that happened. My dad and mom had known each other since high school. They reconnected and fell in love. They got married, and I was born about two years later."

Michael chuckled. "Well, hello, Tyler! Welcome to my world."

Annie's smile returned. "He's a great guy, really."

Annie reached across the table and put her hand on top of Michael's hand. "Your news is so cool, Michael. Thank you for telling me about your conversion. I've been praying for that."

"You have?" Michael asked, eyebrows raised.

"Yes, I have. Some of my friends, as well."

"Wow. No wonder! I've been feeling all this pressure. By the way, I have one more piece of news I need to tell you."

"What?"

"Do you remember me saying in that 'Three questions game' that I was adopted?"

"Yes, I do," Annie replied.

"Well, my birth parents reached out recently to my parents and asked if they could come and meet me," Michael said.

"So, you've really never met them before?"

"No. Never have."

"Cool," Annie said. "That's exciting."

"Yes and no..." Michael trailed off.

"Yes and no? What do you mean by that?"

"The lady, my uh, the birth mother, has terminal cancer."

"Oh, no."

"It's an end-of-life request, I guess. Anyway, my parents are coming to visit here at school, and they are going to bring my birth mom and her husband with them. I will see her for the first... and last time." He paused, then said, "That's weird, isn't it?"

"When will they be here?" Annie asked.

"Next weekend," Michael said. "They will be able to see my game while they are here."

"What are you going to say to them?"

"I don't know. How does anyone know in a situation like this?"

"I'll pray for you, Michael."

"Thank you, Annie, I appreciate that." Michael paused momentarily as he locked eyes with Annie. Then he said, "Can I ask you another question?"

"Of course you can," Annie replied.

"Well, I want you to know I think you are special. I mean really special!"

"Thank you, Michael. I appreciate that very much. So what did you want to ask me?"

"If you would be willing to date me again?"

"Of course I would, Michael. I think that would be neat."

Michael grinned and, with a deep sigh, uttered, "Thank you, Annie."

* * *

A refreshing optimism was in the air Monday afternoon as the Unity Defenders took to the field for practice. The upcoming game on Saturday would be a home game against the Crestwell Capitols, a junior college near Spokane in Eastern Washington. Earlier that day, Coach Cathey had met with his assistant coaches, Fletcher Hoxsey, Bill Redman, and Kyle Patton.

"Men, I need your input," Cathey declared from behind his cluttered desk.

Kyle was surprised and a little confused by his boss's anxiety.

"We just came out of a great win against Findlay. We all should be happy about that, and I know you all are. The team is ready to lace 'em up and go after Crestwell. I sense an excitement we haven't seen for some time. We need to hold on to that at all costs!"

Coach Cathey paused and said, "However, I had two players in my office this morning threatening to leave the team. They are Troy Cobb and Gunther Rigsby, two players we can't afford to lose."

The three assistant coaches were quiet. They glanced at each other, again at Coach Cathey, and back at each other, waiting for someone to comment. No one did. Finally, Cathey looked at Coach Hoxsey and said, "Fletcher, tell me what you're thinking."

Hoxsey paused, placed one leg on the other, and thoughtfully replied, "I don't like it, but I agree. It would be a real setback if they quit the team. But I doubt that they would, really. I know those guys well; they're just threatening. They are senior leaders. They love the team and the school. I may be wrong, but..."

Coach Cathey looked at Coach Redmond. "What do you think, Coach?"

Redmond sighed and said, "Well, these guys have been part of the team for several years. I remember when they both started as freshmen. They're both essential players. I know they felt some humiliation after the game. I would hate to lose them."

Cathey's eyes moved his eyes to Coach Patton. "Kyle?"

"I say, let them go. If they stay, how will their poor attitudes affect the team? The rest of the players may question who's running things. I think we showed Saturday that we had good chemistry with the players who ended the game."

"So," Cathey posed, "You're saying just let them leave?"

"No, sir. I'm saying, *tell* them to leave," Kyle said bluntly. "They are no longer on the team. That would be the best thing for the team and for them in the long run as well."

Coach Cathey responded with, "Hmm. I'm not sure about that. What do the rest of you think?"

"I disagree," Redmond quipped. "We will need those guys down the stretch."

"It's pretty harsh," Fletcher added. "I say we should encourage them to hang in there. We coach, they play, and together, we are a team that represents Unity University. As players, they don't always get it right, and as coaches, we sometimes make mistakes. But we are a team. We win as a team, and when we lose, we lose as a team. In short, win or lose, we are equally responsible."

"Hmm. I like that, Jason. Thank you," Cathey replied.

Coach Cathey leaned back in his chair for several seconds, his hands cupped under his chin, as he thoughtfully surveyed his three coaches. Finally, he stood, put his ball cap on, and said, "Okay, men. We've got a winning team out there waiting on us. Let's get out there and coach them!"

Unity's soccer team looked up as their three coaches emerged from the locker room and ran toward them. The coaches double-timed it across the parking lot and onto the practice field.

"Okay, give me two laps," Cathey hollered to his team. The men took to the cinder track, running in small groups and engaging in small talk as they ran. When the team finished the run, Coach Cathey blew his whistle and motioned for the players to gather around him. Thirty-five players, two managers, and three assistant coaches were anxious to hear from their coach.

"Please take a knee," Cathey instructed. "We have a lot to talk about."

All the players knelt or sat. The coaches stood behind Cathey. Michael and Jake sat next to each other.

"First, your coaching staff wants you to know how proud we are of you," Cathey began. "It's been a tough season, but we have weathered the worst. Even though we are on the wrong end of the win-loss record right now, there are reasons to think the best part of our season lies ahead. We were successful on Saturday because we hung together as a team. I'm proud of all of you. I'm proud of you veterans who have stayed with us over difficult times and you younger players who stepped up under pressure. The coaches and I are excited about our prospects for the remainder of the season. So, hang in there. Trust your coaches. Stay positive."

He turned to his coaches and stepped aside. "Okay, coaches. You've got them."

Fletcher Hoxsey stepped forward and blew his whistle. Thirty-five players rose to their feet and charged onto the practice field.

***

Coach Patton sat at his desk going through his mail that evening. Kayla poked her head through the door, smiled, and asked, "Are you going to stay here all night?"

"Come on in," Kyle offered. "I'm about done."

Kayla entered and sat down in a side chair. She studied her husband briefly and asked, "How's it going, Coach? You seem at odds with yourself this evening."

Kyle pushed back from his desk and replied, "Your intuition amazes me."

"So, can you talk about it?" Kayla asked.

Kyle swung his seat around and faced his wife. He said, "We had a meeting before practice tonight. Coach told us two players were threatening to leave the team because they were unhappy about being subbed out of the game on Saturday."

"Really?" Kayla replied. "Who were they?"

"A couple of the seniors. They didn't like being pulled out of the game and complained to Coach–in his office, no less. The funny thing is, we were down by three goals when they were subbed out, and we ended up winning the game due to the play of the two players who replaced them, who were, incidentally, our kids from Barrymore, Jake Ledger, and Michael Shepherd."

"Wow, how about that? So, what did you all decide to do?" Kayla asked.

"Well, the decision was to keep them on the team. It wasn't my decision, but that's how the vote went. We shouldn't have had a vote to start with. That is a head coach's decision to make."

Kayla came into the room and sat down in an armchair. "So, what do you think is going to happen?"

"It's a sticky wicket," Kyle sighed. "If the guys who stepped up and pulled out the win aren't rewarded with more playing time, the whole team could be disappointed because they won't see effort rewarded. But, if the prima donnas lose playing time, they will be unhappy and likely cause dissension, which could be a death knell for a team that's barely hanging on as it is. No matter which way we go, team morale will be in the toilet."

"How do you think this will affect you?" Kayla asked gently.

"Well, I was the only one who voted for these guys to be dismissed from the team. It turned out my position was not popular. Unfortunately, the coaches seemed more concerned about equity and diplomacy than putting the best players on the field."

"That's too bad," Kayla sighed, shaking her head. "There's no place for that on a soccer team."

"Certainly not one I'm coaching," Kyle replied.

"So, what are you going to do, Coach?"

"Wait it out. See how the season goes."

"Yes, and trust the Lord," Kayla reminded him.

"Yep. That's the main thing. Trust the Lord."

Kayla stood. "So then, no worries, my love. Come on. It's time for story time with your son."

Kyle stood and responded, "Your brother. My son. How does that work?"

"I know it's strange, but it works. Come on, Dad," Kayla replied with a wink.

CHAPTER 23

Michael Shepherd was nervous as he exited Cardinal Hall, home of the English and Literature departments on the campus of Unity University. He was struggling to maintain a "C" average in "Survey of English Literature." He didn't understand much of the dialogue in the classroom, and his one-on-one meetings with Dr. Milton Littlejohn seemed to be a waste of time for both the student and the professor. The prevailing question in the minds of both men immediately after one of their meetings was always: "What in the world was that guy talking about?"

None of that mattered this morning, however. Michael was nervous because he was on his way to the student union building to meet his parents—all four of them. George and Abigail Shepherd had initiated the meeting as a favor to James and Lauren Reynolds, Michael's biological mom and her husband. The senior Shepherds were hosting James and Lauren and had driven from Barrymore to Unity University that morning for the special get-together with her son.

Michael climbed the five steps at the entrance to The Student Union building and pushed through the large revolving door. He immediately spotted his mom and dad standing near the two significant strangers he was anxious to meet.

"Hey, Mom. Hey, Dad," he greeted as he strode over to the foursome.

After exchanging hugs, Michael turned to the couple standing behind the Shepherds. Mrs. Reynolds, with the aid of a walker, stood. She had tears in her eyes. George Shepherd moved aside and said, "Michael, let me introduce you to your biological mother, Lauren Reynolds, and her husband, James."

Michael stepped forward and carefully embraced Lauren Reynolds. Deep emotions surged within his chest as he held her closely. He felt no tension, only a deep love for a lady he had just met, yet strangely seemed to know intimately in these few minutes of tenderness. It was surreal. It was a spiritual moment he would never forget.

As they separated, and with watery eyes, Lauren said, "Oh, Michael. I am so happy to finally meet you, my son. I have prayed for this day for so long." She turned to Abigail as tears gushed down her cheeks. "Thank you. Thank you, dear Abigail and dear George."

Lauren turned back to Michael. "Such a fine-looking boy—or, I'm sorry, young man—and you're so tall!" At that moment, James Reynolds stepped forward and took his turn hugging his stepson. "I'm so glad to meet you, Michael. We've learned a lot about you these past several hours."

"I'm sure you have," Michael responded with a smile. "We may have to get together later to separate fact from fiction."

The five sat in a quiet corner of the Student Union for two hours, getting acquainted, sharing family history, and musing about the future. Even though he was a new believer, Michael could sense the love of Christ in his new-found family. He hoped his mom and dad could see it as well.

"What's the plan, Dad?" Michael finally asked as he checked his watch. "It's closing in on five bells."

George looked at his own watch and said, "It's close to dinner time. Are we ready to find a place to eat?"

"This will be my treat," James announced.

"We can't let you do that," George rebutted.

"I insist," James replied. "You all have been so accommodating to us."

George and Abigail exchanged glances. George shrugged his shoulders in visible acquiescence to James' offer.

"Would it be okay if I brought a friend?" Michael interjected.

"Absolutely," James responded. "Do you have a favorite place you like?"

"Well, I haven't ever been there, but there is a nice seafood restaurant within easy walking distance if you like seafood."

"Seafood sounds good," Lauren replied. "What's the name of it?"

"Surfside Grill. It's just a block and a half to the right down Gloucester Avenue. Let me connect with my friend, and I will meet you there in about a half hour if that's okay with you all."

"Sounds good, son," George Shepherd said proudly as he looked at Michael.

"Does your friend have a name?" Abigail asked, obviously wondering if the friend was a girl.

"Yes, her name is Annie."

"Good," Lauren said, making eye contact with Abigail. "We will look forward to meeting Annie."

As Michael fast-tracked to the front door, he reached into his pocket and pulled out his mobile phone.

Forty minutes later, Michael and Annie stepped through the

front door of Surfside Grill, an upscale restaurant with an extensive cocktail bar and a plush adjacent dining area full of multiple tables adorned with white tablecloths and walls lined with massive booths. Soft parlor music drifted throughout the building.

Michael and Annie walked to a reception counter and were greeted by three young ladies.

"Good evening. Do you have reservations?"

"No," Michael replied. "We are with the Shepherd family. They are probably here already."

"Hmm," a second one said as she scanned her spiral register. "Could that be the Reynolds party, maybe?"

"Yes. That's it," Michael replied.

"Okay, Riley will show you to your table."

On the way to the table, Michael leaned forward and whispered to Annie, "I'm glad I'm not picking up the bill."

Annie laughed over her shoulder. "Me, too. I'm sure it's very expensive," she whispered.

Seated in a large booth and smiling, George and James stood and offered handshakes and warm greetings to Michael and Annie. Confusion surfaced when Michael started to introduce Annie to his parents.

He said, "Mom, Dad—I mean, uh, well, Moms and Dads, I'd like you all to meet Annie Smith."

The men remained standing and introduced themselves and their wives. Abigail and Lauren stayed seated but greeted Annie with smiles and warm salutations as the men returned to their seats. Everyone squeezed together to make room at the table for the newcomers.

A strange feeling swept through Michael's conscience as the

moment's reality struck him.

This is special, really special. This is my family! Thank you, God.

When the meals were served, Michael, overcoming some nervousness, asked, "Would you all mind if I asked the Lord to bless our meal?"

Michael's question created an awkward silence. Abigail gave George a puzzled look, and then both turned their heads toward Michael. George quickly broke the silence and said, "Of course not, Michael. Go right ahead."

Annie reached over and placed her hand into Michael's hand as he began to pray.

***

The Crestwell game opened with intense play by both teams. Both teams mounted multiple attacks on goal as they moved up and down the pitch with quick ball movement and pinpoint passing. Only a stubborn defense by both teams kept the ball from finding the back of the net. Unity forward Vic Haines received a nice cross into the box by right-wing Cameron Mitchell, a recruit from the United Kingdom, but he could not convert due to heavy pressure from two Crestwell defenders. Crestwell worked the ball down to the Unity goal area, only to have it deflected by Gunther Rigsby, who hit a long ball back into Crestwell's defensive end.

The game went back and forth for thirty minutes until Crestwell scored after a rash of heavy action in the Unity goal box. The score was one to nothing. Eight minutes later, Crestwell scored again on a free kick from twenty-five yards out, making the score two to nothing at half-time. Michael and Jake had not seen any playing time.

"What's going on out there, guys? Coach Cathey asked as he paced back and forth in the team dressing room at half-time. "You started fine, finding the passing lanes, one and two-touch passing. But halfway through the first half, you started holding the ball and, frankly, looking like you don't have a clue as to what's going on. Gunther, Troy, where did you guys go?"

Gunther scowled and said, "I'm just not gettin' any help out there, Coach. I'm not gettin' any targets." He looked around at his teammates. "You guys need to be moving around more. Show yourselves."

Michael and Jake sat together. Both frowned at Gunther's comments. Michael's mind was busy. He had the answer. *Put us in, Coach. Jake can find the target because his target would be me!*

As the team left the locker room to start the second half, Kyle Patton caught up to Coach Cathey and said, "Coach, can I have a minute?"

"What is it, Kyle?" Coach Cathey asked with a hint of impatience.

"Coach, please pardon me, but I think you need to make a change in the lineup."

"Oh, really. What do you suggest, Coach?"

"Go back with the players who won for us last week," Kyle said,

"You mean with your two boys back in the game, right?"

"They're not *my* two boys, Coach. They're *your* two boys who pulled the game out of the fire last week and could do it again if they had the chance," Coach Patton replied.

Coach Cathey's countenance changed. His eyes narrowed as he looked at Kyle. "Let me tell you something, Coach: I'll play the players who I think can help us win. That's *my* job, not yours. Now, you need to get out to the field to coach your defenders on how to defend our goal. Leave the game strategy up to me. Got it, Coach?"

Kyle locked eyes with Coach Cathey. "Sure!" He quipped. Then he turned and ran out to the field.

Unfortunately for Unity, second-half play continued at the same tempo as the first half. Selfishness and bickering returned to the team, and there was no emotion or unity in Unity's game. Midway through the second half, Coach Cathey made some substitutions, including Michael and Jake's entry into the game, but by then, a win was out of the question. The contest ended with a final score of five to two in favor of the Crestwell Capitols.

Things worsened for the Unity Defenders by a miserable display of sportsmanship when only a few of their players participated in the customary post-game handshake between the competitors. Dressing room discussion was minimal following the game. Most Unity players were already showered and dressed by the time Coach Cathey and his assistant coaches came into the dressing room.

"Sit down a minute, men. I won't keep you long." Cathay paused as the players found places to sit. Then he said, "I know you are all disappointed at the outcome today. I am, too, of course. However, there is still plenty of season left for us. We can still turn things around. I saw some things today that I liked. I also saw some things I need to change. So, I'm asking you to hang in there. Believe in your teammates; believe in me. I know the buck stops with me. So if you see–or I should say, *when* you see some changes, please know that they are intended to make us a better team. Okay? Now, go home and forget about soccer this weekend. Come back Monday, ready to get back to work!"

As the players stood and began to leave, Coach Cathey tapped on Kyle's arm and said. "I need to see you in my office for a minute, Kyle."

Kyle, slightly surprised, replied, "Yes, sir. I'll be right up."

As Coach Cathey walked out of the room, Kyle's mouth suddenly felt very dry. He walked to the soft drink dispenser and purchased a bottle of water. He took several swallows as he walked out the door and down the hallway to the elevators. His mind was spinning. *I wonder what Coach Cathey has on his mind. Maybe he's going to ream me out over my suggestion to change the lineup, which I'm not sorry I made. He may be the boss, but he's dead wrong. We might have won that game if we had put Jake and Michael in at half-time. I can't believe he doesn't see that, but I'd better not push it. He talked about change. Maybe he's going to agree with me and change the lineup. Yeah, right! Lots of luck with that, Coach.*

Kyle threw his empty water container in the recycle bin outside the elevator shaft and entered the elevator. *Anyway, I hope this is short. I'm ready to go home. Can I forget about soccer for the weekend, too? That's not going to be a problem, Coach Cathey.*

Kyle tapped on the partially open door to Jason Cathey's office, pushed it open, and walked into the office. Cathey rose from his chair and pointed to a side chair. "Sit down, Kyle," he said, then quickly added, "Well, you might not need to sit."

Befuddled by that remark, Kyle placed his hand on the back of the chair, "What's up, Coach?"

"Well, Kyle. I think we have a problem, you and me," Coach Cathey replied nonchalantly. "So I'm going to let you go. You are no longer a part of the coaching staff at Unity University."

Kyle was stunned. Cathey's bluntness and the finality of his announcement caused his body to go weak. His mouth was dry. "I don't understand, Jason. What are you telling me?"

"I'm telling you that you are fired, Kyle. You need to gather up your things and vacate the building."

Kyle felt a surge of anger. He knew he had to quell it before it grew out of control, so he calmly asked, "Would you mind telling me why you are firing me?"

"Kyle, there is a lot of stress on our soccer team. Stress we never had last year. You have expressed your disapproval of my coaching, questioned me in front of my team, and, whether you meant to or not, you have turned my players against each other. I can't have those kinds of high-school hi-jinks on my soccer team, Kyle. It's that simple. I'm sorry, but the chemistry isn't there for me to turn this team around as long as you're part of the program–and by the way, both Fletcher and Bill agree with this decision."

"So you sought their input?" Kyle asked, shocked.

"Yes, I did. It was unanimous."

"So you took a vote?"

"More or less. Anyway, please get your things together and vacate the building. Now!"

Kyle stood for a minute. His anger did not subside immediately. But as he studied his former boss, he began to feel compassion for him. *This guy is beaten. He's like our soccer team—defeated and not taking it well, defeated and looking for a scapegoat.*

Kyle stuck out his hand, looked Coach Cathey in the eye, and said, "I truly hope you find the answers you're looking for, Jason. I'll be praying for you."

Coach Cathey returned the gesture and sputtered a weak, "Thank you, Kyle."

***

Kyle and Kayla sat together on their living room sofa. Kayla was saddened as Kyle went through the details of his encounter with Jason Cathey. She was quiet for a few minutes as she considered what had taken place between the two men. Then she quietly asked, "What are we going to do, Kyle?"

"I'm not sure," Kyle answered. "We'll figure something out. With God's help, it'll turn out for good. I'm convinced of that."

"I know you are, and maybe I will too in time," Kayla replied with a sad sigh. "Right now, I'm having a hard time believing what happened. The coach was wrong, and he will realize it before the season is over."

"We'll see. Meanwhile, dear girl, I need to find a job," Kyle said with a wry chuckle.

"Hmm," Kayla said in agreement. "Do you think you might want to try something besides coaching soccer?"

"Like what, selling insurance or something?" Kyle quipped.

"I'm not so sure about that. Maybe something in computers. You're good with technical stuff."

"I don't know. It could be a good fit," Kyle replied. "We need to pray about it and wait for the Lord to answer. Somewhere, I think maybe in Psalm 30, it says, 'For the Lord is a God of justice. Blessed are all who wait for him.' So, that's what we'll do: trust Him to show us where we go from here."

Kayla reached her hand over and put it on his. "I know, Kyle, and that's what we'll do." She smiled and said, "By the way, I love you... even if you don't have a job."

"Yeah, be careful. I might get used to it. I'll be a stay-at-home dad," Kyle said as he kissed her on the cheek.

"Forget that," Kayla chuckled as she left the room.

***

The termination of Coach Patton reverberated throughout the school and the team, especially among the Barrymore players. Coach Cathey offered no explanation at practice on the following Monday.

His announcement was simple, "You will note that Coach Patton is not here. He is no longer with the team or the school. Coach Patton was a good coach, and we wish him well. Please don't expect any explanation from me. If you are curious, you will have to seek him out. Now, men, we have a schedule to complete. Let's commit to playing our best soccer in these remaining games. Okay?" Turning to his two assistant coaches, he hollered, "You've got them, Coaches!"

The players from Barrymore stood and looked at one another, obviously shocked and confused. They then silently departed to join their teammates on the practice field. After the practice that evening, the four Barrymore players gathered in Michael and Jake's room.

"Did any of you hear anything more about Coach Patton?" Michael asked as he sat on the edge of his bed with his head down.

"Nope, not a thing," Ian muttered.

"He got fired for trying to take over the team," Matt Arnold quipped. "It's as simple as that."

"What makes you think that?" Jake asked.

"Because Rigsby and Cobb were laughing about it before practice. I didn't realize what they were talking about at the time, but I'm sure that was it."

"So what are we going to do?" Ian asked. "None of us are re-spected. We've been working our butts off every day at practice and not seeing anything for it."

Michael turned to Jake. "What do you think, Jake?"

"Well, guys..." Jake began with a sigh, "I feel bad about Coach Patton losing his job. But I can tell you this: Coach would be the first to tell us to stay with the team and finish the season. You all know that. So that's what I'm going to do. We didn't come here because he was here. We came here to play soccer. That's what he would tell us to do, so, again, that's what I'm doing. In the end, it will all work out."

"Romans 8:28," Michael quipped.

"Yep, you got it," Jake said as he grinned at Michael.

"Then that's it," Matt announced. "We'll take one for Coach Patton."

"For the Coach," everyone confirmed. "For the Coach!"

CHAPTER 24

In terms of wins and losses, the Unity soccer team performed no better than before Coach Patton's firing. They lost all remaining games, leaving them with two wins and fourteen losses for the season. It was a record not to be proud of, for sure. At the end of the season, to no one's surprise, Coach Cathey and his entire staff were let go. This was an encouragement for the Barrymore players who planned to return for the next season. With one exception, they all were looking forward to coming back next season. The uncertain one was Michael Shepherd.

Michael had begun devouring his Bible, a gift he received from Jake. He spent every spare minute studying Scripture. His intensity level was no different than what he had put into place a year earlier when he decided to excel at soccer. He joined a men's Bible study for students. He consumed Bible commentaries that explained passages he wanted to understand beyond any doubt. With no soccer commitment, he was able to do so and handle his class assignments as well. He found that his grades were improving even though he was devoting so much time to Christian activities and studying his Bible. He became a regular attendee of Exchange. By the end of the school year, he had become invaluable to the ministry and a big help to Cody Freedman, as well as Cody's likely replacement, Sean Mitchell, an upcoming senior at Unity.

"You've come a long way, Michael," Cody said at the final Exchange meeting of the year. "I'm proud of you, man." Michael was in a final meeting with Cody and Sean which was designed to wrap things up for the end of the school year. "Between the two of you, Exchange is in good hands. Just remember, the Bible is always your authority. The students will be looking to you for leadership, especially the new ones. Your job is to model Christ on and off campus, where people you don't know will be watching you. I'll be praying for you, brothers. You're the leaders now. Godspeed."

Both Michael and Sean gave Cody strong embraces as they told him goodbye.

***

These remembrances had been racing through Michael's mind all evening, and were still there the following Sunday morning as he, Jake, and Ian Gregson walked back to campus from church service at Redeemer Bible. His deep dive into Scripture was impacting his thoughts about the future.

Am I in the right place? Is God trying to tell me something? Is Civil Engineering really what I want to do? I hate calculus. God knows that. And what about Annie? Where do I stand with her? I've got to find out. But how? Well, freaking ask her, dummy! You mean, ask her if she loves me? Yes, ask her if she loves you. But you must tell her how you feel first. Can you do that?

***

The three young men were excited about an invitation they received that morning from Coach Patton.

"Kayla and I would like you to come for dinner this afternoon," Coach Patton had offered when they happened to come together in the foyer after the service.

"Awesome," Jake said, responding for all three. "What time?"

"How about three to three-thirtyish?" Kyle said.

"That's great," Jake replied. "Thanks for the invite!"

Three hours later, Kayla poured the last cup of coffee and began to clear away dessert dishes. Kyle rose to give her a hand, leading the three guests, including Joshua, to clear away their own dishes.

"I can take care of this," Kayla insisted. "You guys go sit down in the living room. I'll be fine."

"No, come on, Kayla. Please join us," Kyle insisted. "We can take care of the dishes later."

Everyone was soon seated in the living room. All eyes were on Kyle as he pushed back in his leather chair. As his gaze completed the circuit and the silence became uncomfortable, he smiled and said, "I think I can guess what is on everyone's mind today. Do you want me to try?"

"Give it a shot, Coach," Jake said.

"What's Coach Patton going to do now that he is unemployed? Am I right?"

"Goal!" Ian blurted.

Michael shifted his body, placed one leg on the other, and asked, "What are you going to do, Coach?"

"Well, I am going to look for a job. I've got a family to support."

"A coaching job?" Michael asked.

"If possible. However, I'm open to any opportunity."

Jake quickly opined, "Coach, you'd be good at anything you tried. The Lord has the right spot for you. He'll reveal it to you soon. There's no doubt about that."

"Thank you, Jake," Kyle responded.

Sitting on the floor next to the coach, Joshua blurted out, "Coach Kyle can do anything!"

Kyle smiled and said, "Thank you, Joshua."

Jake then suggested, "It's about time for us to leave, but before we do, let's have a short round of prayers for Coach and his family. I'll start, then Ian, you follow me, and Michael, why don't you finish? Okay?" With no hesitation, Jake put his head down and began to pray, "Dear God in heaven, we lift Coach Patton up to you...."

Jake's suggestion triggered a surge of anxiety in Michael. *Uhmm, I'm not sure I can pray alongside these giants. I'm not comfortable praying out loud. Jake knows that. Why does he always do this? What can I say that won't sound stupid? Nothing. Anything I say is going to be stupid. Lord, give me the words.*

In a moment, Jake said amen, and Ian Gregson began to pray. He prayed a few short sentence prayers for Kyle and his family and soon said, "Amen."

There were a few seconds of silence before Michael began his prayer. His heart was thumping. His voice seemed to be coming from out of nowhere. He heard it say, "God, this looks to be an awful moment for Coach. He has lost his job, a job he was really good at. But we know, Lord, that you cause all things to work together for good for those who love you, for those you call together for your purposes. So, God, please make this situation turn out for the good of Coach and his family. I ask this in your great name. Amen."

Michael breathed a sigh of relief and looked up at Coach Patton, who winked and gave him a quick thumbs-up. Kyle "Thank you, men. Those prayers mean more to me than you can imagine."

The players walked up to Kyle and embraced him. Then, they each said goodbye to Kayla and Joshua before departing the Patton home.

At first, there was very little discussion on the way back to the campus in Jake's pickup. The young men were undoubtedly silently conjuring memories of playing soccer for Coach Patton and learning from him in the classroom.

Ian Gregson finally broke the silence. "He did so much to help us. I wish there were a way we could help him. He's going to need a job, even if it's temporary, and like Joshua said, Coach Kyle can do anything. I think he's right about that."

"I've got an idea," Michael said.

"What's that?" Came the unanimous response.

"I can't say, at least not right now, anyway. But Jake, I need a favor."

"What's up, bruh?" Jake asked.

"I'll need to borrow your wheels for a couple of hours tomorrow."

"No problem, man. The gas tank is on the passenger side," Jake said with a chuckle.

"Yeah, I know. Thanks, bruh."

The next morning, Michael walked out of Brompton Hall, where he had just spent two hours in a calculus class. He paused for a moment on the front porch. *You know what, I don't really care what the difference is between differential calculus and integral calculus, Dr. Christopher. That's not important to me right now, sir. And what's more, I pray it never is. Besides, I've got some important business to take care of today.*

The air was cold and biting as Michael walked to the student parking lot. In twenty minutes, he cranked the engine in Jake's truck and quickly noticed that the fuel gauge showed less than a quarter of a tank of gas was left in the vehicle.

Come on, Jake. You're killing me, man. I've got ten bucks for gas and lunch. How am I going to handle that?

Michael drove the car off campus and down Gloucester Avenue. There were several service stations, so his eyes locked on the one that looked the least busy. As he slowed down to turn into that station, an orange, green, and rusty pickup truck pulled out from the service station and sped down Gloucester ahead of him.

DEREK!

Michael's heart jumped into his throat as he whipped his steering wheel back to the right and began to accelerate until he was riding the ugly truck's rear bumper. Michael stayed close as the pickup and its single occupant threaded along, weaving in and out of the three lanes available. After several minutes, Michael noticed the driver glancing frequently into his rear-view mirror, obviously wondering who was riding his bumper. After another ten miles of this bizarre game of road-tag, the lead vehicle pulled off the road and onto the parking lot of a small grocery store. Michael followed and parked inches behind the pickup truck.

In a few seconds, Derek Steinman got out of his vehicle and walked back toward Michael.

Michael pushed open his door and emerged from Jake's truck.

"What's going on, dude?" Derek asked as he studied Michael's face. "Do I know you?"

"Yeah, you do, as a matter of fact," Michael replied. "I'm the guy you and two goons beat up and left on the side of the road outside Barrymore a year ago. Do you remember that dude?"

Derek's eyes moved up and down Michael's body. Then he said, "You don't look like that guy."

"Well, I am that guy."

"So, what about it?" Derek said, crossing his arms over his chest.

"Well, for starters, you stole my coat. I want it back."

Derek took a deep breath and, once again, with a thoughtful eye scan, sized up his accuser.

"I don't have time for this, man. I got your coat at my house, about three miles from here."

"Good. Let's go get it. I'll follow you."

Michael followed Derek as he pulled back onto the main road and then down a two-lane gravel driveway to a single-story dreary-looking farmhouse with a metal roof, shake siding, and a deteriorating front porch. A dried-up garden patch lay alongside the driveway. The driveway itself was riddled with potholes and deep ruts. Michael parked Jake's pickup behind Derek's and followed Derek onto the porch.

Turning to Michael, Derek said, "Wait here. My Gramma's inside. Uh, she's not doing too good." Derek disappeared inside the house. Michael turned and gazed at the area. Signs of poverty were everywhere. He felt a flicker of compassion for this one-time adversary.

In a few minutes, Derek emerged through the front door. He walked to Michael and handed him the coat. Michael took the coat and held it up for a close examination. Then, he tucked it under his arm, looked Derek in the eye, and asked, "So what's wrong with your gramma?"

Derek was obviously surprised by the question. He pondered for a minute and then said, "Not sure. She's old. In a wheelchair."

"I'd like to meet her," Michael said.

Derek paused and gave Michael a puzzled look. Then he said,

"Okay, I'll bring her out." He disappeared into the house and re-appeared seconds later, pushing a wheelchair across the threshold and onto the porch.

Derek said, "Gramma, this is Michael–a friend of mine. He wanted to say hello to you."

The lady was frail-looking and appeared to be in her mid-eighties. She had thinning white hair, which was neatly combed. She wore a flowered dress and wool slippers.

Michael took her outstretched hand. "Hello, ma'am. My name is Michael. I'm glad to meet you."

Showing some mild confusion, she said in a raspy voice, "Are you a friend of Derek's?"

"Yes, ma'am, I am."

"Well, you certainly are a nice-looking young man, not like... Well, never mind. My name is Edith, Edith Steinman. You can call me Edith."

"Thank you, Edith," Michael grinned. "It's a pleasure to meet you. Have you lived here for a long time?'

"We moved here from Minnesota about twenty years ago. My husband was a millwright. Derek was two years old. We raised him here."

"That's good to know, Edith. Maybe I can see you again some-time." Suddenly, Michael heard himself ask Edith, "May I pray for you before I go?"

Did I ask that? I can't believe I asked that.

"Yes, I would like that," Edith responded. "I'd like that very much."

Michael bowed his head. Edith bowed her head. Derek looked at both of them with uncertainty and then bowed his head, too.

Michael prayed, "Father, our great God in heaven. I pray for Edith today that you will bless her, encourage her, and help her feel your presence in her life. God, I seek your will for Edith and her grandson, Derek. Bless them both in Jesus' name. Amen."

Edith looked at Michael with an appreciative smile and said, "Thank you, Michael. You are a nice young man. Come back anytime."

"Thank you, ma'am. I'd like to do that. It's a pleasure to meet you."

Michael then said to Derek, "Is there a gas station nearby? I'm running on fumes."

Derek pondered for a moment, then said, "Not that close. But I can get you some gas."

"Oh? How so?" Michael asked.

"I'll show you." Derek jumped into his truck, started the engine, and backed it next to Jake's pickup. He got out of his truck, holding a five-foot rubber hose. He removed the gas cap from his truck and stuck one end of the hose deep down into the cavity of his gas tank.

Realizing what was happening, Michael removed the gas cap from Jake's truck and stood aside. Derek put the free end of the hose in his mouth and started sucking. When gas began to flow, he poked the hose into the open gas tank and grinned sheepishly at Michael.

Michael returned the grin. "Very professional."

"No comment," Derek murmured.

Michael studied Derek thoughtfully for a moment, then said, "Derek, would you mind sharing your phone number with me?"

Derek gave Michael a quizzical look and asked, "What for,

bruh?"

"Just to stay in touch, maybe. You never know."

The two men exchanged phone numbers, and thirty minutes later, Michael was on the road to his parent's home in Barrymore. He chuckled as he thought about how different things were from what he had imagined they would be if he ever encountered Derek Steinman again.

So, what's the deal? What happened to my plan to get revenge on the guy for what he did to me? But that didn't happen. Why not? Because he's changed, somehow? Yeah, maybe. But so have I. I don't hate the guy anymore. He gave me enough gas to get all the way back to the campus. That was cool. Anyway, I'm going to talk to him and his grandma about Jesus in the near future. In the meantime, he has my phone number, and I have his. Who would have thought this a few months ago? Only God.

Michael pulled into the parking lot of Ponderosa Pine Lumber Company, one of the major businesses in the Tu Valley region in Eastern Oregon, and where George Shepherd had been employed for the past thirty-seven years. Michael was proud of his dad. George had started many years earlier as an accountant when it was a brand-new company. He was now the General Manager and Chief Executive Officer. *Something he never talks about. He's a good dad. I should tell him how I feel. But I'm not sure I can.*

The familiar whine of the planer mill filled the air, along with several forklift trucks moving from stacks of lumber to tractor-trailer rigs waiting to be fully loaded and dispatched across the country. Michael grew up listening daily to those sounds and realized how much he had missed them since leaving for college.

"Well, hello, college boy," Sonja Parrish exclaimed from behind the receptionist's counter at the front entrance as Michael entered the office.

"Hi, Sonja," Michael responded, giving her a quick hug. "Is Dad in?" Michael nodded toward a corner office at the end of a long hallway.

"Yes. He's been waiting for you. Go on down. His door is open."

Michael walked to the end of the hall, where he stopped at the open door and leaned against the doorjamb. Sitting at his desk, which was decorated by several stacks of paper, George Shepherd looked up, smiled, and said, "Come in, Michael." He then stood and held out his hand. "It's good to see you, son. Sit down, please. He pointed to an open side chair, which Michael moved to and sat down.

Michael looked at his dad and said, "Thanks for seeing me, Dad. I know you're busy, and we were just together, so let me get right to why I'm here, if that's okay."

"Certainly. But first, I've got to know what's happening with your coaching staff and your soccer team," George asked, eyebrows furrowed.

"Umm, good questions, Dad. The team will be fine, but the coaches are all gone. They were all fired. And that's the reason I'm here."

"Oh?" George leaned back in his leather chair and mused, "Let me guess. You want me to come and coach the team."

"Yeah, that's it, Dad. Maybe Mom could come in and be the head cheerleader. What do you think?" Michael laughed.

"No, I don't think that's a formula for success, son," George laughed alongside his son. "So, tell me, what's on your mind?"

"Okay, here it is in a nutshell. Coach Patton needs a job. He's a good man, Dad. You know him, of course. He has a wife and a son now. He needs a job."

"So, what do you have in mind for him? Can he drive a fork-lift?"

"I'm sure he can. But Coach is very smart. He's good with computers. He's a great teacher and maybe could be a trainer or something like that. He is personable and maybe could do a sales job of some kind. You do have a sales department, don't you?"

"Not really, son," George said.

"Uhm, bummer. Maybe you could start one, and Coach could head it up." Michael's eyes dropped for a moment. Then he looked his dad in the eyes and said, "Seriously, Coach Patton has done a lot for me, Dad. I want to help him if I can."

"I know you do, Michael. And I do too. Hold on for a minute."

George stood, left the office, and returned shortly with a manilla folder. He handed the folder to Michael and said, "Here's a job application. Give it to your coach and ask him to fill it out. There's an envelope inside with my name on it."

George then sat back down at his desk, looked at Michael, and said, "No guarantees, Michael, but I'll see what I can do."

Michael stood, walked around the corner of the desk, and uncharacteristically engulfed his dad in a bear hug. "Thanks, Dad. I love you."

Surprised by the sentiment, George rose unsteadily, put his hand on Michael's shoulder, and with a voice suddenly gone hoarse, said, "I love you too, son."

On the return trip to the Unity Campus, Michael's heart filled with emotion. *Lord, that was the best moment I have ever had with my dad. Thank you. What a blessing it is to know and feel the love between us now. What a difference. Thank you. And then how all of it went down this afternoon with Derek. That was awesome. Thank you, Lord.*

Michael reached down and turned on the car radio, tuned into a Christian radio program he had found recently, and cruised on to Unity University.

CHAPTER 25

Unity's school year came to an end with final exams, goodbyes, packing, and promises to stay in touch. To the students from Barrymore, the significant goodbyes were not traumatic. They knew the separation was just a mere twenty miles on the highway. However, other issues, such as summer jobs and moving back in with Mom and Dad, caused concern.

Jake had no problem. He took a job off-bearing a cut-off saw inside the planing mill at Ponderosa Pine Lumber Company. A job for Michael was another matter. Because George Shepherd was CEO of the company, he would not allow Michael to come to work for the plant for fear of claims of favoritism. So, Michael had to look elsewhere. Fortunately, he landed a job pulling lumber from a green chain in a small sawmill on the outskirts of Barrymore, Oregon.

Kyle Patton also found employment. After an in-depth interview and a series of tests, Kyle was hired by Ponderosa Pine Lumber Company as a computer technician, whose job was to coordinate and upgrade, where necessary, the company's data processing systems.

Kyle was at home reviewing his first day on the job with Kayla.

"I can't believe how great everyone is," he said. "I have a lot to learn, but I have a pretty good trainer. I'll be working some nights and Saturdays, but that's no different than coaching a soccer team."

"What's your boss's name, and what's he like?" Kayla asked.

"Tom Task. Great name for a boss, right?" Kyle laughed. "He seems to be a decent guy. He's the operations chief over the whole plant and a busy man. I think he's very happy I am there to give him some relief.

"Is he a believer?" Kayla asked.

"Not sure," Kyle replied.

At that moment, Joshua burst through the door and ran and stood beside Kyle.

"Hi, Coach Kyle. Can we play some soccer?"

"We sure can, buddy." Kyle paused for a minute, then asked, "But do you know what?"

"What, Coach Kyle?"

"We need to give you a new name to call me. I'm not a coach anymore?"

"You're not?"

"Nope.

"Aren't you going to coach me anymore?"

"Oh yes, I'm still going to coach you, but you will have to start calling me something else."

"What should I call you, Coach Kyle?"

"Well, I don't know. Let's see here.... Wait, I got it. How about calling me Dad?"

Joshua looked at his sister, who was smiling with a tear in her eye. He looked back at Kyle. "Do you want me to call you Dad?"

"Yes, Joshua. Or Daddy will work as well. I'd like that very much."

"Wow! Thank you, Coach---I mean Daddy. I can do that. Now,

can we go play some soccer?"

"We sure can, son. We sure can."

Kyle winked at Kayla, who now had tears in both eyes, and he and Joshua left to go outside.

***

On a warm Friday afternoon, Derek Steinman punched off the clock at Sullivan Lumber in Tomika. He then headed home to shower and get ready for a get-together with his two running mates, Joker Duff and Nick Foster. It had been several weeks since the three of them had been together.

"I've got something you might be interested in," Nick had informed him during their phone conversation the night before.

"What is it?"

"Can't tell you on the phone, but it's big," Nick said. "Let's meet tomorrow night around seven o'clock at Barney's Barbeque. Okay? I'll pick up Joker."

Derek was silent for a few seconds, then agreed to the meeting. *This better be worth my time*, he thought as he hung up the phone.

The following evening, Derek was in his house, in the living room with his gramma, watching a Western movie on television. He glanced at his watch, stood, and said, "Gramma, I'm going out for a while. I might be late, so don't wait up."

"Where are you going, son?" Edith asked.

"I'm just going to a movie with some buddies," Derek replied.

"But what about dinner?"

"I'll grab something on the way, Gramma. Don't worry, I'll be fine."

"Oh dear, I hope you aren't going out with those boys I don't like; Jockey or something like that? Or his friend, Nick something. You know I don't like those boys, Derek."

"Yeah, I know, Gramma," Derek sighed. "Sometimes I don't like them either."

"Well then, why don't you invite that nice boy back? The one who was here the other day? What was his name?"

"Michael? Ha! Not much of a chance that's going to happen, Gramma. Anyway, I'll be fine. Don't wait up."

***

Forty-five minutes later, Derek, Joker, and Nick were seated in an isolated booth in Barney's Barbeque. There was a near-empty pitcher of a dark beer in the middle of the table.

Joker and Nick were sitting across the table from Derek. Nick, in a hushed voice, said, "I'm telling you, Derek. This is a no-brainer. I've been there a couple of times. There are only two attendants: a guy and his son. There's a cash register and a money box below the counter. We could be in and out of there in less than two minutes."

"What's the name of this place? And where is it?" Joker asked.

"Try Buy Market," Nick replied. "It's on Yancey Street. Near the airport."

"Oh yeah. I know the place," Joker said. "Were there many people there?"

"Not many. But by the end of the day, that cash register has got to be full. And we could be in and out of there in...."

"Yeah, you said that already," Derek interrupted.

"Here's what I'm thinking, Derek." Nick was excited. He leaned over the table and spoke in a whisper. "Next Thursday is the end of the month. You know what I mean? Payday for a lot of people. Friday will be a big day for the store. People will be spending money like crazy." Then he sat back in the booth, looking proud.

The boys across from Derek waited for Derek to speak. But Derek said nothing. He sat emotionless and sipped his beer. Finally, Joker asked, "What do you think, Derek?"

Derek remained quiet for several more seconds. Then he looked at Nick and asked, "A guy and his son, eh? How old do you think the boy is?"

Nick paused and rubbed his chin. "Maybe about sixteen or so. He shouldn't be a problem."

Again, Derek was unresponsive as he slid his thumb up and down his beer mug, wiping away the condensation. Four eyes on the other side of the table never left his face as they watched him intensely. Derek waxed total indifference to the question on the table.

Finally, Joker said, "So how do you see this, Derek? I think Nick's on to something here. I'm ready to go. Are you with us or not?"

Derek picked up his beer mug, drained the contents, and placed the vessel back on the table.

"I don't like it."

Joker and Nick exchanged glances and then looked back at Derek. "Why? What's the problem?" Joker was blunt. "This deal's a gimme! You know that!"

"To start with, we've never done nothin' like this before," Derek began. "This is different. If you don't pull it off, you're lookin' at serious slammer time. Are you ready for that?"

Nick leaned back in the booth. "Come on, Derek. Are you suddenly turnin' gutless on us?"

"No. Just being real." Derek leaned forward and glared at Nick. "Look at your plan, Nick. Your picture has already been taken at the location at least twice, and it will be again, only this time with a gun in your hand. This sixteen-year-old is probably not going to let you hurt his old man and vice-versa without putting up a fight. So are you going to shoot him, Nick? They also have pictures of your car and will have them again unless you drive Joker's car, which they will then be able to trace. So you probably should steal a car to use, which is another ten to twenty years if you get caught."

Derek stood, picked up his car keys, and said, "You know what, men? I'm thinking there's another life out there somewhere. Actually, I know there is. I've seen signs of it." As he stepped away, he looked at their stunned faces and said, "That's it for me. I'm moving on." As he stepped away from the booth, he said, "I hope you don't do this job. If you do, I believe you'll be making a big mistake."

Joker and Nick stared at each other in unbelief as Derek left the restaurant.

***

Michael and Annie were sitting in Michael's car near a lookout point outside LaGrange, a popular location for young lovers to hang out. The scenery was peaceful, and there was a nice view of the Grande Ronde River quietly flowing through the west end of Tu Valley below. Saturday night was cool and, with the stars and full moon above, quite romantic. Michael pulled Annie into his arms and kissed her. Holding her tight, four words suddenly spilled out of his mouth before he could think about them. He whispered, "I love you, Annie."

"I love you, too," Annie responded.

An awesome sense of relief flooded Michael's senses when he heard those words from Annie's mouth. *She loves me. I can't believe she said it. But she did. Thank you, Lord.*

After several more tender moments of embracing and kissing, Michael was prompted to ask, "Are you happy, Annie?"

"Yes, I am very happy. Are you happy, Michael?" Annie asked.

"About us? Yes. I couldn't be happier, but...." Michael hesitated.

"But what?" Annie replied.

"I'm not sure I am where God wants me to be."

"Why do you say that?"

"I think that God may want me to go to seminary."

"Wow! Really? Like, become a pastor?"

"I guess."

"You guess? Michael, that's something that has to be certain." Annie exclaimed.

"I know, Annie. I would also guess that time is of the essence to get accepted."

"Michael, dear, you need to stop guessing and get some answers."

Michael grinned, "God tells us to pray, be patient, and wait on Him. That's what I'm doing." He paused for Annie to respond. When she didn't, he asked, "What about you? Are you going to stay at Unity for three more years?"

"Well, I guess I am," Annie said slowly.

"Now you're guessing."

"I know. I can get a degree to teach in three years, but I will probably need to get a Master's Degree, which will be two years more, and then maybe a PhD after that." Annie paused, then added, "So we are facing a lot of uncertainty, aren't we?"

"Yes, we are," Michael replied. But one thing we know for sure is, 'But God.'"

"But God?" Annie asked.

"Yes. But God directs our steps and brings us into compliance with His will for us. He leads. We follow. That takes care of the guesswork, doesn't it?"

"Well, yes, I guess it does," Annie said with a chuckle.

Michael laughed, "You are too funny, Annie Smith."

***

It was late when Michael arrived home from his date with Annie that night. Michael pulled his car onto the far right side of the Shepherd household's driveway. The house was quiet as Michael entered. He noticed a desk lamp with a sealed envelope propped against the lampstand was on. The envelope was addressed to him and bore the return address of James and Lauren Reynolds in Vancouver, British Columbia, Canada.

Michael picked up the envelope, walked down the hallway, and went into his bedroom. He sat on the edge of the bed, opened the envelope, and read the letter.

"To my dear son, Michael. This letter is being written by my good friend and nurse, Melissa, who has been with me for several weeks while I've been in the hospital. I am giving her the words to write, but it's a struggle. James is here and helping as well. He sends his regards, along with mine. By the time you read this letter, I will no longer be here. I am in such pain now, but I asked them to withhold all my pain meds for a time so I could write this letter to you, my precious son. Soon, they will take me off life support, and I will be gone. Sadly, I'm not sure where I will be. I hope in heaven, but how does one know for certain?"

"Goodbye, for now, Michael. I am so happy I was able to see you and tell you I love you." The letter was signed, "Mom."

Michael held the letter to the side, bowed his head for several seconds, and thought about this lady who was his birth mother. She had come into his life so suddenly and was gone just as suddenly. *The saddest part was that I wasn't there to answer her question, "How does one know?" How could this wonderful lady, who knew her life was ending soon, not have someone talk to her about Jesus and his gift of eternal life? Where was I? Why didn't I see that?*

As Michael lay his head on his pillow that night, his thoughts were a mix of questions. *What about Annie? Is she the one? Where is God leading me—back to college or on to seminary? Or maybe into an outreach ministry of some kind? And how can I follow up with Derek and his gramma? Should I be doing something there? It seems to feel that way. I need to call Jake and see how he's doing. A lot is going on right now.*

" I need wisdom, Lord."

* * *

Kyle, Kayla, and Joshua were the invited guests of Michael, Annie, Jake, and Olivia for breakfast the next morning at Wixx Cafe. They had driven down from church service at Redeemer Bible Church and were sitting in a large circular booth. The conversations bounced from the sermon by the Senior Pastor Josh Lincoln to styles of music and to the upcoming men's fish fry on Tuesday night.

Then, Kyle Patton looked at Michael and Jake and asked, "Have you all heard from the new coach at Unity yet?"

Jake looked at Michael, who remained quiet and said, "Yes, we have. We both were notified we were on the scholarship list and should be receiving confirmations soon."

"That's great news guys," Kyle said with a smile. "I'm proud of you both. When is the first practice?"

"I don't know," Ian replied. "Late August sometime."

Kyle looked at Michael and asked, "Do you know Mike?"

Michael paused, shook his head, and looked uncomfortable when he answered. "I'm not sure I'll be going back this fall, Coach."

Kyle was surprised. "Really, Mike? What are you thinking of doing?"

Michael locked eyes with Kyle and said, "I haven't decided yet, but I'm thinking of going to seminary."

Kyle turned to Jake, who returned an acknowledging nod. Then he said to Michael, "That's a big decision, Mike. I'm glad you told me. Kayla and I will pray about that for you."

Joshua put his hand up and yelled, "Me too, Mike! I'll pray about it, too!"

Michael grinned and, looking at Joshua, said, "Thank you, buddy."

"What seminary are you thinking about, Michael?" Kayla asked.

"I'm not sure. I have applications in for three of them," Michael explained.

Kyle said, "Please keep us posted. Okay?"

"Yes, sir. I will. How's your job going, Coach?" Michael asked.

"It's going well. Thanks for asking. I do have something you all might be able to help me with. I need to bring in an assistant to help me with the detail stuff I don't have time to do. A young guy who won't mind doing grunt work and getting his hands dirty. With all of your contacts at Unity, do you know anyone who might fit that description?"

Michael immediately declared, "As a matter of fact, I do. Let me check it out and get back to you."

"Sounds good, Mike. Let me know."

***

Late Sunday evening, Michael was sitting on his bed, propped up against the headboard, reading from chapter 43 in Isaiah. Michael had set himself a goal of reading through the complete Bible before school started again. It read, "I, even I, am the Lord, And there is no savior besides Me. So you are my witnesses, declares the Lord, And I am God."

Michael sat back for a thoughtful moment, then put his Bible down and picked up his phone. He dialed the number Derek had given him.

"Yeah, you got Derek," Derek's voice echoed through the speaker.

"Derek, this is Mike. What's going on?"

"Everything's cool. Why the call, man?"

"Well, I've got something you might be interested in."

"Really, what's that?"

"More than I can tell you on the phone. How about meeting me for pizza tomorrow after work?'

"Sounds good, man. Where?"

"How about Pierro's in LaGrange?" Michael asked. "Have you ever been there?"

"Oh yeah. I know the place," Derek replied.

"Okay, see you at Pierro's Pizza tomorrow night at six o'clock."

"Who's buying?"

Michael laughed, "The last guy there. How's that?"

"Hmm," Derek said in agreement. "Sounds like a plan. See you there."

At 5:40 p.m. the next evening, Michael pulled into the parking lot of Pierro's Pizza. He immediately caught sight of Derek's ugly pickup, prominently resting in a handicapped parking space in front of the pizza parlor.

This guy has a long way to go, Michael sighed as he walked across the parking lot to the restaurant's front door. Four vehicles were parked in handicapped, and all four had handicap placards on their inside windshields, including Derek's. Michael shook his head, opened the restaurant's front door, and went inside.

Michael spotted Derek at a table covered by an oilcloth, sporting a half-empty beer mug. Derek stood and waved. Michael walked to the table and shook hands with Derek. Both men sat down. Derek took a drink from his mug and sat his still frosty mug on the table.

"Want a beer?" He asked.

"No thanks. I can't drink alcohol. Too young."

"Oh, sorry." Derek was surprised. "That never bothered me," he chuckled. "I can fix you up with some I.D. if you want."

"No, thanks."

Fifteen minutes later, the two guys were annihilating a large pizza. Derek was on his second mug of beer, and Michael was washing his pizza down with a soda.

Derek pulled a wedge of pizza onto his plate, quaffed down a gulp of beer, and looked at Michael. "So, what's up, Michael Shepherd?"

Michael wiped his mouth with a paper towel from a roll on the table. "A friend of mine is the I.T. guy at a large lumber company. He is looking for someone to come in and help him with some of the detail work as well as a lot of the grunt work to free him up to do his job better. I thought you might be interested in talking to him."

Derek wiped his hands and face on a paper towel, immediately ready to ask his first question. But before he could ask it, Michael lifted his hand, palm out, and said, "No, Derek. I don't have any idea what they pay."

"Hmm. So you don't think the pay is important?" Derek asked, derisively.

"Sure, pay is important, Derek. But I don't think what they pay is the most important aspect of this job, not in your case anyway."

"Why not for me?"

"This job would give you the chance to get out of the rut you're in and give you a new start," Michael explained. "I know this company. It's a good company and could be a great opportunity for the right person. The job you're doing today, pulling lumber off the green chain, that's what you'll be doing ten years from now or until you're too old to do that heavy work anymore. Then what will you do?"

Derek shrugged his shoulders and took another slurp of beer.

Michael continued. "You do know, I hope, the other stuff you do is criminal and will probably land you in jail someday."

"I've stopped doing that stuff," Derek said gruffly.

"Really? Wow! What brought that about?" Michael said as he took another bite of pizza.

"I don't know," Derek replied. "Let's say I got tired of it."

"Well, hallelujah. That's quite a decision, bruh. Do you mind telling me about it?"

"There's not much to tell. I just decided I needed to change. Maybe it was something you said. Or something another guy said to me several months ago."

"Really! Who was that?" Michael asked.

"I don't know. Some guy I met." Then he chuckled and looked around the room. "Right here, in fact. In this very restaurant. We were sitting right over there." Derek pointed to the table where he was sitting when he met Kyle Patton. "Anyway, he let me know I was a dirtbag and needed to straighten up. And then he said he would pray for me. I thought the guy was nuts at the time, but now, I'm not so sure. He may have been right. Anyway, I doubt that anyone would hire me for the job you're talking about. Not with my background."

"I'm not so sure about that, Derek," Michael said. "I could have some influence on the deal."

"Really? After what I did to you? Why would you do that?"

"Well, for one thing, I believe you when you say you've made a change. You've still got a ways to go, but I'm betting you're not the same guy I met a year ago. I see some good in you, Derek." Michael paused, noting Derek's receptive smile at that remark. Then he continued, "I'll tell you what, Derek. I'll see if I can get an interview set up for you sometime this week. What time do you get off work?"

"Four o'clock."

"Can you make it to Barrymore by 4:30?"

"No problem."

"Okay, Derek. I'll get it set up and text you the details when I have them."

"Sounds good, bruh. Thanks. By the way, what do you mean? 'I still have a ways to go. Like what?" Derek asked.

"Well, things like using a false handicap placard to get a close parking spot, for starters."

"It's not false. It belongs to Gramma. She got it when she was still driving."

Michael wiped his mouth and hands on a napkin, stood, and said, "That's what I mean, bruh. You've still got a ways to go. But we'll talk about it. I promise."

Derek picked up the ticket for the meal and put it in his pocket.

Michael looked at him and said, "I was the last one in."

"My treat, bruh."

Both men stood, shook hands, and departed Pierro's Pizza.

CHAPTER 26

Derek had a lot on his mind as he drove to his home that night. He considered his conversation with Michael. *Yeah, maybe I shouldn't be using Gramma's handicap card, but it'd be stupid to park a long way from the front door when I have the card. She ain't using it. Yeah, I know; what about the real handicapped person who can't find a place to park because I'm taking up his spot? What about that, Derek?*

Derek peeked at his gas gauge and noticed the needle was near empty. He maneuvered to the outside lane and pulled into an all-night gas station. He got out of the car and walked into the concession area. Everyone inside was fixated on the television perched on a high shelf. The picture on the screen displayed the parking lot of a small food market. There were police vehicles, an ambulance, and an emergency vehicle parked in front of the market. A split screen displayed the news anchor inside the studio and a news reporter inside the store. The camera swept through the store, exposing a sheeted body on the floor, and then quickly moved to the news reporter.

"The incident is apparently over," news anchor Alan Johnson announced. "We are here at the Try Buy Food Mart, where an alleged robbery attempt took place about forty-five minutes ago. It appears one of the alleged robbers is deceased, and we understand that one police officer has been taken to the hospital. Evidently, a store employee was also wounded and taken to the hospital. A second alleged robber has been cuffed and is sitting in a squad car outside the store. Katie Sunrich, our on-the-scene reporter, tried to interview the apparent store owner, but he was pretty distraught. We weren't able to learn much from him."

The image of Katie Sunrich then filled the entire screen. Katie was a diminutive young lady who looked to be in her late twenties. "That's all we have from here, Alan. Back to you."

News anchor Alan Johnson appeared full screen again and said, "That's all for now folks. Please tune in again at 10:00 p.m. for any updates on this and other breaking stories, as well as sports and weather. Thank you for listening to this special report on WTHL Evening News. Goodnight."

Derek was stunned and sickened as he watched the news report unfold. Here were who appeared to be his close friends in a world of trouble. One was possibly even dead, and the other on his way to prison. Derek continued to stare at the television as it ran through a gauntlet of automobile and insurance ads.

How could they do this? I warned them! It has to be somebody else. These can't be my guys. Please, somebody. Maybe God, if you exist. Whoever you are, don't let this be my guys.

"Can I help you? Sir, can I help you?" A clerk behind a cashier counter raised his voice, trying to get Derek's attention.

A young man standing behind Derek tapped Derek's shoulder and said, "You're up, dude."

Derek snapped back into reality and walked to the counter. "Yeah. Five on six, regular."

"You got it. Have a good one!"

"Yeah, you too. Thanks," Derek muttered as he moved like a zombie through the exit door.

* * *

Derek's mind was still numb when he parked his truck and walked up the steps to his house. *What am I going to do? I tried to warn them. I hope it wasn't them. But I'm pretty sure it was.* He felt sick to his stomach and totally helpless. His head felt numb. His heart was pounding in his chest. Derek knew one of his friends was probably dead, and the other one was in a lot of trouble, and there was nothing he could do to help them.

"Derek!" Gramma screamed when he stepped inside the house. "Thank God you're home. I've been prayin' and prayin' you were okay. Did you see what was on the news tonight?"

"Yeah, Gramma. I did."

"Weren't those guys your friends?" Edith asked.

"Maybe, Gramma," Derek said hesitantly. "What makes you think that?"

"The car. They showed the car. It looked just like the one one of them drove when they were here."

"Did they give any names?"

"No, they didn't. Oh, Derek. I'm so glad you weren't with them." Gramma rolled her wheelchair over to Derek and threw her arms around him. "I've been so worried about you."

"I'm fine, Gramma," Derek said reassuringly.

* * *

Two days later, Derek punched off work, climbed into his pickup, and drove twenty miles to Barrymore. Following Michael's instructions, he pulled into the Ponderosa Pine Lumber Company parking lot for visitors. He exited his truck and walked toward a white single-story office building. It was 4:30 p.m. when Derek opened the door and stepped inside the office. He immediately came face to face with Kyle Patton. Both men were momentarily stunned and speechless.

Kyle cringed as his mind connected to their last meeting on a lonely gravel road leading to a city water tank. Now, here they were, face to face again, in his office.

"You're *that* Derek?"

"Yes, sir. I'm, uh, Well... This is really weird. Do you want me to leave?" Derek asked.

"No. Of course not. Come on into my office." Kyle led the way into his office, a room full of computers, computer screens, cameras, and file cabinets. He sat down behind a neatly ordered metal desk and motioned to Derek to sit in a chair near the desk. Derek could not hide his nervousness as he sat down and stared at Kyle. He let out a huge sigh. "I can't believe this, Mr. Patton. I'm sure I'm wasting your time. I get it if you want me to leave. I really do."

"It's not a problem, Derek, but it is weird. So you're a friend of Michael Shepherd?"

"Well, sort of, I guess," Derek replied. "We're just getting acquainted, you might say."

"Interesting. I want to learn more about that. But right now, what's important is that I need to hire someone to help me do my job better. And we need to find out if you are the best candidate for the job."

For the next two hours, Kyle went through the basics of the job requirements, gave Derek a tour of the administrative areas of the facility, and reviewed his completed job application. At the end of the formalities, the two men were relaxing in Kyle's office.

Derek said, "I thought you were a coach."

"I was," Kyle replied. Until I got fired."

"You got fired?"

"Yep. I sure did."

"Why would anyone fire you?"

"I guess because I wasn't getting the job done," Kyle said with a shrug.

"Hmm," Derek replied. "Do you think you will ever go back to coaching?"

"I'm not sure. I really like what I am doing here. There are a lot of interesting challenges here. Besides that, it's different, and I'm enjoying the change. So far, anyway."

Kyle paused and picked up the application Derek had completed. "One last thing I need to ask you, Derek."

"Yes, sir."

"I see your formal education ended after the tenth grade. Tell me about that, please."

"Well, my dad made me quit school and take a job because we were barely getting by," Derek explained. "To tell the truth, he was drinking up most of what we were making. Then he up and passed on us. I didn't have any choice after that."

"Did you try to further your education in any way?" Kyle asked.

"No sir, I didn't."

"Would you consider taking some night classes and going for your GED?"

"Yeah, that's where you can work on getting a high school diploma, right?" Derek asked.

"That's right," Kyle replied.

"Yes, sir. I'd like to do that someday."

Kyle leaned forward in his chair. "One more question, Derek. Do you remember what I said to you that night about getting your life squared away?"

"Yes, sir."

"Well, have you thought about that?"

"Yes, sir. A lot, lately."

Kyle straightened up and pondered for several seconds as Derek sat quietly.

Then he stood and said, "Derek, that's good. I hope you continue down that path." After a brief Pause, Kyle said, "I need to get home to my family now, Derek. Thank you for coming in. I'll be making a decision about the job in the next few days." He extended his hand to Derek. Derek stood and responded with a handshake.

"Thank you, Derek. One piece of advice, if I may."

"Yes, sir."

"Spend some time with Michael," Kyle grinned. "He would make an excellent mentor for you."

* * *

"I really had to force myself to shut up," Kyle said to Kayla as they sat together that evening in their living room. "I wanted to pursue the spiritual issue with him, but the circumstances weren't right for that."

"Because it might sound job conditional, right?"

"Right. But I keep asking myself, what's the high road here?"

"I think you took it, Kyle," Kayla encouraged. "Let's just pray he doesn't get hit by a truck before he makes a commitment to

Christ."

"He's ready, I'm sure of that. But I didn't want to put him in what he might regard as an either/or situation. I'm hoping Mike will pick up on it when he sees him again."

"How did the actual interview go?" Kayla asked.

"He did well. Actually, very good considering the circumstances," Kyle replied. "You should have seen the look on his face when he saw me."

"It was probably no different than yours, dear," Kayla laughed.

"I'm sure you're right. "God's on top of His game, isn't He?"

"Twenty-four seven, dear husband. Twenty-four seven. So, is he your man?"

"I'm not sure. I have a few more applications to look at. I'll let you know."

"I hope he is," Kayla replied. "I can't think of a better place for the young man to be than under your leadership."

"We'll know in a few days. Meanwhile, I'll call Mike tomorrow and update him."

"Yeah, you're going to sic him on Derek, aren't you?" Kayla laughed.

"I won't have to," Kyle replied. "In my mind, Michael has become very much like a man I told him about once, a man named Joseph."

"Joseph? Joseph, who?" Kayla replied.

EPILOGUE

Over the following months, Michael and Annie married and moved to Portland, Oregon, where Michael entered Multnomah Biblical Seminary. Kyle continued his career at Ponderosa Pine

Lumber Company. He and Kayla welcomed a daughter, Cate, into their family, so Kayla quit her teaching job to stay at home and be a full-time mom to Cate and Joshua. Jake continued playing soccer for Unity. Under new coaches, he developed into an outstanding player who received "All Conference" recognition in his final two years in league play. He and Olivia were married, and Jake continued studying for an advanced degree in business. Derek became a valued employee at Ponderosa Pine Lumber Company and became a follower of Christ under the guidance of his supervisor, Kyle Patton.

Four years after his entry into the Seminary, Michael Shepherd stood in a line with 31 men and women who were waiting to walk to a podium and receive their Master of Divinity degrees. As each person's name was called, the graduate walked across the stage and received their degree. As he waited to receive his degree, Michael's eyes and thoughts were not on his fellow graduates or on the large contingent of black-robed educators assembled on the stage. No, his eyes and thoughts were focused on his family and friends who had come to participate in the event.

What a great moment, Michael thought as he looked out at the audience. *There's Annie, my beautiful wife for whom I'm ever grateful. There's Mom and Dad. God bless them. I was so upset when they told me I was adopted. How cruel that was of me. They actually chose me to join their family. What an honor and a privilege! There's Coach Patton and his family. I remember how he encouraged me after that Langford game when I felt so bad about costing us the game. He was there at one of the lowest points of my life, and here he is with his family at one of the highest points of my life. God Bless Coach Patton. I see Derek is here with Emily. That's amazing. Derek, who overwhelmed me with his badness, and Emily, who overwhelmed me with her goodness, standing together in their oneness because of Jesus Christ. God bless Derek and Emily and whatever He might have in mind for them. Finally, there's Jake. My best buddy. He was unrelenting in chasing me down for Christ. God bless Jake and Olivia.*

"Mr. Michael Shepherd," boomed through the speakers surrounding the stage in front of the Johnson Academic Building of Multnomah University.

Michael's mind snapped into real time as he heard his name announced. He grinned widely as he walked across the stage and received his Master of Divinity degree from Dr. Robert Driscoll, President of Multnomah University. Michael was excited about the prospects of his first job as Assistant Pastor. He had received and accepted an offer to serve as Pastor of Student Ministries and Biblical Studies at a mid-size evangelical church located near Eugene, Oregon.

THE END

THE BACK OF THE NET

The following friends and family provided special encouragement and insight, including much-needed technical assistance in writing this novel:

Fred and Elise Freimark provided much of the classroom reality
and dialogue, including help with all facets of this nation's
Constitution and Bill of Rights.

Hope Dover.
This fantastic lady handles all the intricate details of my
relationship with my publisher.

Brittany Hagmaier, a neighbor and friend, was always available
to help me with any issues related to Microsoft Word.

Gary Fearon, a fellow author with Collierville Christian
Writers, designed and set up my website.

Rad Andrews provided medical expertise.

Daughters Ona and Cathy, voracious readers, proofread my
novel several times.

Son Patrick, an excellent soccer player and coach, provided
insight into the soccer strategies prevalent throughout the
novel.

Pam Stein, Bartlett Christian Writers provided much-needed
initial proofreading help.

Many friends extended words of encouragement along the
way. I cannot list them all, but I give special thanks to Mickey
Bowden, Annette Teepe, Frank and Kay Dibianca, Martha
Banks, Gil Brandon and my wife and
best friend, Erdeen Fitzgerald.